The Legacy of Deer Run

Elaine Marie Cooper

To Barb —
May the Lord
bless your Legacy's
In His Grace,
Elaine Marie Cooper

Book Three of the Deer Run Saga

Sword of the Spirit Publishing

ISBN: 978-0-9838836-7-8

Published by Sword of the Spirit Publishing
www.swordofspirit.net

This book is dedicated to my husband, Steve

"Sometimes we just go where the pieces of our heart live. They are not always in one place. It helps us appreciate the times when our hearts all beat as one together, in one place."

Acknowledgments

No book is birthed through the hands of one. So many have contributed to this novel that it would be neglectful on my part to leave any contributors unmentioned. I hope they all know how much I appreciate each of them.

Once again, my husband, Steve, has been an awesome force behind this book. My first editor for each chapter, you check every detail mercilessly! And you're usually correct. You can sometimes even do it with humor. You are a gem.

To Donald J. Parker of Sword of the Spirit Publishing, thank you for believing in my work. I feel honored to be working with you.

To my editor, Lisa J. Lickel, what can I say? You are wonderful. With your knowledge of both editing and history, your skills prodded me to go the extra mile to re-check facts and fill in any gaps. I cannot tell you enough how great it has been to work with you. "Thanks" does not seem sufficient.

To my loyal and encouraging first draft readers, Julie Walters, Jenni Wilson-Cooper, and Linda Wilson, thanks for all your input and enthusiasm. You deserve special recognition for plodding through the rough version!

The large amount of detailed research into life in Springfield, Massachusetts in 1800 and the Springfield Armory was made available to me by the best group of historians I've ever worked with. In alphabetical order, I send a *huge* thanks to Richard Colton, Historian at the Springfield Armory; Margaret Humberston, Head of Library and Archives at Museum of Springfield History; Guy McLain, Director, Connecticut Valley Historical Museum, Museum of Springfield History; and Dennis Picard, Historian at Storrowton Village Museum in West Springfield, Massachusetts. Your incredible knowledge and resources for the era, as well as the details of production at the armory, have added invaluable detail to this book. Thank you for sharing your rich knowledge with me and for your support. You are all so appreciated.

To Katie Leporte, my wonderful cover artist—this design is so perfect for the story. You have captured the feel of this tale with your paintbrush and I am in awe of your talent. Thank you for your wonderful artistry painted for the Deer Run saga!

To all of my faithful and encouraging friends, both authors and readers, thank you from the bottom of my heart. A writer's life can feel so solitary but you have filled me with your uplifting friendship and support. You are all a blessing and I thank you.

To the best sons a mom could ever have and their lovely wives—Ben and Kristen and Nate and Jenni—I love you all so much. You all make my life rich with love. As do Jack, Chloe, and Luke. ☺

To my Mom, Lucy Prince Mueller: I am so pleased that I can present you with this last book in the Deer Run Saga, based on your great, great-grandfather. It has been a delight discovering family history.

And thanks, as always, to my Lord and Savior Jesus Christ, from whom all blessings flow.

Chapter 1
Danny

April 1800

It was James's wife who died. But Danny's heart grieved in unison with his brother. An observer might even wonder which man was the grieving widower.

Convulsing waves of sobs from his twin surged through his being as if they were his own. Danny had always been close with James but never before had their common day of birth made their connection more palpable. James's loss tore at every sinew of Danny's being. Observing his brother hold his newborn daughter while staring at the young wife's coffin brought a fresh wave of despair to Danny.

He stared blankly at the grave marker that had been quickly chiseled.

Anne Lowe
Born 1780 Died 1800

So few words to memorialize so much heartache.
She was only twenty. She did not deserve to die.
Deserving or not, his young sister-in-law had labored to deliver her firstborn far too long. In a letter to Danny, his mother wrote that, after finally rallying to deliver the healthy girl, Anne's heart gave out in exhaustion.

Danny could see that the light of joy from James's eye had been extinguished with his wife's last breath.

Now, standing next to the hungry hole that was ready to swallow the wooden box, Danny worried that James would leap into the pit with the baby and beg the mourners to throw the dirt over them as well. While he readied to grab his brother's arm in the event of such an act, Aunt Sarah approached James and touched his arm.

"James. Let me nurse little Rachel. See how she hungers." Sarah pointed to the infant who thrust a fist into her small, searching mouth.

Still sobbing, James handed the infant to Sarah with trembling hands. The child began to wail, as if giving voice to the sadness on each face at the gravesite. Sarah bundled the baby in her shawl and scurried back to the Lowe's cabin to feed her.

The boys' mother wrapped her arms around James. Tears poured down her cheeks as she clung to him.

Reverend Hollingsworth finished the Scripture reading and the men in the crowd took turns sifting dirt through their fingers onto the pine box. Whispers from behind him became clear as the crowd dissipated. Danny turned to look.

"It's a curse." One of the older women from Deer Run spoke closely into the ear of her friend. "She never should of married that Redcoat's son. 'Twas bound to bring heartache to the young fool. A curse, I tell ya."

Danny clenched his fists so tightly his nails dug into his own flesh. Heart pounding and face burning, he edged closer to the gossipers.

If his eyes were arrows they would surely have pierced the two women upon whom he focused his gaze. He used his most menacing voice to grab their attention.

"My dear Missus Endicott, perhaps you should this day thank the good Lord in heaven."

Missus Endicott cleared her throat nervously. "Pray, what for, Mr. Lowe?" Her voice sounded strained.

"You must thank the Lord that He chose to create you a female, Madam. Because, had He so chosen to create you a man, I would surely thrust this fist into your lying mouth."

The women gasped and lifted their skirts off the ground as they scampered away from the gravesite. Danny watched them with utter contempt.

Pathetic gossipmongers.

A sudden commotion directed Danny's attention back to the graveside. Anne's father was shaking a fist at Daniel Lowe Sr., his face contorted in pain and anger. Daniel Sr.

stared wordlessly at the grief-stricken parent.

Danny recalled how Anne's father had objected to the marriage in the first place. He had been a most loyal patriot during the war and never quite trusted Danny and James's Redcoat father, even after he had become an American. Anne's father was never able to forgive Daniel Lowe for being a King's soldier during the Revolution. And now the anger of the distraught man appeared to smother any grief he might feel about losing his daughter. He stared with glowering eyes at the engulfing grave. Without speaking a word to the Lowe family, he silently turned his back on them and strode away with unforgiving steps.

Danny wiped the dampness from his face as the mourners slowly ambled back to the Lowe cabin.

The younger man's thoughts wandered back to James and Anne in happier times. How excited they had both been about the coming baby. How his brother's eyes lit up whenever his wife walked into the room.

His father, for whom Danny had been named, drew near. "Are you all right, son?" He welcomed his parent's arm across his shoulders as they left the graveside.

Anger melted from Danny's heart, replaced by renewed pain as the finality of this loss pierced his soul.

"No." He could say no more as his father held him while he sobbed.

When he thought the tears could flow no more, Danny looked up. "Why? Why does James have to suffer so? He loved Anne. Why?"

Daniel was silent for a moment before speaking. "I have no words of wisdom to impart to you." Danny noticed tears welling in his parent's eyes. "I know not the why. I just know we must trust God, despite not knowing the answers."

Danny stared silently at his father, then they trudged side-by-side back to the cabin.

A few neighbors from Deer Run brought the grieving family pans of freshly made bread and stews. Danny stared numbly at the offerings. The empty pit in his belly could not be filled due to the constriction in his throat. It was all he could do to swallow his tears.

His sister Polly, her face reddened from crying, sat beside him. She did not speak but she briefly squeezed his hand. That was how it was with his sister. They were there for each other, in good times and bad. Words were usually not necessary.

"Danny." The gentle voice of his Uncle Nathaniel stirred his dulled senses. "You asked me to tell you when the sun was low. You need to return to Springfield, lad."

He forced himself to his unsteady feet.

"Yes, of course. Thank you, Uncle."

He approached his brother James and threw his arms around him. Neither spoke — neither could. After a moment Danny forced his arms to release his twin and he turned sadly away.

Their mother reached out toward Danny and hugged him tightly. "I wish you did not need to go."

"I know." Danny kissed her cheek and gently forced his way out of her arms. "I love you, Mother."

"God speed, my son." The words sobbed from her throat.

Danny's father followed him out to the barn.

"So…you must return to the armory."

"Yes, Father. They only let me have the day off for the burial."

Daniel Lowe seized his son's shoulders and held him tightly. Danny clung to his father for a long moment then released him.

Climbing onto the rented mare, Danny glanced down the road toward Springfield, then looked at his father. There was so much he wanted to say but words would not alleviate the pain they all felt. And discussing their loss would not change a thing. It never did. He tipped his hat and set his eyes on the road ahead, before urging the roan onward.

Galloping along the hardened dirt road toward Springfield, he could not get out of his mind the words spoken by the gossiping attendees at the burial:

"It's a curse, I tell ya."

Was there a curse? Did his father's past as an enemy soldier carry with it a tragic destiny for the family? Would anyone daring to love a descendent of Daniel Lowe be declared anathema and rejected by God? First it was Deborah. And now Anne.

Rage surged through him anew. He kicked harder at the sprinting horse. Chilled evening air made his teeth ache as he breathed with his mouth open, tears flowing down his cheeks. He hoped that every pounding gallop on the road would distance him from the pain of his brother's loss, as well as his own painful loss four years before.

Deborah. If only I had not cared for her, perhaps she, too, would still be alive.

After a mile or two, he slowed the laboring horse to a steady trot.

Feeling numb in his emotions, he stared at the road ahead as if in a trance.

Nearing his destination, a good twenty miles from Deer Run, Danny coaxed the animal to a slow walk. Entering the stable near his barracks at the armory, he made a decided resolve.

I may be only twenty-one, but I shall never marry. I'll not take the chance that Missus Endicott was right. Perhaps there is a curse on us because of our father. Perhaps we do bear the mark of condemnation on us forever. Maybe we are the accursed ones.

He dismounted the sweating animal, removed the saddle from the fatigued horse, and began brushing her with swift, hard strokes.

Footsteps approached behind him — a shuffling, familiar gate. *Ezra Pritchard.* This was just the person Danny did *not* wish to see.

Ezra stopped near him, uncharacteristically quiet.

"So…how fares your family, Danny? Your brother?"

Danny paused in the brushing to observe his fellow workman at the armory.

"As well as can be expected." Danny turned away and resumed his task.

Ezra's large hand grabbed his arm to slow down the frantic strokes on the horse's withers.

"Come on, lad. Let's go to the tavern. I know you're always sayin' it's not for you, but let us quaff a couple of ales and you'll be smilin' again."

Danny looked at Ezra, who stood as tall as himself, with suspicion.

Since when did Ezra ever want to do anything for me?

"I spent all I had on my journey. I've nothing left for visiting the tavern." *Why doesn't he just leave?*

"Hey…it's on us. Your mates want to help. Join us. You'll forget your family's sorrow after a few swigs of the good creature."

Danny filled the feeding trough with fresh hay, then gave the mare a bucket of water. He stood for a few moments and stared at the open doorway that revealed a waning spring sunset.

Why not? A few ales will help me forget – at least for one night.

"All right, then. When do we leave?"

Ezra beamed. "The lads are getting together now. Come on."

He put his arm around Danny's shoulders and they walked toward the barracks.

Tomorrow is Saturday – only a community day anyway helping raise the new meetinghouse. What's an ale or two before an easy workday?

Chapter 2
Susannah

Susannah Dobbins surveyed the outline of the rooftops outside her bedroom window. Try as she might, she could discern nothing even remotely familiar in their shadowed shapes.

And why should it be? Springfield is nothing like Boston. Springfield – despicable place.

It was easier being angry than sad about the move. Leaving the only home she had ever known, it helped her to feel outraged rather than give in to tears. Sometimes.

Why did Father make me leave everyone?

While she knew he was still grief-stricken over her mother's death eight months before, did he not understand that this move was the final nail in her own heart's coffin? Not only was her best friend, Verity, not within visiting distance, but Susannah's maid, her constant companion since childhood, was unable to accompany them. Fanny's upcoming nuptials prevented her from moving the hundred miles to stay with Susannah.

And now I will miss her wedding.

She wanted to cry. Wondering if her source of tears had dried up like the lake during the drought last summer, Susannah rubbed her cheeks below her eyes. Still no tears.

I am drought-stricken.

The open window welcomed in swirls of cool breezes, which caused her to shiver through her thin chemise. Stepping back from the chill, she draped a grey shawl across her shoulders. Playing with the folds of soft wool, she sauntered back, this time perusing the stars. There was some comfort in the knowledge that her friends in Boston might be gazing at the same stellar canvas.

I wonder if Elias is looking at the stars. I wonder if he is thinking of me.

Elias Hopkins was the handsomest lad in her northside neighborhood. Verity loved to tease Susannah about the long gazes that Elias fixed upon her when she was not looking. Susannah always protested, saying that Elias had eyes for every girl. But she still wondered if Verity was right.

He does have the most gentle brown eyes.

Sighing, she pulled the shawl closer around her shoulders.

If I had stayed behind in Boston, perhaps we would have become promised to one other. After all, I am nineteen now. Old enough to be courted.

A tendril of hair fell across her eyes and she blew it away.

I wonder what Mother would think about Elias.

The instant her thoughts turned to her deceased parent, the drought in her eyes was replaced by a flood of tears.

"It is not fair, God. Why did you take my sweet mother away? Father, Stephen, and I need her." Sobs wracked her whole body.

It took her a moment before she realized that she had cried out loud. She threw her hand tightly over her own mouth, allowing hot tears to coat her fingers.

She heard a gentle knock on the door. "Susannah, are you well?"

Father!

Wiping her nose with the edge of her shawl, she swallowed back the tears in her throat.

"Yes, Father. I was just…reading aloud. I am sorry if I disturbed you."

"Are you certain, my dear? I can call Modesty if you'd like."

Modesty! A misnomer. A slovenly hill person if I ever saw one.

She immediately regretted her harsh thought.

"I am well, Father. Please do not disturb Modesty." *Please. She is the last person I wish to see.*

"Very well, then. Goodnight, my dear Susannah." His voice sounded tired and filled with defeat.

"Good night, Father." She wiped the drying tears from her face. Sniffing sharply, she was drawn once again to the open window by voices. Loud, raucous voices.

The armorers. Ghastly creatures, the lot of them.

Despite her disgust, she crept toward the sounds emanating from the street. The boisterous male voices grew louder the closer they came to the dirt road in front of her home.

She pushed up with her hands on the sill and looked out the window, forgetting to keep a grip on her shawl, which slid to the floor.

Fascinated yet appalled, she curled her lips into a frown, glaring at the drunken revelers.

One of the drunkards seemed to have more difficulty walking than the others. In the dim streetlight she could see his two companions supporting him, one on each side. The dark-haired man in need of assistance appeared more ill than rowdy.

Susannah leaned farther out to get a closer look and shook her head.

I do not know why this town tolerates such a public display. This daily drunkenness is shameful. Armory workers or not, they should be arrested. This would never be allowed in Boston.

She huffed at the thought that these workers should be considered so valuable that their nocturnal binges were coddled.

Insufferable.

Suddenly, the sickly-looking man carried by his friends looked up at her. He gazed at her for several seconds before she realized he could actually see her. Her mouth gaped in surprise and then shock when she discerned that her chemise was pulled lower than it should have been.

Gasping, she drew away from the window, flattened herself against the wall, and threw her hands over her bodice.

How much did he see?

Heat infused her cheeks as she grabbed her shawl off the floor. Throwing herself onto her bed, she blew out the candle and pulled her covers over her head.

I am so humiliated. Thank the good Lord that I shall never mingle in society with such a rogue.

Chapter 3
Church Raising

The wind near the river disrupted Susannah's carefully coifed curls. The voluminous brown tresses often vexed her on such blustery days, but today in particular.

Why did Father insist I help feed the workers? She inwardly groaned at the task and wished she were at home, consumed in her reading. Enmeshed in one of her favorite novels, Susannah could pretend she was elsewhere. Anywhere but here.

Standing near the loading ramp, she impatiently awaited the arrival of the ferry. Modesty's incessant chatter began to irritate her. The new maid was not shy in the least, and often lacked discretion.

Would she ever stop talking?

"Such a lovely day, is it not, Miss Susannah? Why, a finer April I've never seen. Even the river is fair peaceful. The ferry should be smooth as French silk—not that you'd want to be seen wearing French silk, mind you. Not with those frogs giving our fine sailors such grief on the high seas. My cousin in our fine Navy must be near beside himself with those seafaring Frenchy ruffians."

She paused for a moment and Susannah grabbed her opportunity.

"Perhaps, Modesty, we can put aside such political meanderings. After all, this church raising should draw our minds toward our work for God, should it not?"

Modesty's face turned a bright red, emphasizing the Irish auburn color of her hair even further.

"Aye, miss, you do speak God's truth." She looked at the ground as the ferry drew closer to the landing.

"Well, Modesty, here it is. Do watch your skirts on the damp wood." Susannah hiked up her gown a mere inch or

17

two. Looking back at Modesty, Susannah inwardly groaned as she observed the maid draw hers upwards several inches, exposing a sufficient amount of her stocking-covered legs to draw the obvious attention of three men stepping onto the ferry behind them.

Susannah blushed with humiliation when she heard them whispering and chuckling in a manner that one hears from workmen with their minds in the gutter.

Scoundrels.

She glared at the three, which promptly arrested any further laughter from the working class fellows.

Hill people. She huffed.

Standing next to the railing, Susannah glanced at her maid.

"You can let your gown down now, Modesty." She kept her voice low.

The maid quickly opened her chubby fingers and released the material, apparently oblivious to the stares she was getting. She was too busy taking in the surroundings, grinning from ear to ear.

"It's been many a day since I've ridden this ferry, miss. I so love an adventure."

Susannah rolled her eyes. "It's just across the river, Modesty. Not much of a journey."

"Aye, but it's such a delight." Her gaze wandered incessantly from the scenery to the faces of those on board. Suddenly her eyes seemed to lock on something. Or someone.

"Well, looka there, miss." Her lips slowly curved upward into a wide grin. "Now a finer face on a man I ne'er did see. Look."

Much to Susannah's horror Modesty pointed right at the last passenger boarding and spun Susannah to face him. After he boarded, he leaned over the ferry rail next to a friend, looking for all the world as if he would lose his breakfast into the swirling water of the river.

Susannah swung away, seething. "Do not do that again, Modesty. You have embarrassed me beyond words."

Intense heat flooded both cheeks as she stared down at the water, trying to appear aloof. Her bonnet flapped slightly in the wind and she grabbed the crown to be sure it would not lift from her head. Retying the ribbons holding the striped linen bonnet in place, she was startled by a slight commotion.

"Blast! There goes my cap." The dark-haired man who had caught Modesty's attention reached toward the water as if his hands could will the head covering back into his desperate grip. But the woolen hat sailed downstream, seemingly intent upon its own adventure.

Looks like someone in Hartford will be wearing that now. Susannah smirked.

"Poor lad. That'll cost him a half dollar at least." Modesty shook her head.

"It's only a hat. I'm certain he can replace it quite easily at my father's store."

"True enough, miss. But I wager that fifty cents will cost him dear." Modesty revealed a sly grin. "Perhaps I might comfort the man with some sympathy."

Susannah recognized that glint in her servant's eyes and she pulled back on Modesty's arm.

"We shall not approach that man. That is most unladylike."

Modesty snorted. "No one's ever accused me of being a lady, miss."

Not surprising.

"Even so, we shall not approach him. We have work to do today. Let us concentrate on how we may serve the workers raising the new church building."

Although Modesty appeared to disengage from the man and his friend, Susannah knew she had best keep an eye on her. It had been only two weeks since Susannah's arrival in Springfield, but Modesty's ways were easily recognized.

The ferry slowly made its way across the Connecticut with a lulling sound.

Modesty is right about one thing. This lovely day is a balm to my soul.

Inhaling the fresh spring air, Susannah's gaze slowly wandered toward the back of the ferry and, against her better judgment, came to rest on the now-hatless passenger.

With his cap gone, his dark brown hair gleamed in the

bright sunlight. Masses of curls stopped just past the nape of his neck, encompassing a face that was astonishingly handsome. He did not seem to notice her staring at him as he surveyed the water. His fine nose was straight, his jaw firm, and — what she could see of his lips in profile — were so full that they appeared to pout.

Susannah did not know how long she lingered on his visage, but when he turned her way, her stare was met by the greenest pair of deep-set eyes she had ever seen. His eyebrows furrowed and she snapped out of her trance, turning her face toward the far shore.

"So you noticed him too, miss." Modesty smirked playfully.

Susannah pretended to focus on something of interest on the far shore. "I've no idea what you mean."

Modesty snorted, but remained mercifully quiet.

It seemed like an hour had passed, but it took a mere fifteen minutes for the wooden ferry to reach West Springfield. As the ferry workers unfolded the ramp, it landed with a thud on the shore. The passengers disembarked. Susannah refused to look at the man who had monopolized her attention and followed the others on the pathway leading up the hill toward the building site. A group of men were being served breakfast on long tables set up for the gathering.

A middle-aged woman with cherubic cheeks and an impish smile approached Susannah.

"Good day, my dear. We have not been formally introduced but I have met your kind father and I do so see your resemblance to him. I am Missus John Ashley, consort of Deacon Ashley who is behind this inspiring project. Thank you for agreeing to help serve our workers on this noble construction of First Church."

The woman's smile was so engaging, Susannah could not help but feel her heart warmed.

"Good day, Missus Ashley. I am most anxious to be of service in this fine project. This is my maid, Modesty."

"Welcome to you, as well. And such a lovely day we are

blessed with!" The woman fairly oozed enthusiasm. "My dear husband says it is not just a fine project but a most necessary one. Why, the last meetinghouse was worse in the rain than if we'd been standing underneath an open cloud! But come, let me show you where you'll be helping."

Missus Ashley gently drew the taller young woman to the huge kettles of simmering stews.

"Here is an apron, my dear. No sense in soiling your fine dimity."

Susannah left her bonnet on to protect her skin from the sunlight, but removed her pelisse and laid it carefully on an empty chair. Tying the linen apron around her slender waist, she smoothed the crisp material and looked around, wondering where to start.

"Several new workers have just arrived, Miss Dobbins. Why don't you carry these plates to them?" The older woman handed her two plates and then two more to Modesty.

Walking toward the long cloth-covered tableboard, Susannah slowed her walking pace as her heart quickened. *The man with the green eyes.*

Modesty saw him at the same instant.

"Oooo, miss, there he is." She giggled, far too loudly.

"Hush, Modesty." Susannah whispered harshly, her cheeks flaming.

Taking a deep breath, she approached the hatless man and his friend.

"May I serve you, gentlemen?"

Why I am calling these workers "gentlemen"?

Susannah was all too aware that these men were not of her class.

So why am I so nervous?

"Thank you, miss." The blond-haired worker who still had his woolen cap intact grinned awkwardly. "Not exactly used to such service from a fine lady."

Susannah noticed Green Eyes furrowing his eyebrows sternly at his friend. Then those eyes met hers.

"Thank you, miss." He took the plate carefully and stared up at her before setting it down. Picking up his pewter fork, he gingerly moved the food around, as if afraid it might be poison.

She tried to smother her rising irritation. "Is the food not to your liking, sir?"

He looked up at her again and stared for a moment.

"'Tis fine, miss."

Where have I seen that face?

She started to move away, but the blond-haired friend gave an embarrassed grin.

"He's not quite himself today. Had too late a night with the boys. Didn't ya?" He poked his hatless friend in the side and laughed. The man turned a deep shade of red but did not look up at Susannah.

So that's where I've seen that face. The drunk in the street! Wretched man. And now here to help in the Lord's work? Outrageous.

She stalked away, followed closely by Modesty. The servant girl turned toward Susannah as soon as they were out of earshot.

"Did you see those fine green eyes? Wouldn't you like to look at those every morning?" Her enthusiastic giggles threatened to turn the conversation downright bawdy.

"Modesty! If you please! We will not indulge our salacious natures in our thoughts or our speech. Is that clear?"

The servant's countenance fell. "Yes, miss." Her voice lowered almost to a whisper.

Susannah turned back toward the kettles to collect more serving plates.

Why did Father ask me to come here. I just want to go home.

At the thought of home, Susannah nearly burst into tears.

I cannot cry here. Certainly not in view of complete strangers.

She turned away from the kettles, widened her eyes and sniffed sharply. Refusing to give in to her grieving heart, she refocused on the task at hand.

The satiated workers began to vacate the tables one-by-one. Susannah watched most of the men stretch their limbs and pat their leather work belts before heading toward the wood frame of the new church building. But Green Eyes remained at his table, eating slowly.

Clearing away the dirty plates, Susannah felt someone's

hands gently grab her arms from behind. Missus Ashley was at her side, her sparkling smile brimming with mischief.

"Miss Dobbins, why don't you sit for awhile? You've been working so hard and you are still recovering from your long journey to Springfield. Come sit here, my dear."

Much to Susannah's horror, Missus Ashley navigated Susannah over to the table where Green Eyes sat. He was obviously laboring to finish his first plate when Missus Ashley plopped Susannah down on the bench next to him, much too close.

She quickly inched away.

"Miss Dobbins, I would like you to meet Mr. Daniel Lowe. He is one of our fine workers at the armory as well as a regular congregant of First Church. A fine Christian man."

Susannah narrowed her gaze.

She wanted to say, "Is that so?" Only her mother's training in manners rescued her from inflicting insult.

She cleared her throat.

"So pleased to meet you, Mr. Lowe."

"Miss."

"There. Now you are acquainted, I shall return to my tasks." Missus Ashley gave a positively mischievous grin to the two before heading back to the kettles.

An awkward silence followed the departure of Missus Ashley, though Susannah could hear the woman giggling in the distance with another cook.

Side-by-side, they both looked down at the table. Susannah fidgeted with her thumbs and Mr. Lowe nervously rubbed his hand through one side of his hair. Just when Susannah thought she could not take the tension any further, the workman spoke up.

"Miss Dobbins, it is quite obvious how…uncomfortable…you are in my presence. Please do not feel obliged to remain here and entertain me." His voice was surprisingly smooth and well spoken. Not at all what she imagined.

She glanced up at his eyes, which were fixed upon her. She cleared her throat.

"Mr. Lowe, it is not that I am uncomfortable..." She closed her mouth when he began to shake his head and gave a low, dismissive grunt.

"Please, Miss Dobbins. There is no need to explain. 'Tis quite obvious that I am not...shall we say...well-suited to your station in life." His face grew sober and he rubbed his head as though it were in pain.

"It is not just your station, sir..."

"Ah, see, I was right."

She flustered and sat up straighter. "That you are a workman notwithstanding, your behavior of last night was appalling. I find it quite shocking that you would carry on with your drunkenness and then make a mockery of helping to build a church. The Lord's meetinghouse!"

Mr. Lowe glared back. He kept his voice low but his words were pointed.

"Is it your custom, Miss Dobbins, to display yourself at your window for all to see?"

Susannah gasped and threw her hands across her bodice.

"How dare you accuse me of such behavior! I...I...was merely preparing to retire for the night when I was disturbed by you and your drunken friends."

His gaze penetrating her to the core, Mr. Lowe leaned closer.

I wish his eyes were not so disarming. He was leaning so close she could feel his breath.

"You seem to so easily pass judgment on me, Miss Dobbins."

She thought she saw pain glaze across his expression. He continued. "You know naught of me. And perhaps it is better that way...for both of us."

He grabbed his cloth napkin and wiped it fiercely across his mouth. Throwing it on the table, he stood up and lifted his long legs one at a time over the bench. Grabbing his hammer from his work belt, he stormed toward the construction site.

She sat there for a moment, heart pounding and temples throbbing.

Insufferable man!

Within moments, Missus Ashley appeared.

"I see you two were getting to know one another." There was that impish smile lighting up her soft face.

"Yes. We certainly were."

Susannah's throat felt parched, making it difficult to swallow. She grabbed a tankard of cider and took a long, unladylike swig.

Still shaking from the encounter, she barely concentrated on listening to Missus Ashley.

"...such a shame about his family..."

Susannah was suddenly alert. "Shame? What shame?"

She noted the older woman's sad expression.

"Why, his brother's wife—his twin brother, no less. The wife died giving birth, poor lass. Dan has not been himself since he got the news. Rode twenty miles to and from the burial just yesterday, I hear."

Deep regret swarmed over Susannah's heart.

Looking down at her lap, she stammered. "No. No...I did not know."

"Dan is very close to his family. But work was not to be found in his village of Deer Run so he had to leave and find work at the armory. And a right fine worker he is, says Mr. Ames. He's the superintendent, you know."

Missus Ashley paused briefly.

"Are you alright, my dear? You seem rather pale. Perhaps you should sit under the chestnut tree and rest."

"Yes, perhaps I should."

She rose with difficulty and managed to make her way to the shade of the overhanging limbs, despite her tremulous limbs. She sat on a blanket that Missus Ashley laid on the ground. Leaning back on the trunk, she exhaled slowly.

So he grieves as well. What have I done?

Chapter 4
Shop

The swift breeze slammed the door so hard, the glass nearly shattered.

Danny glanced sheepishly at the merchant. "I am sorry, sir. I did not realize the wind was so blustery this noon."

His greeting was met with the man's friendly smile. "Good day, Mr...."

"Lowe. Daniel Lowe Jr. I fear I was in too much of a hurry. Please forgive me for nearly ruining your entrance."

The merchant smiled even wider. "No harm done, Mr. Lowe. Charles Dobbins at your service." He extended his hand but Danny hesitated.

"I have just come from work and my hands are soiled, to say the least. There is just a short break before I must return, so please forgive my appearance."

"No need to apologize for hard work, Mr. Lowe. My father often came home for his noon meal with grit on his face and hands."

"Mine as well." Danny began to relax. "I see by your new sign that you are now partners with Mr. Stratford."

"Yes, my brother-in-law. He is getting on in years and...well...his health is not what it once was. I moved here a few weeks ago from Boston with my daughter Susannah. Perhaps you became acquainted with her at the church raising?"

Heat rose in Danny's cheeks and he knew it was not because of the brisk walk from the armory. He wondered if his red skin was visible beneath the caked grime from work.

"Yes. Yes, I believe we met."

He tried to think of something else to say, but further words choked in his throat.

Mr. Dobbins glanced at his clean fingers as if studying them and then met Danny's eyes. "I hope my daughter was pleasant enough. She...she is still much-aggrieved over the loss of her mother last year." He paused briefly and, in a lower tone, said, "I know that I am." Mr. Dobbins then busied himself straightening out a pile of cravats sitting on the counter, awaiting display.

"I am very sorry, sir. I can only imagine your great loss. As well as your daughter's." Danny licked his lips nervously and wiped a finger across his nose, further spreading black soot.

"Thank you, Mr. Lowe." Appearing to recover himself, Mr. Dobbins continued. "When I received word that my brother-in-law was looking for a partner, I grabbed the opportunity to relocate. My son, Stephen, is a lieutenant stationed at the armory. I thought it would do us all good to be together. At least, until Stephen's next assignment." He smiled wryly.

Danny raised his eyebrows.

"Lieutenant Dobbins? I know him well. A fine soldier and one all the lads admire and respect."

Mr. Dobbins beamed. "Thank you, Mr. Lowe. Those are words to please a father's heart. Now, forgive me, you said you were in a hurry and I am detaining you. What may I help you with today?"

"A wheel cap, sir. I lost mine a few days ago. It fell in the river."

"Oh, my. Difficult to be without one, I dare say. Let's see what we have." Mr. Dobbins pulled down two different styles, one woolen and the other duck cloth.

"I'm afraid I need the woolen one, working around the fire and all. I've already lost one in the water — I don't need the next one burned up!"

Wiping his hands on the back of his breeches, he picked up the black hat carefully so as not to get any soot or grease on the new wool. Danny donned the cap and set it down on top of his mass of dark curls, pushing down slightly on the short bill.

"Fits well." Taking it off, he looked at the price posted and his eyes narrowed. Fumbling in his pocket, be drew out several coins and began to count them. He stopped and then counted them again.

Mr. Dobbins cleared his throat. "You have just the right amount there, sir. A fair trade for one of our fine armorers."

Danny shot his glance upward and shook his head. "No sir, I am short several pennies."

Mr. Dobbins glanced back at the stack of hats.

"Oh, I see the confusion. I neglected to put up the sale sign. I have lowered the price in celebration of our grand opening of Stratford and Dobbins Mercantile. I apologize that I neglected to post it hastily enough." He grinned amiably. "You have the exact change, sir."

Danny blinked. He could not believe the man's generosity.

After a few seconds, he recovered himself. "Thank you, sir. A most fortunate sale." He nervously put the new hat on his head and grinned. "I am grateful, sir." He stretched out his hand to shake the merchant's and then withdrew it quickly, remembering the state of filth on his fingers.

Mr. Dobbins put his hand out and warmly grabbed Danny's. He shook it tightly.

"I hope to do business with you again, sir."

"I hope so as well, sir. Good day." He doffed his new cap at Mr. Dobbins and exited, just as Susannah entered. He nervously doffed his cap at the merchant's daughter. "Good day, Miss Dobbins."

She blushed a deep shade of red. Her voice was so low, Danny had to bend near to hear her.

"Good day, Mr. Lowe."

Danny fairly ran out the door, though careful to close it gently this time.

It was a half-mile climb to the armory. He raced up the dirt road faster than usual, in a hurry to return to work.

But he was even more anxious to get away from Susannah Dobbins.

* * *

Susannah winced and covered her nose with her perfumed kerchief after Mr. Lowe's retreat. Recovering from the odor of heavy labor, she breathed in deeply as if fresh air were necessary to revive her.

Mr. Dobbins frowned.

"Is that truly necessary, Susannah?"

"Father, he was filthy. Did you not notice his face and hands? And that smell! Do they not provide soap and water at the armory?"

"The lad has been working since four-thirty this morning. Stephen tells me these armorers are hard at work well before sunup each day and usually after sunset as well. They forge iron over hot fires and on grinding stones, file the stocks for muskets, hammer day and night—all to make arms to protect our country. To protect *you*, Susannah. Do you think they can work this hard without a bit of sweat and grime?"

Susannah glanced at the floor, feeling the heat of shame rising in her cheeks. "I suppose someone must do the laborious tasks. It is fortunate that the hill people are here for just such labor." She returned her kerchief to her pocket. When she looked up again, the disappointment on her father's face took her aback.

"Susannah, you are becoming positively pompous. It is the root of pride, you know, assuming you are better than they."

Susannah bit her lip at the sting of his words. Tears welled and she tried with great difficulty to hold them back.

"I am sorry, Father. I did not mean to be prideful. I am just…" She could not go on as her face flooded with the moisture from her grief.

Mr. Dobbins walked around the counter and put his arm across her shoulder. "I did not mean to upset you, my dear. It's just…since your mother left us, you seem to be so sullen, so bitter. I miss your gentle disposition. This unpleasantness does not suit you." He kissed the top of her bonnet.

She sniffed and searched his face. "But Father, you must know how much more difficult it is for me now coming to a strange, new place. Being torn from my friends, from Verity and Fanny. And…and Elias. The core of my heart is wounded and lonely."

Mr. Dobbins squeezed her shoulders.

"And that is why I have invited your friend Elias to our party this weekend at our home."

Susannah gasped. She finally found her voice and jumped up and down. "Elias? Coming here? Oh Father, thank you!"

She could not contain her joy as she threw her arms around his neck and kissed his cheek.

Just then, Susannah heard the shop door close and she whipped around to see who had entered. Standing proud, a young officer bowed politely, sweeping his tall lieutenant's cap into a graceful bow.

"Good day, dear sir and kind miss." A mischievous grin widened. "I must say, if those female kisses are available in this shop every day, I will indeed visit this fine establishment regularly."

Blushing, Susannah giggled and glanced at her father. She noticed with dismay that he frowned.

The young officer grew serious. "I jest, sir. Under the circumstances, I hoped a bit of humor would provide a respite from our long work day."

Mr. Dobbins continued to frown as he held out his hand to the young man. "My name is Dobbins. And you are?"

"Lieutenant Morris, sir. At your service." He gave a slight grin as he shook hands.

He's trying to appease my father's irritation.

"And this is my daughter, Miss Dobbins."

The officer turned toward Susannah and winked on the side facing away from her father.

"Enchanted." He bent down to kiss the back of her hand.

Susannah's face stayed warm. She could feel her father bristle, so she pulled her hand away. "Thank you, sir."

Despite her father's reaction, Susannah could not help but be enthralled with the officer's charm and good looks. His skin was olive and his hair nearly black, which gave him an exotic look, only enhanced by the flamboyance of his attitude. Penetrating brown eyes practically wooed her to distraction.

She shook herself. "Well then, I must look for more ribbons. That is, after all, why I came in." She twisted herself away from the gentleman and walked back to the corner of the store where she tried to keep her occasional glances at the officer discreet.

Lieutenant Morris purchased some tobacco and, with great flair, sniffed the sweet new wad and inserted it into his pouch. Flipping his coattail aside, he elegantly stuffed the pouch into an inside pocket. Susannah glanced toward the man briefly when she heard him complete his transaction.

He gave a most charming smile as he clicked his heels together and bowed.

"Miss." He winked again, then sailed out the door, leaving a scent of flowers behind.

Susannah stared after him, then heard her father clear his throat brusquely.

"Found your ribbons, my dear?"

"Yes, yes, several." Deep in thought, she paused. "Do you suppose the officers of the armory might be invited to our party after the Sabbath? In celebration of the church being raised, of course."

Her father looked down at the jar of tobacco he was putting away, then glared at her.

"If your brother wishes to invite anyone, he may." He plopped the jar back onto the shelves. "I must also inform you that all the workers who raised the church are invited Sabbath next to celebrate."

Susannah stood there numbly. "All the workers?" She swallowed nervously.

"Yes. All." He stared at her pointedly.

"Father, must you invite all the armorers, as well?"
Please, Father, not Mr. Lowe.

"Must we go through this again? You will treat others as equals. It is the Christian thing to do."

Susannah sighed. "Very well. But I shall soak my kerchief in perfume before the night's events. Just in case they forget to bathe." She strutted over to her father and he kissed her face gently. "Thank you for the ribbons, Father." Her defeated voice was tinged with sadness.

He tilted her head up toward his.

"Who knows? You may have a joyous evening, after all. Remember, Elias will be there."

"Yes. Elias." Just the thought of him warmed her heart. "Thank you, Father."

Turning away, she exited the door and held her bonnet close to her head in the breeze as she walked the two blocks to their home.

Lord, help me to tolerate the presence of the hill people – right in my own house!

Shaking her head she walked with her head down the rest of the way home.

Chapter 5
Party

Susannah squirmed in the new church pew and dabbed her kerchief against her damp upper lip.

Did Father speak to the reverend about me?

Conviction twisted her soul as the reading from the second chapter of the Book of James continued:

"For if there came unto your assembly, a man with a gold ring, in goodly apparel, and there came in also a poor man in vile raiment; and ye have respect to him that weareth the gay clothing, and say unto him, Sit thou here in a good place; and say to the poor, Stand thou there, or sit here under my footstool: Are ye not then partial in yourselves, and are become judges of evil thoughts?"

"Evil thoughts." Tears overflowed her eyelids and fell onto her lap. *I have been entertaining evil in my heart.*

Her brother, Stephen, nudged her arm. He leaned close and whispered. "Are you all right?"

Meeting his concerned gaze, she nodded "yes" and blotted the moisture with her kerchief. Stephen gently squeezed her arm and looked up toward the pulpit again.

Lord, I beg your forgiveness.

Glancing toward the far side of the newly-erected meetinghouse, Susannah noticed Dan Lowe sitting next to two of his friends. She recognized one of the fellows as the worker who had accompanied him the previous week for the church raising.

The message of the sermon now complete, the reverend shifted to a new topic. He praised all the fine workers who had helped with the building, in particular the surrounding farmers, armory workers, and especially the nearby ship builders who had hoisted the belfry and steeple to its new home atop this "glorious new meetinghouse."

Smiling faces throughout the new interior nodded assent. A musician set up his bass viol on the stage and led the congregation in a closing hymn. Everyone stood for the song and Susannah tried not to be obvious with her stares toward the handsome armory worker.

I must ask him for forgiveness. I have been prideful beyond words. Of course, I must not let him think that this is anything more than an apology. I will make my confession brief and to the point.

As the music ended, Susannah donned her Indian wrap and followed her father and brother to the main door. The pleasant smell of fresh cedar from the new pews seemed to waft through the air the more churchgoers moved from the benches. Seeing she was about to approach the doorway at the same moment as Mr. Lowe, her pulse quickened and her throat dried.

Why am I so nervous?

"Mr. Lowe."

"Miss Dobbins." Though his mouth was unsmiling, his green eyes held a hint of warmth.

She cleared her throat. "May I speak with you? Just for a moment, that is."

A look of confusion crossed his countenance. "Certainly. Let us discourse outside."

He allowed her to exit ahead of him and she stiffly walked down the stairs and onto the dirt walkway. Turning toward him, she glanced just for a moment at his face and then stared at her feet.

"Mr. Lowe. I...I do not know where to begin." She fumbled with the tie on her purse.

"My father always says 'Just start at the beginning.'"

At his half-smile, her emotions lurched from fear to embarrassment to intense attraction.

Why does he have to be so handsome? This is difficult enough.

Taking in a deep breath, she blurted out, "I am sorry."

He looked at the ground and then gazed at her with a meaning she could not discern.

"I am sorry as well. I had no cause to be so rude. Please forgive me." His green eyes mesmerized her.

Her own eyes widened, and she opened her mouth, but could not find words to respond. She forced her surprised thoughts to the back of her mind, and continued with her apology. Her face felt like it was on fire.

"It was I who was rude. And my heart, more treacherous still." She bit her lower lip.

He put his hands on his waist and glanced to the side, before looking back at her.

"You were right about me going to the tavern that night. You may not believe this, but it was my first time out with that group. And it will be my last."

Her heart filled with compassion.

"I extend my sympathies to you and your family. Such a tragic loss."

"To you as well. I am greatly saddened by your loss."

She noticed his mouth tremble slightly; then, with great effort, he seemed to stop the movement.

Meeting her gaze, he appeared to recover himself. "Well, then, both our consciences should be assuaged."

She drew in a sharp breath in anticipation of her next words.

"You will be coming to the evening party, will you not?"

He readjusted his new cap and cleared his throat.

"I do not know, miss. I have to work early tomorrow. Besides, I am certain you will be more comfortable with your own friends."

The heady scent of bayberry soap emanated from his clothing when his arm moved, completely changing her mind about their last encounter.

If only his lips were not so full. She pinched her arm. *Stop this!*

"All the workers from the church raising are invited. My father would be most regretful if you and your friends did not come."

Smiling warmly at him, she thought she noticed a look of panic in his eyes.

"I've nothing to wear, save this attire." His jaw twitched.

"You are welcome in this or any other attire." She felt her heartbeat flutter in an odd rhythm and she could not take her eyes from his.

She saw him swallow. "Very well, then. My friends and I shall be there at dusk. After Sabbath."

"Very well."

She gave a slight curtsy and turned around, her heart racing from the encounter. Approaching her father and brother, she saw they both smirked.

Narrowing her gaze, she huffed. "What are you both grinning about? I was merely paying heed to the reverend's sermon."

She whipped around and headed for the ferry that would take them back to their home across the river.

* * *

Shuffling through his clothes chest at the foot of his bed, Danny tossed aside one shirt, then another. He sighed in exasperation.

Nothing.

Ezra walked in and interrupted Danny's frantic search.

"Got a special evenin' with a lass, old boy?" He slapped Danny playfully on his shoulder.

The exasperated man sunk onto the side of his bed, shoulders stooped.

"Just an evening party. A celebration of the church raising. But my clothes are remarkable for how pathetic they are." Danny shook his head as he stared at the stained shirt in his hand—one more reminder of his meager income.

"Maybe I got somethin' for ya." Ezra went to his own box and looked through a pile of linen garments. "Here. This should fit ya." He threw the brown linen smock at his friend.

Danny held it up and inspected it for stains. Not a mark or hole could be found.

"Where'd you get this?" Danny eyed him suspiciously.

Ezra grinned.

"Well you may not agree with my gamblin' but last game o' cards I came home with the shirt from someone's back. But don't worry, I had Cassia wash out the smell."

Danny sniffed it and his eyes narrowed.

"Perfume?"

"Hey, Cassia said 'twas the only means to get out the stink. Take it or leave it."

"I'll take it." Danny silently whispered a prayer of thanks for the boarding house washerwoman.

He shed his white linen shirt and put on the borrowed one over his head.

"Well, look at you. The ladies will be beside themselves." Ezra grinned wide enough to expose a missing tooth.

"They'll have to look but not touch. This lad's not available." He buttoned his wool waistcoat over the shirt.

Ezra frowned. "What? You never said you had a lass back home."

"I don't. And I don't intend to ever have a lass — or get married." Danny pulled a comb through his thick locks.

"Then why ya primpin' like a schoolgirl, man?"

"It's a church event. I need to be looking my best. But not for the ladies."

Ezra grinned knowingly. "Right. And my name is President John Adams."

Danny threw his dirty shirt at his friend. He left Ezra laughing uproariously at his own joke.

Shaking his head, Danny threw his jacket over his shoulder, settled the wool cap, and headed for the party.

The air was still warm and smelled like the sun-drenched earth. In the waning sunlight, Danny could make out the buds on the maple trees starting to open. Passing the main armory building, he rounded the bend and saw two figures whispering to each other. He could not make out their faces but one of them was an officer, the other a workman.

They did not seem to notice Danny plodding on the soft moist earth nearby, but Danny perked his ears at their conversation.

Are they speaking French? He strained to listen, but the two must have seen him because they quickly parted and went their own way.

Danny did not know what to think. America was not on good terms with the nation of France.

Why would an officer of the United States Army be speaking

French? I must be mistaken.

Perhaps he was too far away to hear clearly enough.

Putting thoughts of political intrigue behind him, his mind drifted to another intriguing contemplation: *Why am I so nervous?*

The rising sweat on his brow was not from the strain of walking to the Dobbins house.

I am just anxious about this "gentry" affair. He scoffed. *Gentry.* Yes, he had already been on the receiving end of gentrified airs, directed at his mother by his paternal grandsire. Danny was proud of the way his father had stood up to his parent, not allowing their family to be separated. Had Danny's father relented, Danny and his twin brother would have been raised in the upper class in England while his mother and sisters would have been left behind in America.

Danny's cheeks burned with indignation. And sadness. Had his father agreed, the last four Lowe siblings would not even have been born.

He shook his head. *Get these thoughts out of your head.*

Voices floated toward Danny as he approached the two-story house. Right about now, he wished that his friends had agreed to come with him but none of them had the courage.

Danny looked up at the window where he had first seen Susannah the night he was coming home from the tavern. He had difficulty erasing the thought of Susannah as she hung out the window staring at the drunkards. Her hair draped around her shoulders, her chemise pulled low…

Better get that image out of your head. He swallowed and knocked at the door.

The effervescent laugh of the housemaid greeted Danny at the opened door.

"My, but are ya not handsome, Mr. Lowe. Come right in." Susannah's brazen maid, Modesty, grabbed his arm and led him in to the large parlor.

Danny suddenly wished he had not come. Elegant ladies were dressed in diaphanous gauze material layered in multiple tiers of muslin draped from below their bodices, and streaming down into soft folds to just above the floor. While their bodices were likewise covered, the point at which the material began its coverage was so low as to cause Danny's heart to leap and miss a beat.

Clearing his throat, his heart leapt again when Susannah approached him. It was all he could do not to glare below her bejeweled neck. Danny struggled to stay focused on her eyes. He bowed slightly, closing his eyes as he did so.

"Miss Dobbins."

"Mr. Lowe." She curtsied. "Thank you for joining us. Please come and greet my father."

Danny noted the outstretched hand of Mr. Dobbins and was once again struck by the man's friendliness.

"Welcome, Mr. Lowe."

"Thank you kindly, sir."

"Please come have some refreshment. In celebration of the new meetinghouse."

Danny followed him to a table where a large cake was decorated with an image of the new building. He grinned at the artwork on the sweet cake, as he gingerly took a piece from Modesty.

He swung around and noticed the stares of several attendees. Several of the ladies whispered to each other and giggled.

His appetite melted away faster than a chunk of ice on a summer afternoon. A feeling of nausea gripped his stomach as he set the uneaten piece of cake on the table.

Smiling at Modesty, he said quietly, "Thank you, but I am not hungry."

Modesty lowered her eyes then looked up at him. "I am sorry, sir." She gave an angry glance at the whispering women.

For the first time, Danny noticed the long fitted trousers of the gentleman guests. Glancing at his old woolen breeches that clung just below his knee and his homespun stockings, he felt heat rise in his cheeks.

The men's overcoats were finely tailored, long and form-fitting with wide collars. The attire looked as formal as the coats of the Army officers.

What am I doing here?

He barely noticed a somber Susannah staring at him from across the room as he excused himself to no one in particular.

Walking briskly toward the foyer, he grabbed the doorknob but felt someone's hand on top of his.

Susannah.

"Please stay, Mr. Lowe." Her blue eyes pleaded with him and her voice was a whisper. "Please—forgive my friends."

She squeezed his hand with her small fingers. A shiver warmed through his spine and awakened a hunger deep within him. But it was not a hunger that food could satisfy.

He tried to speak to her but the words caught in his throat, strangled by the pink fullness of her mouth and the earnest kindness of her eyes.

Just when he thought the paralysis in his voice would ebb, a tall, thin man with hair swept forward along his cheeks approached.

"Do you need any help, Susannah?" While the voice was directed at the woman, the glaring eyes bored into Danny's. The stranger drew Susannah's hand into the crook of his elbow. He only glanced away from Danny long enough to leer at her décolletage.

Something inside Danny reared with rage.

Susannah broke the tension.

"Elias Hopkins, please make the acquaintance of Mr. Daniel Lowe. Elias is a friend from Boston, Mr. Lowe." Her voice sounded strained during the introduction.

Elias nodded curtly and Danny doffed his hat to the unfriendly suitor. Neither exchanged pleasantries so Susannah spoke up.

"Elias, I was just trying to convince Mr. Lowe to stay and enjoy the refreshments. He did a great deal of work helping to raise the church."

"I daresay, Susannah, perhaps Mr. Lowe has other obligations, such as laboring before sunup. I hear the workmen are in such a habit." Elias practically sniffed when saying "workmen."

Susannah glared at him and quickly turned back to Danny with wide, apologetic eyes. She seemed to swallow with difficulty.

"Mr. Lowe, please feel welcome to stay." Her lips trembled.

"It is all right, Miss Dobbins. As the man says, we workman are up before sunrise." He tipped the short brim of his hat once again and exited, trying not to slam the door shut.

He paused on the stoop and closed his eyes for a moment.

I shall never come back here again.

Determination in his steps, he strode back up the hill toward the armory.

Go back where you belong.

Cool night air rustled his hair and felt soothing against his inflamed cheeks. He kept his eyes on the ground so as not to trip in the dark. But as he approached a tavern on the corner, he heard giggling from both a woman and a man. Then the soft undertones of a male voice and the unmistakable phrase: "Enchanté, ma chérie."

Whipping his head toward the sound, he observed in the dim streetlight the swooping motion of an officer's hat greeting a lady of the night.

More giggling ensued as the unidentified officer grabbed the woman and began kissing her neck before navigating the receptive female inside the tavern door.

The door closed and Danny stood with his mouth agape.

Could there be a spy in their midst? And to whom should he report this suspicion?

Normally he would not hesitate to go to one of the officers about this possible enemy infiltration. An armory could be a prime target for subterfuge and theft of valuable weaponry.

But knowing the spy could be an officer in the Army, which one could he safely approach? This new quandary only added confusion and despair to his already hopeless outlook.

God help me.

He returned on the path back to the barracks. There was a weight on his spirit heavier than a blacksmith's anvil.

Crawling into his bed amidst his sleeping, snoring

comrades, Danny pulled the quilt up to his neck. Clutching the blanket wrought lovingly by his mother four years before, Danny rolled onto his side.

I wish I had never had to leave Deer Run.

Chapter 6
Return

Mary Lowe stared at the letter from her oldest son.

Sitting on an old tree stump, she put the parchment on her lap and tried to control her trembling lips.

Lord, Danny needs Your comfort. Please be his strength.

Wiping a single tear, she glanced at nineteen-year-old Polly pushing the front door of the cabin open with her hip while lugging a basket of dirty clothes outside.

"I cannot bear this odor one more moment." Polly set down the load. "Do we have to wait for Monday next to wash these?"

Mary sniffed away a remaining tear and forced a subdued smile. "No. I daresay spring planting has increased the dirt beyond the need for only one day of washing. Let us fill the kettle."

Both women began lugging bucketfuls of water from the nearby well to the huge outdoor kettle perched over a pile of kindling.

Mary could feel Polly's intense gaze.

"Are you well, Mother?"

"You can always sense my mood, can you not?"

"I saw you reading the letter from the postrider. Is all well with Danny?"

The look of concern on Polly's features only enhanced her beauty. Mary paused in her task, enjoying her daughter's sweet expression that was so like the girl's father. Polly received green eyes from her mother and blond hair from her grandfather, but the overall appearance of the young woman revealed to anyone who paused long enough to notice that she was indeed the daughter of Daniel Lowe, Sr. At times the resemblance was startling. Like now.

Mary reached out with one hand and stroked her

daughter's cheek. "Danny says he is well, but a mother knows her child. I can tell he is burdened." She smiled bravely although her heart was not in it.

"I shall pray for him. Is it because of Anne's death?"

"Yes. But something more seems to be wrong. I cannot say what. And he did not reveal it." She stroked away strands of hair from Polly's face. "It is difficult when children are so far that we cannot wipe their tears away any longer."

Polly dropped her bucket on the ground and flew into her mother's arms.

"I hope to never be that far away from you." Polly squeezed Mary for several moments before they kissed each other's cheeks and resumed their work.

* * *

As late afternoon brought diminished daylight, Mary watched Daniel and their sons, James and Ephraim, drag their feet up the road toward the cabin. James drove the team of oxen past their home and down the road toward the Eaton house where the animals were stabled. James spent most evenings there so he could be with his infant daughter, who was cared for by Mary's sister Sarah.

Mary opened the door and greeted her men.

Waving at James as he strode by with the huge beasts, she yelled, "Give my love to Mother and Sarah...and all the rest."

"I will." James held the reins lightly as the oxen needed little encouragement to head back to their home.

Her attention was drawn to ten-year-old Ephraim who was heading for the front door.

"Ephraim! You are covered with dirt. Wash up at once," Mary ordered.

Daniel smiled at his youngest son. "Thought you'd get away with it, eh? Your mother's eye is quite sharp." He laughed and tousled the boy's dark hair.

Ephraim twisted his face. "Nothing wrong with dirt. I'm hungry."

Mary walked toward him and checked his fingers. "Keep scrubbing, young man. Then you can find a bit of dried fruit to stay your appetite 'til the girls get home from school."

She could hear the girls giggling in the distance as Polly walked them home from the schoolhouse. Mary placed her hands on her hips and shook her head. She could not help but smile at the sound, although she knew without Polly's prompting, they would dawdle the entire way home. The sound of their laughter approaching always warmed her heart.

Prissy came out of the house and looked in the direction of the voices. "They're a bit late today. I was wondering where they were."

Mary watched the group emerge from the woods on the well-worn path. Polly had an especially large grin on her face and was more jovial than usual.

"Polly has a boyfriend, Polly has a boyfriend." The words were being chanted by all three girls: Sally, Alice and eight-year-old Betsey, Daniel and Mary's youngest.

Polly turned a bright shade of red and protested the chant.

Mary glanced quickly at Daniel, who had nearly finished washing up at the basin. His face was somber.

"What is this?" Mary smiled inquisitively.

Betsey blurted out before the others could spill the news.

"Polly likes our new schoolmaster! She was doing this." Betsey batted her eyelashes and stared adoringly at Mary, causing her mother to burst out laughing.

"Is this so? And tell me about this new schoolmaster." Mary tilted her head at Polly, who looked at the ground and blushed as red as a harvest of new beets.

"They are being ridiculous." Polly glared pointedly at her younger sisters as she tucked a wayward strand of hair back under her linen cap.

Prissy joined in the sisterly fun. "Pray, tell us about him, Polly. We are all ears."

Polly met her mother's gaze. There was an unfamiliar look in Polly's eyes that revealed the truth to Mary. She knew it would be there someday. And that day had now arrived. She was clearly enamored with a young man.

Mary glanced again at Daniel and noticed he stood still as stone. The look in his eyes told her that he knew it as well. And she saw the pain in that knowledge. They had both tried to prepare themselves for the day their children would marry and leave home—perhaps leave Deer Run. Although they wanted their offspring to find love, the thought of them departing the family fold always left a void in their hearts.

She met Polly's eyes. "So tell me about him." Mary swallowed with difficulty.

"He's the new schoolmaster. He and his father recently returned to Deer Run. His father has been away a long time, he says, and is unwell so he wished to come home. His mother passed away several years ago and he and his father lived in New York, where he just finished his schooling. When his father saw the advertisement in the newspaper for a new schoolmaster, he quickly applied. He is so smart, the town hired him immediately."

Fourteen-year-old Sally smirked. "So smart—and so handsome!" All the sisters burst out laughing and began to bat their eyelashes in a mocking manner.

"Stop it, please." Polly rolled her eyes in exasperation.

Daniel walked over to the group of females. "Lassies, go inside." They immediately responded to his tone and ran to their cabin, giggling the entire way. Daniel stared at Polly. "Is this young man a Christian?"

"Yes, Papa. He said he was anxious to attend our services at the meetinghouse every Sabbath. He said his mother always took him to church from the time he was a child. His father, too, after he returned from war to their home in New York."

Mary tilted her head. "But you said his father was from here."

"Yes, before the war. Afterwards, they all lived in New York."

Daniel looked pointedly at his oldest daughter.

"So then what is his name?"

"Jonathan. Jonathan Grant."

Daniel drew in a sharp breath and blanched. Mary felt her own throat tighten.

Finally she was able to ask the next question with difficulty.

"And do you know his father's name?"

"Josiah," Polly said innocently. "He says his father's name is Mr. Josiah Grant. What a wonderful name from the Scriptures, is it not?"

Mary could not speak as her heart lurched uncomfortably.

Polly's expression twisted in discomfort.

"What is the matter?" Her question was fraught with consternation.

Jaw twitching, Daniel turned on his heels and limped with heavy steps back to the house. He turned around only briefly. "We shall discuss this later."

Entering their cabin, he slammed the door shut.

"What is wrong?" Polly asked. Her lips trembled.

"*You* have done nothing wrong, Polly. It is the situation that is most distressing." Mary gazed into the distance.

"Why? Because I like a man?" She gently grabbed Mary's arm. "Why is that distressing? You do not even know him."

Mary slowly turned back to her daughter. "No. But we know his father. And that is why your Papa is upset."

"Has he wronged Papa in some way?" Tears flowed down Polly's pale cheeks.

"Let us discuss this tonight — after the younger ones are in bed. Come. Let us serve up the victuals to our hungry men." Mary's attempt to smile failed as she returned to the house, followed by a distraught Polly.

The evening meal was nearly silent. Occasional somber glances by the girls at each other told Mary they knew better than to speak or mention the new schoolmaster. The only one unaffected by the tension was Ephraim who gobbled down two portions of venison stew. Polly picked at her food and occasionally wiped a tear that escaped. Daniel said not a word. Mary's stomach lurched with nausea.

All the girls grabbed the trenchers and tankards from the table and whisked them away faster than usual. It seemed only moments to Mary before the tableboard was clean and the girls enmeshed in their schoolbooks. Prissy helped Betsey with her homework.

Daniel spoke for the first time in nearly an hour.

"Mary. Polly. Come outside."

All eyes in the room grew wide as the three headed outdoors in the waning light.

"Let us take a stroll." Daniel's voice was controlled but firm.

Heading toward the barn, Daniel turned around and leaned against the wood siding. Putting his hands in his pockets, he faced Polly.

"Polly, I need to know your intentions toward Mr. Jonathan Grant."

The young woman shook her head in bewilderment. "Intentions? Of what do you speak? I only just met him."

"Good. Let me make this quite clear. You are not to form any attachment to this man, is that understood?"

"But Papa...why?" Tears brimmed once again.

"Because I said so. Your mother and I are well acquainted with this young man's father. That is sufficient for you to be told."

"Papa! You are judging him by his father? You do not know him."

"Polly, there is an old English proverb that I believe to be true. 'Like father, like son...How many sons inherit their father's failings.' I have known this to be so, many a time."

Polly glared at him through moist eyes. "Are you like your father, Papa?"

Her words appeared to jolt Daniel. "That is different. The circumstances are so different. I am talking about character, Polly."

"Could you just meet him, Papa, and judge for yourself?" Her voice was small and strained.

A look of pain crossed Daniel's countenance. "I am certain that I will be meeting the man if he is living in Deer

Run. But, I must insist—no attachments to the man. Is that clear?"

Polly's face fell. "Quite clear."

There was silence for a moment.

"May I go to bed, Papa?"

Daniel's face wrenched. "Yes, Polly. Rest well." He went to kiss her but she whipped around and hurried toward the house.

Staring after his daughter, Daniel stood silently for several moments before Mary spoke.

"I know we both dreaded the moment when Polly would notice a young man. But neither of us ever foresaw this." Mary sighed. "Daniel, are we doing the right thing?"

Daniel jerked his face toward her. "What choice do we have?"

Mary gaped at him. "What choice? Daniel, we have not even met the man. We have not even see Josiah after all these years. How do we know the situation? Are we so fraught with a lack of forgiveness we are not being rational?"

Daniel's jaw set. "Have you forgotten, Mary? The words he spoke? The bruises on your arms? The wretched way he treated us all?"

Mary touched his arm. "I have not forgotten, Daniel, but I have forgiven. And I have not forgotten the scarred and beaten-looking man who returned to war, never to come back. Until now." Mary squeezed his arm. "Daniel, please do not be so harsh."

He looked at the ground.

Mary took a deep breath. "Daniel, if Polly should be drawn to this Jonathan—as you and I were drawn to one another—how can you stop it? Can you destroy the love between a young man and a maiden? I was ready to run away with you if my mother forbade us. Remember, Daniel?" She put her hands around his waist. "Remember?"

"That was different." He wrapped his hands around her waist.

"Not so different. And I was the same age as Polly is now."

Daniel narrowed his gaze. "That cannot be. She is a child."

"She is not."

"Well, I am quite certain that Polly will listen to her papa. I have stopped any romantic attachment before it could begin. That should put an end to the concern."

"Are you so certain, Daniel?"

"No. But that is what I have to believe if I am to get any sleep this night."

Arms around each other's waist, they ambled back to the cabin.

* * *

The meetinghouse was abuzz with the news: A town war hero, Josiah Grant, had returned. To add to everyone's joy, he had brought his grown son with him, now settled in as the new schoolmaster.

Jubilant chatter seemed to burst from everyone in Deer Run—everyone except Daniel and Mary. Their somber faces were a stark contrast to the rest of the community. But the rest of them did not know the real Josiah Grant. Daniel's stomach clenched with bitterness at the memories.

The more the neighbors fawned over the Grants, the more rage consumed Daniel's thoughts.

How dare he return. I nearly put the thought of him out of my mind. And now he is back...with his son! The next generation ready to abuse an innocent woman — my daughter! This will never happen. Not while there is breath in my body.

"Daniel. Are you all right?" Mary held his arm and stared at him with concern. "We must go greet them. It is not right to ignore newcomers, especially not a revered veteran from the war." When Mary gently pulled him toward the friendly throng, Daniel caught a glimpse of Josiah.

Even though he recalled the ravages that smallpox inflicted on the man, it startled Daniel to see the devastation once again. He had nearly forgotten. The deep pockmarks had etched so cruelly into the war veteran's face; it was heartrending to view even in one's enemy. Josiah Grant was frightening to behold.

How did a woman see past the horror to love him — and bear him a son?

But there, standing next to Josiah, was the fruit of that union. And almost more startling than the vision of Josiah was the discovery that the young man was the image of his father before the illness. That resemblance was unnerving.

It looks like his father spat him out of his mouth.

Daniel could barely speak, he was so taken off guard.

Suddenly, he and Mary were face-to-face with the two and Daniel was forced to recover himself.

"Good day, Josiah. I see you have returned." Not a welcoming statement but it was all he could manage.

Josiah grasped Daniel's hand. "So good to see you, Daniel. After all these years." He turned toward the younger man. "Please say hello to my son, Jonathan." He looked at Daniel in gratitude. "Jonathan, this is Daniel Lowe, the man who helped your grandsire and me when we were ill. I am forever indebted to him."

Jonathan broke into a grin. "I am so pleased to meet you, sir. Father always speaks so highly of you." He shook a startled Daniel's hand.

"Yes. Well, I was only saddened that your grandsire did not survive. Your namesake, I assume."

"I hear he was a fine man."

"Yes, yes he was." Daniel remembered his manners and turned to his wife. "This is my wife, and my sons and daughters." He could not help but notice the inflamed look on Polly's cheeks during the introduction. She bloomed with happiness as Jonathan smiled at her.

"I have had the pleasure of meeting most of your daughters. I must say that Sally, Alice, and Betsey are fine students. Diligent workers."

Daniel was surprised that Jonathan already recalled his children's names.

"Their mother and I have taught them to be diligent — and obedient." He gave a sideways glance at Polly. She turned away.

"Well then, let us proceed into the meetinghouse."

Daniel encouraged his family forward, watching Polly carefully. She stole a glance at Jonathan and his gaze at her was far from just friendly. Daniel recognized that look all too clearly.

This is going to be a battle. One I am determined to win.

Chapter 7
Visit

It was a brilliant Saturday in early May, with warm air beckoning the Lowe children outdoors for play. With most of the chores already completed, chants of "Ring Around the Rosie" wafted through the open window.

Polly looked up from the chair where she was sewing a new shirt for her brother Danny. Her voice full of compassion, she broke the silence between her and her mother.

"Mother, did you hear Mr. Grant coughing at the meetinghouse Sabbath last?"

Mary looked up from kneading the bread dough.

"Yes, I did. I also noticed that you waited until your papa was gone to work in the field before discussing it." Mary met Polly's eyes with a pointed stare.

Polly looked intently at her sewing. She pricked herself with the needle by mistake and scrunched her face in pain. "Ouch!" Sucking on her finger she glanced at her mother.

Mary winced. "That is painful."

Removing her finger from her mouth, Polly spoke again, this time more boldly.

"Mother, Mr. Grant is quite ill."

"And how do you know this, Polly?" Mary paused in her kneading and put her hands on her hips.

Polly blushed. "Because Jonathan told me."

Mary's eyes narrowed. "And when exactly did he tell you this."

Shifting in her chair, Polly sat up straight and looked directly at her mother. "When I met the girls after school yesterday, I asked Jonathan about his father. It seems he does not have many months to live."

The news startled Mary and her face grew as pale as the wheat flour on her hands. "I see." Swallowing with difficulty, she then took in a deep breath. "And what would you like me to do?"

"The same thing you do for anyone in Deer Run who is

ill or dying. Send food. Send help." Polly grew flustered then blurted out, "Send some compassion!"

Mary's eyes widened. "You will speak to me with respect, daughter."

Lowering her eyes, Polly appeared remorseful for the outburst. "I am sorry to speak without respect, Mother. But please...I have never seen you lose your heart of compassion before."

An uncomfortable memory from years before pricked at Mary's conscience — similar words of accusation that she had directed at her own mother when Daniel had been ill and wounded. He also had been their enemy at the time.

Conviction wove its way across Mary's soul.

Lord, have I become so hardened as to be cruel? Forgive me.

Mary met her daughter's eyes. "No. No, I have not lost my compassion. I just misplaced it for a time." She attempted a brave smile. "You are right, of course. We must send some victuals and see if they need any other help. But please, do not say anything to your papa. I will tell him in my own time."

Prissy came in from planting the garden. "'Tis warming up quickly out there. I love the spring weather."

"It is lovely." Mary formed the raw dough into its final shape, set it on the floured bread peel, and opened the beehive oven. Sliding the wide wooden pallet into the warm enclave, she plopped the lump of dough onto the hot bricks and closed the door.

"Mmmm...I cannot wait to taste that fresh bread." Prissy licked her lips.

"Hold onto that appetite, Prissy. This loaf is going to a sick neighbor."

"Who is ill?"

"Mr. Grant."

Mary could not tell if the girl was more alarmed at the news her mother was delivering bread to the Grant home or the report about the man being ill. Prissy stood there quietly for a moment then appeared to come to a decision.

"I shall not inform Papa. About delivering the bread to the Grant's, that is."

"Good." Mary hurried to prepare another loaf for her own family. "Some things are best unspoken. I shall inform him at the proper time."

* * *

Approaching the old Grant homestead sent chills through Mary. It brought back so many memories of her youth, the war, and most alarmingly, the day of the encounter twenty-three years ago.

That day in 1777 remained unforgettable for both Mary and Daniel.

British soldier Daniel Lowe had been seriously wounded at the Battle of Saratoga. Mary and her widowed mother were hiding him in their cabin when the brash Josiah Grant came home for a visit, reportedly to visit his dying mother. It soon became obvious to Mary that he had come with other intentions. With her midwife-mother away delivering a child, Mary intercepted Josiah outdoors. He sought her embrace, assuming she wanted him physically as much as he desired her. When she refused him, he grabbed her arms, leaving bruises behind. Josiah threatened to rape her and Mary had been terrified that he would, until she accused him of learning his vile behavior from the British troops. He left her in anger, while Mary suffered from the terror of the moment. Daniel was inside the cabin the entire time, listening to the whole encounter. Wounded and weak, he'd fallen on the floor in an unsuccessful attempt to rescue her, and nearly reversed his slowly improving condition. Neither Daniel nor Mary ever forgot.

* * *

Mary shivered at the sickening memory.

I must not think about this. I will show compassion to a dying man.

Glancing at Polly who accompanied her, Mary prayed that her beautiful daughter would never know the fear that she had experienced that day so long ago.

Polly lifted her face up toward the sunlight, as if relishing the warmth. "I've never been to the Grant's cabin before."

"That's because it was closed up for over twenty years. You would have no cause to come here." Mary squeezed her daughter's arm. "Thank you for informing me about Mr. Grant. I am certain these recent years have been most difficult for him."

Polly's face grew inquisitive.

"So you knew Mr. Josiah Grant's father? Jonathan's namesake?"

Remembering the older gentleman elicited a smile from Mary. "Yes, I remember him well. Your papa does, too."

The young woman's eyes widened. "Papa? How?"

"When Mr. Josiah Grant came down with the smallpox, your papa was the only one in Deer Run who had already had that dreaded disease. It became your father's opportunity to show the townspeople that he was on their side — no longer loyal to the Crown. It was a daring venture for your papa as Mr. Josiah Grant had tried to turn him in to be hung as an enemy soldier."

Polly's eyes widened even further. "No!"

"Yes. But God watched out for your papa. Josiah Grant was won over by your father's kindness. And your father and the elder Jonathan Grant became fast friends. Sadly, Jonathan died of the disease, much to your father's distress."

Eyes narrowing, Polly appeared confused. "So if Mr. Josiah Grant and Papa became friends, why this hatred on Papa's part?"

"I would not call them 'friends' exactly. And there is more to the story that I do not choose to share. But your father has never gotten over his mistrust of Mr. Josiah Grant. And the fact that young Jonathan favors Josiah Grant when he was younger only revives dreaded memories further."

Polly was silent for a time, then spoke with courage.

"The reverend always says that we must forgive in our hearts. Is Papa's heart so unforgiving?"

Mary sighed deeply. "I cannot speak for your papa, nor

see into his heart. But we should all listen to the gentle prodding of the Holy Ghost when we need to examine ourselves, should we not?" She pointed a finger outward. "There is the cabin. We are here."

Jonathan hoed in the garden. Numerous weeds were piled high in a corner of the yard, still green from their recent scything. When Jonathan saw Mary and Polly, an excited smile erupted on the young man's face.

"Polly!" As if remembering his manners, he wiped his dirty hands on his leather breeches and approached the women. "Missus Lowe. Polly. How good to see you."

Bowing slightly from the waist in greeting, Jonathan stood and stared at the younger woman. Polly self-consciously curtsied and grinned from a face that was three shades redder than a moment before.

Mary cleared her throat.

"Mr. Grant, I have come to bring you some fresh bread from my oven. Not just to welcome you but to offer some sustenance for you and your father. I understand he is quite ill."

The exuberance on Jonathan's face faded as he glanced briefly downward. Meeting Mary's eyes, he replied, "Yes. Quite ill."

Sounds of a gut-wrenching cough followed this exchange and Jonathan jerked his head toward the cabin. "Let me check on my father. One moment, please." Running to the door, he flung the portal open and walked inside. Mary heard their voices but could not understand the conversation.

Jonathan ambled back outside and approached the women. "My father will be out forthwith. He is somewhat embarrassed by the state of our cabin." He looked at the ground sheepishly.

Polly perked a reply. "That is alright. My mother will wait to speak with him. Please...show me what you are planting." Walking side-by-side to the garden, Jonathan pointed to the various rows explaining what he'd planted.

"Hello, Mary."

She startled and spun to view the doorway. It took every

ounce of her strength to smile at the visage that greeted her.

Will I ever cease my shock?

"How are you, Josiah? I have brought you some bread."

Josiah smiled slowly, revealing a hint of his former handsome grin.

"So you must have heard." His grin faded.

Mary swallowed with difficulty and bravely faced him.

"Yes. Polly informed me of your illness."

He huffed. "Illness. That is one name for it. I prefer to call it what the doctors have told me." He looked up at her, pain filling his eyes. "'Tis a scirrhus that has spread to my lung. And there is nothing they can do."

Mary's face contorted in shock.

"Cancer?" The horrible diagnosis felt like a knife. "I am so sorry."

Josiah gave a mocking laugh. "A fitting end for a fool, some would say. I know I do." He looked at his feet while leaning weakly against the splintered doorway.

Mary quelled the nausea that threatened to overtake her.

"I would not call you a fool, Josiah."

He smiled wryly. "Well, you should. And I am quite certain your husband does."

Mary did not know how to answer.

Spasms of coughing racked Josiah. After a moment the cough relented. Mary moved swiftly to the well to grab a ladle of water. Approaching him, she ached at the deep pain in his eyes.

He drank the water carefully, savoring every sip. Handing the ladle back to Mary, his rheumy eyes glistened with emotion and regret.

"I am sorry, Mary. For everything. I have waited all these years to tell you in person. I prayed to God that I would be able to ask forgiveness of you before dyin'."

Mary's legs swayed until she forced them to stand firm.

"You are forgiven, Josiah. I forgave you a long time ago." Tears welled in her eyes.

"I do not deserve your mercy, Mary. But I am grateful for it."

Mary struggled to restrain her emotions. "None of us

deserves mercy, Josiah. For we all have sinned."

Josiah wiped off the tears that had fallen into the pockmarks on his cheek.

"Some of us worse than others." He glanced over at Jonathan and Polly. They were chatting amiably and Polly giggled at something he handed to her. "My Jonathan. I've naught seen him so smitten before." Growing serious, he continued. "I suppose your husband objects to him. Bein' my son and all."

Mary looked at the ground, struggling to find the words. "He is not pleased with the prospect of Polly becoming enamored of Jonathan."

The reality of the spoken words seemed to cause physical pain in Josiah, which sent him into further spasms. Wiping his face with the back of his hand, his eyes pled with Mary.

"Please. Do not let my son bear the curse for my sins. He is a good lad…the best. My wife — his mother — raised him to be disciplined and good, something my mother never did with me. I beg of you…" Tears poured unhindered with his plea.

Mary could no longer hold her own tears back.

"I shall speak to Daniel, Josiah. And I shall pray for you."

Wiping her moist face with the back of her sleeve, she handed him the fresh bread.

"Please accept this. And do let us know what else we may do to ease your pain."

Josiah looked at Jonathan and Polly.

"Give grace to my son."

She drew in a sharp breath.

"I shall try. Be well, Josiah."

Calling for Polly to come, she scurried back up the path toward home.

Dear Lord, only you can bring about this miracle.

Chapter 8
Information

Tearing the brown paper wrapping from the package, Danny held up the shirt.

"Thank you, dear Polly!" He unbuttoned his woolen waistcoat and all but ripped off his old linen shirt that, up until now, was the best he had. Slipping his arms through the smooth, woven sleeves, Danny shrugged his shoulders until the garment felt well placed.

"Now this is a decent shirt." Tucking it into his breeches, he glanced up to see his friend, Ansel, stop by the doorway to his barracks. Ansel grinned.

"Gift from a lady friend back home?" He winked at Danny.

"A gift from a lady, all right—my sister!"

"Ah, is she pretty and unmarried, then? I wouldn't mind meeting her—unless, of course, she resembles her ugly brother."

"No she does not. Poor lass if she did. But you may *not* meet her as she is far too pretty for your ragged face." They both laughed and Danny tucked his old shirt into the chest by the foot of his bed.

"Let's be off to the meetinghouse, then. Today of all days, I am grateful they continue the post rider on Sabbath. Else I'd be wearing my stained shirt."

The day was ripe with spring as the two traversed the steep hill down toward Boston Road and on toward the river. Maples and hickories budded everywhere and, even in the distance, the small erupting heads on each branch combined to paint a green landscape. Danny breathed in deeply, refreshed by the air. It was a stark contrast to the past six days of smoke-filled shops, where the fires continually spewed out choking ash.

Out of habit, he tossed an imaginary tail of long hair that for years had draped across his shoulder.

"Still missing that queue, eh?" Ansel smirked.

"Not exactly missing it. Just habit. At least, I no longer worry about it catching fire."

"Hey, did you hear about Congress?" Ansel's face brightened to share the news.

"What?"

"We are now officially exempt from military or jury duty as armorers employed by the United States Government. What d'ya think?" Ansel slapped Danny's shoulder.

"I think, 'Thank you, dear Congressmen of the United States.' Huzzah!" The friends laughed as they approached the line awaiting the ferry that would take them across the river to the meetinghouse.

Danny automatically glanced around for any sign of Susannah. He at once caught himself.

Don't be a fool. There is nothing to say to the lady anyway.

Watching the ferry draw near to the shoreline, Danny determined to forget about the winsome Miss Dobbins — no matter how alluring she was.

* * *

She knew she should be concentrating on the reverend's words from the pulpit. But Susannah could not erase the memory of Dan's face when he had left her party the week before. The guilt of that moment clung to her, causing the muscles in her neck to clench like an iron vise.

Her thoughts continued wandering.

How did I not see that side of Elias?

Then the realization struck her: She was blinded to his haughtiness because she had become exactly like him. She despised herself for the revelation.

God forgive me.

She knew she had already confessed to Him, but the pain she had seen in Dan Lowe's eyes as he left a week ago haunted her as she tried to sleep at night. Her father was right. She *had* changed. Now she was guilty by association.

After Dan had left that night, Elias bellowed a mocking laugh at the pathetic armory worker wearing those "wretched breeches so fashionable in the hills." A group at her father's party joined in the mockery. Susannah turned a scornful look at Elias, begged a headache, and excused herself. By the time she had finished crying alone in her room, the headache had become a reality.

She was jolted from her thoughts by the congregants standing up for the final hymn. Picking up her parasol, she somberly inched her way out of the seat following her father's lead.

"Are you well, my dear?" Her father touched her arm tenderly.

I hate to worry him.

Forcing a smile, she squeezed his arm back. "Yes, Father, quite well."

"Then let us enjoy this glorious weather with a picnic on the lawn."

She took her father's arm and the two walked out the double doors. They were alone today, since her brother was on duty at the armory.

"I wish Stephen were here."

Her father gave her a quizzical glance.

"Not Elias?"

Susannah firmed her jaw. "No. Not Elias." She inhaled deeply. "I have written him a letter, Father. I do not wish to further engage in friendship with him."

Mr. Dobbins grinned. "Good."

Glancing at her father sideways, she opened her mouth in surprise. "Why did you never tell me you did not like Elias, Father?"

"Had I done so, I might have pushed you toward him. That was the last thing I wished to do."

Susannah paused in their walk and looked intently at him. "Father, please promise me you will tell me what you think of my suitors. I wish to know."

"I will. It is just that, after losing your mother, I feared hurting you further by revealing my concerns about Elias. As far as his reputation and integrity, I had no cause for concern." He looked off into the distance. "But as far as his humility..." Mr. Dobbins slowly shook his head.

"What humility?"

At Susannah's words, they both burst out laughing.

Looking up from her outburst of giggles, Susannah caught a glimpse of Dan Lowe looking at her briefly before turning back toward his friend. Mr. Dobbins leaned close to her ear.

"Perhaps Mr. Lowe and his friend could join us for the picnic."

Her lips felt numb with fear.

"Father, I am so embarrassed about the party...can I face him?" She bit her lower lip and fluttered cool air onto her face with her Chinese fan.

"Yes, you can."

Sucking in a deep breath, she awkwardly strode to the shade below the large chestnut.

"Mr. Lowe, my father wishes to invite you and your friend to join us for the picnic." There. The words were out but she could barely breathe.

Bravely looking up to meet his gaze, she was captured by his green eyes that progressed from embarrassment to gratitude to warmth. He started to speak but his tongue appeared to falter.

"Of course, we accept!" The blond friend doffed his hat. "My name is Ansel Dickens. We met at the church raising."

She smiled self-consciously. "Of course, Mr. Dickens. So pleased to make your acquaintance."

Danny remained tongue-tied. Ansel chuckled. "Forgive my eloquent friend here. He was moved speechless by the reverend's words."

Twisting his face, Danny seemed to recover himself. "I am sorry. I was just not expecting your invitation."

"I do not know why. You are always welcome." She pointed to where her father was sitting on a sun-drenched blanket. "My father already has a spot. Today is the deacons' wives' turn to serve so the rest of us ladies get to sit and visit."

Danny looked around the crowd. "So is your friend Elias here?" His face was drawn tightly as if ready for a fistfight.

"No. He has returned home." She waited a moment before adding, "He will not be back."

Swirling around as dramatically as she could, she propped up her parasol over her bonnet and strode toward her father, swishing her crisp petticoat as loudly as she could through the tall grass. She could practically feel Dan Lowe's gaze taking in her femininity. A quick glance backward rewarded her with a look in his eyes that made her blush.

Missus Ashley was serving a plate of chicken and cooked garden vegetables to her father. Susannah noticed the older woman's eyes widen conspiratorially as she saw Danny and his friend approaching over Susannah's shoulder.

"Look sharp, fair maiden." Missus Ashley's voice was a whisper. "The troops have arrived for the conquest." She giggled mischievously and scurried away to get more food.

Susannah warmed feverishly as she searched for a corner of the blanket, and deposited herself.

She could barely pay attention to the conversation between her father and the young men, so distracted was she by Danny's long, lean leg so close to hers. She nibbled at the food, trying not to chomp onto any green vegetables that might linger on her teeth. She delicately tore off small bits of bread and swallowed them with difficulty.

"Do you know, Susannah?"

She jerked her head toward her father.

"What?"

"I said, do you know about the history of this common?"

"No, I do not." She wiped a crumb off of her linen gown and flicked it directly onto Danny's breeches. She started to reach for the crumb before she realized what she was doing and stopped her fingers.

"I apologize. I did not mean to inflict my crumbs upon you."

His smile bedazzled her. "That is quite all right. No harm done." He wiped the crumb onto the grass next to the blanket and gave her another heart-stopping grin.

She stared mutely at him, attempting to recover from the assault on her feminine senses.

Finding her voice, she willed her eyes to connect with her father's and blurted out something that was close to discernible: "Father...history...this common?"

Unsuccessfully smothering a smirk, her father answered. "Yes, my dear, this is the very common that the British troops came through during the war. Deacon Ashley informed me earlier that several of Burgoyne's soldiers stopped here after their defeat at Saratoga. Whilst eating a picnic at this very spot, many of the Hessian soldiers became enamored of the local lasses and decided to stay. I imagine their children now live in this community. Isn't that quite the story?" He took a large bite of the chicken that was still on his plate.

Susannah's mouth dropped open.

"Redcoats? Right here in West Springfield? How frightening! And to think their children might be here in this very town. Is that not appalling?" Looking at Dan Lowe, she expected to see him nodding in agreement. Instead the armory worker had grown pale and silent. His grin of only a moment before had melted into a tortured countenance.

He started to speak but his words appeared to lodge in his throat. His jaw worked tightly back and forth as he wiped his hand across his forehead feverishly.

Is he ill? Is the food not agreeable? Am I not agreeable?

After a moment's silence, Danny stood up.

"Please excuse me."

She watched the tall, lean man walk slowly away.

"Did I say something wrong?" She flitted her gaze between her father and Danny's friend, Ansel.

Ansel gave her a sympathetic grin.

"You didn't mean nothin', miss. He'll be all right."

Susannah looked down at her food, losing what little appetite she had.

What have I done now?

* * *

Danny's heart wrenched at the young woman's words.

What was it she said? "Appalling." I am appalling.

Shaking his head slowly, he looked out toward the river, once again wishing he was somewhere else. The beauty of the day was lost on him. It might as well have been pouring rain with the dreariness that soaked into his spirit.

"Mr. Lowe?"

Danny startled and spun toward the voice.

The Superintendent!

"Good day, Mr. Ames."

The man smiled at him. Slightly shorter than Danny and perhaps forty years of age, the head of the Springfield Armory was known for his amiability with the workers. He was not always as courteous to the others in higher position at their workplace, but David Ames was always a fair boss to the factory workers who labored with gritty sweat to produce the quality weapons that the armory was known for producing.

The superintendent looked at the view Danny had just been staring at.

"This is truly a look at God's creation." Moving his gaze several degrees to the south he added, "And there is the necessary evil that darkens the beauty." Looking at the blackened smokestacks atop the buildings on the hill across the river, Mr. Ames smiled ruefully.

"The blight from the sin of man." Danny stared at the wooden structures that, on every day except the Sabbath, spewed out smoke and coal ash into the air.

The superintendent looked at him in surprise. "Yes. I daresay it is. But, thankfully, we have the machinery and skill to arm ourselves against those intent upon harming us. And I am grateful for it."

His eyes narrowed. "I am glad I saw you alone where we can speak in private. I understand you came to my office earlier this week because of a concern. My secretary said you were hesitant to share it with him. He thought it might be pressing."

"Mr. Ames, I am not certain if this is anything to be alarmed about. I was not certain to whom I should relay this information or if it was even necessary to do so."

The man stared at Danny intently. "Go on, Mr. Lowe."

"A week ago, I attended a party at the home of Mr. Dobbins. It was a celebration of the church raising." He paused, uncertain if he should proceed.

Perhaps I was alarmed for no reason.

"Go on, sir." Mr. Ames was fully engaged now.

"Whilst walking down the hill from the barracks, I thought I heard two men talking—an Army officer and a worker—and...I thought they might have been conversing in French."

Mr. Ames scowled and he put his hands on his hips. Danny continued.

"They stopped so quickly, I thought perhaps I had not heard correctly. But then, on my way home, I passed by the tavern on Boston Road. There was an officer—I could not see who it was—engaging with a lady, sir." Danny cleared his throat. "This time, I know that I heard him speaking in that language."

The superintendent appeared frozen in thought and his eyebrows were deeply furrowed.

"You say it was an Army officer? And you could not see his face?"

"No sir, I could not tell who it was. But I am certain it was an officer."

After several moments of silence, Mr. Ames spoke.

"You have done right by telling me. Have you relayed this information to anyone else?"

"No, sir."

"Do not speak of this to anyone else. But if you see or hear of anything suspicious at all, come to me immediately. I will investigate on my own in the meantime."

Turning toward Danny, he gave a half smile. "The armory is lucky to have you, sir." He appeared to be lost in thought for a moment. "I remember when you first came on as apprentice. Just a skinny, lanky thing you were...you and your twin brother. I remember your father signing you on. He had quite the military bearing about him. I remember he had a limp as well. Was he in the war?"

Danny paled and then forced himself to recover.

"Yes. Yes he was." He swallowed hard.

"What regiment was he in?"

"I...he never told me, sir." Sweat formed beads on Danny's forehead. "I only know he was injured in New York."

The superintendent smiled.

"Well, he did a fine job raising both of you boys. Your brother...James, is it? He left after working here a year, did he not?"

"Yes, sir. My father needed help on the farm. His leg pains him much from his war injury and we have a large family."

"Well, I am most grateful you stayed on. Especially now." The superintendent's face grew sober and thoughtful. "Remember, report to me anything else you see that seems suspicious. Wars are never over for good. Not so long as men's hearts are evil."

"Yes, sir."

Danny watched him stroll away, as casually as if they'd been talking of the weather.

He recalled his superintendent's parting words: "Wars are never over for good so long as men's hearts are evil."

Then I suppose they are never over.

Chapter 9
Probing

Thirst drove Danny to the well that blazing morning in early June. He had been working in the finishing shop since four-thirty in the morning. On an ordinary day, the heat from the indoor forge alone was stifling enough. Today was unbearable.

After guzzling several ladles of water, he wearily sauntered to the nearest tree and sat in the shade. It was not cool, but at least he was protected from the merciless intensity of the noon sun. Plopping himself on the ground, he was too tired to even wipe away the flies swarming around his head.

He closed his eyes but he could not do so for long without envisioning Susannah. He forced them open again.

Forget her, you fool. Even if she could look past your meager purse, she could never tolerate your heritage. No wife wants her children carrying on the sins of the grandparents.

Danny had struggled with his father's history ever since he was old enough to understand the word "Redcoat." He could never forget his mother sharing the story of finding his father who had been wounded during the war, only to discover the shocking truth that Daniel Lowe was an enemy soldier. Recovering from his wounds and then falling in love with Mary Thomsen, Daniel Sr. soon became an American. But in many patriots' eyes, Danny's father was always under suspicion. Danny was acutely aware of that mistrust when, as a youth, friends mocked him for his unpatriotic parent.

I feel like I've been fighting my father's past my whole life.

Pulling his cap from his head, he wiped the sweat from his forehead with the back of his forearm. He had already rolled the linen sleeve up above his elbow for relief from the heat. It did little to relieve the moisture on his face when his wet arm made a vain attempt to wipe it away. Danny pulled the tail of his work shirt from his breeches and wiped his face with it.

He closed his exhausted eyes again, only to envision the look on Susannah's face at the picnic last month when she spoke of the enemy soldiers who stayed behind in America. Her horrified countenance was only equaled by the subsequent words that spat from her tongue. "Appalling" drummed its three syllables into his thoughts.

At least I shall not have to inflict my "appalling" self upon her. My curse will protect her from such ruination.

Recalling that day on the common brought to mind his conversation with the armory superintendent. Danny was grateful he had been able to reveal his concerns to someone he trusted. It seemed by Mr. Ames's reaction that Danny's suspicions were perhaps well founded. That thought was not a comforting one.

Even more disturbing was the feeling that he was being watched the whole time he spoke to Mr. Ames that day. It was an eerie feeling that even now sent chills through him. Ever since that day, he guarded his every step and conversation. Suspicion became his invisible companion.

He was startled to hear approaching footfalls, but grinned sleepily at the sight of his friend, Ansel. "So they let you off the water shops for a bit?"

"I let myself off. Needed some victuals from Missus Parker." He wiped his arm across his head and took off his cap. "This heat is murderous."

Ansel landed on the hard ground under the tree, wincing at the erupting root that bruised the back of his thigh. "That smarts." He shifted his legs. "You found the perfect spot, didn't ya? I'll have to sit first next time."

Danny grinned. "Almost lost your future generations there, eh?"

"My progeny is safe for now." Ansel grinned with his eyes closed, then opened them to look more seriously at Danny.

"So, Dan, speaking of progeny, when might we expect Cupid's arrow to find you?"

"I'm afraid his arrow is not strong enough to penetrate

my iron heart."

"Come on, lad. I've seen the way ya look at that Miss Dobbins. And believe me, she's lookin' back." Ansel winked knowingly.

"Are you serious? You heard what she said...and you know my past. Enough said right there."

Ansel shifted to face Danny. "Why do you not speak with her about it? She was just spoutin' off. It won't matter to her who your father was. What matters is who *you* are."

"Ah, yes...a poor armorer with enough sense to know I cannot provide so grand a future as her ladyship is accustomed to. What a fine prospect I am." Danny shook his head, holding his grime-covered hands in front of him. "Can you picture her looking at this every day? You must be daft, man."

"Well, you must be daft if you do not notice the way she takes you in with her eyes. I only wish someone looked at me that way." Ansel's teasing banter turned more serious. "You gotta put aside your fears. Else you'll never be content."

No one knew Danny better than Ansel. They had been inseparable since Danny's brother, James, had returned to Deer Run to help on the farm. Besides James, there was no closer friend.

"Look, I know you're trying to help. This just wouldn't work—Susannah and me."

They were interrupted by the sounds of the wooden cart filled with the metalwork of muskets being hauled up the hill to the proving house. Pulling the wagon laden with new barrel assemblies, the two oxen obviously labored in the intense heat. Their breathing was louder than usual and their steps slower.

"Poor animals. They never get a break even in this heat." Danny wiped his face with his shirttail again.

Ansel stood up. "None of us does. I need to get back to the mill. See you at supper."

Danny watched his friend start the mile-long walk to the water shops, where he spent hours a day seated at a grindstone shaping iron gun barrels. It was no cooler there, despite the presence of water from the large stream.

Slowly trudging back to the finishing shop, Danny tucked his damp shirttail back into his breeches.

Ansel knows nothing about women.

* * *

The proving house was one of the most important buildings on the armory grounds. It was here that the integrity of the muskets was put to the test. If the barrels could not withstand the force of the heated gunpowder exploding and sending the ball to its intended destination, the gun was useless.

To test the worth of these gun barrels, two dozen or so were placed side-by-side in a row, pointing toward a hill of sand inside the building. A metal tube that funneled gunpowder to each barrel extended the length of the long row.

The walls of the building were a foot thick and windowless. After the proof master readied the barrels for testing, he sealed the thick, wooden door closed. The next moments proved the most dangerous for this worker as he went to the end of the metal tube extending to the outside, carefully lit the line of gunpowder, and raced away to safety.

The explosion of the line of muskets always shattered the relative stillness of an afternoon. It could be heard over the harsh hammering of hot iron submitting to a forger's forceful blows even through the proving house walls.

Somehow today's explosion carried a different tenor to Danny's ears and every worker stopped momentarily from the sound.

"Someone's ruptured."

Eyes narrowed throughout the shop where Danny worked.

The newest armorer, recently promoted from the water shops, nervously wiped the grime from his forehead. "Hope it wasn't mine."

Danny noticed the man's demeanor. "I'm certain yours stood the proof. I checked it myself. You're doing well."

The grateful employee gave an appreciative look to Danny. "Hope so. My lass and I intend to marry soon. Canna' afford to have my pay docked."

A smile emerged on Danny's face.

Cupid's arrow had found its mark.

Returning to spinning the musket barrel and checking each seam for any aberration, Danny was soon lost in his work again.

The afternoon passed so quickly that Danny was surprised when his stomach churned with hunger. His thoughts veered toward the stew he had seen the cook preparing at the noon meal.

Not quite as fine as from home. But it will fill the hole.

A sudden shadow appeared in the doorway. A burly man nearly filled the opening, considerably diminishing the now-dwindling daylight.

"Lowe."

Danny stood up straight from his work.

The proof master.

"Lowe, see me in my office."

His heart lurched at the announcement. The eyes of the dozen workers in the shop bore into him. No one spoke.

"Yes, sir." His voice sounded foreign to himself. Removing his leatherwork apron, he almost lost his balance when he turned toward the doorway.

He glanced at the soon-to-be-married worker and read pity in the man's eyes. Danny set his jaw firmly and strode to the office of the man who tested their muskets for strength and durability.

Danny's mind began to race.

How is this possible? I know mine was sound. I've never had a ruptured barrel before.

Following the stocky man to the small building, he stepped in the doorway and immediately saw the musket in question on the proof master's table. It was an ugly spectacle of shattered iron.

The large man put his hands on his hips and glared.

"I'm surprised at you, Lowe. This is a disappointment. Are you losing your touch?"

It took all of Danny's will to quell the anger that rose in his spirit. His heart raced in an odd pattern.

"I am not, sir. To the best of my knowledge, my musket barrel was sound. I have never been called into your office before."

The man held his eyes on Danny with such harshness, it felt like a physical force bearing into him.

"Well, now, does that mean you're getting careless? Thinkin' yours are so good you need not inspect them closely enough?"

Again, Danny fought the urge to strike back with his tongue. He could hear his pulse pounding in his ears.

"No, sir. I check them carefully — every time." He wanted to swallow but his throat was parched.

"Well just how sound do you think this one is that bears your initials? You are the only "DL" on these grounds, are you not?"

"I am." Danny felt weak.

What is happening here?

He looked up at the proof master. "May I look at the musket, sir?"

The large man's eyes narrowed. "You may." He spit a wad of chewing tobacco toward a bucket on the floor and missed. The sight of the brown saliva increased Danny's nausea.

Picking up the shattered piece, Danny stroked his fingers over every inch. Something about it was unfamiliar. He had made so many muskets through the years, he could practically tell his own handiwork in the dark, just by feeling the pieces of metal. Turning it over, he looked at the roughened metal where the worker's initials were always stamped. DL. They were there all right. But looking further, Danny searched for the small mark that was his own. He always stamped a small cross farther down the underside of the gun. It was so small that most would not notice it.

It was not there.

What is happening? Terror gripped his heart.

Slowly drawing his gaze to the proof master, Danny handed the ruptured piece back to him. "Yes, my initials are there."

The man tossed it onto the table, where it landed with a loud thud.

"You'll be docked pay for this. No cavortin' for you this month."

"Yes, sir."

"You're dismissed. Better look sharp." At Danny's surprised look, the man added, "Look careful at your work." A half sneer crept across his face.

"Yes, sir."

Danny whipped around and left the stuffy office, breathing deeply of the humid air outside. It was not much better than the close air in the building he had just left, but at least he was away from the proof master. Their encounter had nearly taken all the breath out of him.

I can never prove that is not my musket. Who would believe me?

Outrage and fear intermingled in his thoughts. But then complete terror gripped him as he realized the obvious.

Someone is trying to frame me.

Chapter 10
Tour

Susannah drew in her breath at her father's announcement.

"You're going to the armory grounds today?" Her mouth curved slowly upward.

"Yes, my dear. The shipment of wood came in on the flatboat yesterday and I want to oversee its arrival at the armory. This is the first sizable purchase the armory has made from our mercantile and I want to ensure that Mr. Ames is satisfied with the quality. I know he was quite pleased with the purchase price that I offered." He smiled suspiciously. "And why exactly would the daughter of the merchant be so interested in this particular client?"

She flushed and looked down at her nearly empty breakfast plate. "I…I just thought I might accompany you. After all, we have lived in Springfield some months now and I have never toured the grounds. It would be…educational. Is that not so?" She tried to keep her gaze as innocent as she could. "Besides, perhaps we might run into Stephen and greet him."

Her father leaned his head back and guffawed. "Susannah, you are terrible at trying to hide your intentions. Please be honest with me. I know why you wish to visit there—perhaps to catch the eye of a certain armorer?" He looked at her with amusement.

She turned warmer yet. "Father, I do not mean to deceive you. And I do not know why I am so attracted to him." She bit her lower lip. "I am certain that Mother would have desired someone of a different station in life for me to become enamored with. She would probably have been quite disappointed that I feel like a pathetic schoolgirl whenever I am around him."

Mr. Dobbins's face sobered and he grew quiet. After a

moment he took her hand and looked directly at her. "Susannah, perhaps you did not understand your mother so well as you think."

"Whatever do you mean?" Her inquisitive eyes searched his.

"Your mother and I did not exactly come from the same background, Susannah. In fact, your grandsire rather objected to our attachment. The war was still going on. I had been wounded and was unfit to return to duty for a time. I had returned to Boston only to find my family had left, their whereabouts unknown. Your grandsire took me on to work in his shop. But I had nothing.

"When I met your mother, the attraction between us was so strong." His eyes misted. "I...I had nothing to offer in the way of worldly goods. But if my deep affection for your mother were valued in pounds and schillings, I would have been a wealthy man indeed." He paused for a moment.

"But I was willing to walk away, I loved her that much. She insisted, however, that if I left, she would run away and find me. She told your grandsire as much and he finally relented."

He dabbed at his eyes with his linen napkin. "The love that your mother and I shared never diminished all the years we were together. And though she is gone, my love for her remains."

Susannah's dampened eyes widened. "Why did you or Mother never tell me this before?"

"Perhaps because we hoped that you would find love — as well as a comfortable future." He paused for a moment. "Yet, I know that, more than anything, your mother wanted you to pick a good Christian man who would treasure you in his heart, regardless of his treasures here on earth. *That* is what we would both want for you."

"And how will I know when I have found such a man?" Susannah felt so confused.

Her father squeezed her hand. "You will know."

* * *

The four-wheeled wagon drawn by two horses hurtled Susannah back and forth on the seat as she struggled to maintain her balance. Sitting next to her father, she grabbed his elbow to keep from being jerked uncomfortably close to the edge.

Although it was difficult to focus on the scenery, Susannah strained to take in the view. Once they had turned off of the main street where most of the stores were situated, there was little building to be seen. Long grasses and weeds in want of a sickle and occasional trees that had escaped a farmer's hatchet lined the dirt road directly uphill to the armory. Turning around once, she viewed the Connecticut River from the higher vantage point. The sun glistened on the waterway like shimmering jewels.

'Tis lovely – like heaven's streets of gold from afar.

"Sorry this road is all uphill, Susannah. We shall be there forthwith."

"I am fine." Her words were braver than she felt. Breathing a sigh of relief as the wagon stopped at the gated entrance, Susannah watched the armed sentinel reach for the acquisition order her father handed him. The soldier read the orders and, without speaking, waved the wagon through. She watched him return to standing stiffly at attention as soon as he had permitted their entrance.

"This heat is vexatious. That woolen uniform looks most disagreeable for any man to endure." Susannah shielded her face from the glaring sun with her parasol.

Driving past the large two-story building on the left, Susannah saw several workmen accompanied by armed sentinels carrying heavy-looking muskets into the doorway.

"That's one of the arsenal buildings, Susannah. That's where the finished arms are stored until ready to be dispatched to the army."

"Is this the only place in all of America where muskets are made?"

"It's the most important facility. There is one other — a smaller one — at Harper's Ferry farther south."

He steered the horses toward the open drive that turned onto the grounds. Pulling up the reins, the horses complied, nodding their heads and flicking their tails against the onslaught of flies. Mr. Dobbins climbed down from the wagon seat and walked around to assist Susannah.

She carefully took hold of his hand while lifting her fine muslin gown up just far enough to avoid getting caught on the front wheel. She delicately placed her silk, high-heeled shoe onto the narrow step and held her breath as she lowered her leg to the ground. Safe once again on the hardened earth, she drew a deep breath and smiled with relief.

"Such a long way down."

"Mr. Dobbins, welcome, sir."

They both turned toward the voice and Susannah saw the man that she recognized from Sabbath services in West Springfield.

"Good day, Mr. Ames. Have you met my daughter, Susannah?"

"I have not had the pleasure, sir. Welcome to the Springfield Armory, Miss Dobbins." His grin was accompanied by a stiff bow from the waist. "I regret the weather is not more comfortable but, alas, we are deep into June and the summer appears intent upon making its presence felt—most humidly!"

Susannah curtsied. "Thank you, Mr. Ames. But you need not apologize for this delightful season. Although quite warm, it is brilliant and uplifting to one's spirits."

"I see you have raised your daughter to be a gracious and charming woman, Mr. Dobbins. You must be quite proud."

Mr. Dobbins grinned. "I am, sir."

Susannah blushed but was anxious to tour the grounds before the intense heat caused a less-than-ladylike moisture to invade her freshly washed garments. "I am looking forward to seeing your grounds, sir. I have already been in Springfield some months, but have yet to tour your most noble facility."

"Well then, we must rectify that situation post haste. Let me find a sentinel to give you a tour." He looked around without success. "I fear they are otherwise occupied. I would ask Lieutenant Dobbins to do the honors, however, he is overseeing the transport of arms today."

"Perhaps there is someone—obviously a dependable man with integrity—from the shops who can show my daughter around." Mr. Dobbins's innocent-sounding question nearly forced a laugh from Susannah, but she controlled herself.

Mr. Ames paused with his finger on his cheek. Then his eyes widened. "Ah yes. There is a man whom I would entrust my life to. Let me see if he is on duty. Come with me."

Traversing the long path a hundred yards or so, they passed by a shop on the right that, Mr. Ames pointed out, belonged to the weapons inspector. Approaching two long buildings on either side of the road, he veered toward the one on the right and put his hand in a halting motion. "Wait here, if you please. I do not wish you to get too close to the fire." The superintendent walked inside the building, then reappeared a few moments later, accompanied by a dirt-and-sweat-covered Dan Lowe.

The young worker could not have looked more surprised as he stood there mutely for a moment. Removing his work hat, Dan fidgeted with it between grime-covered fingers.

"Mr. Lowe!" Mr. Ames was shouting at him above the forger's hammers inside the building. "I said, can you take Miss Dobbins on a tour of the armory grounds."

As if snapping out of a trance, he looked at his boss, and nodded.

"Well then, Susannah, I must discuss business with Mr. Ames. I hope you enjoy your tour." Winking at her so the others did not see, her father, accompanied by the superintendent, walked back to the wagon.

Susannah stood there awkwardly, shifting her legs, regretting the choice of shoes that pinched her toes. "Good day, Mr. Lowe."

She saw Dan lick his lips and look down at the ground while slowly approaching her as she stood several feet from the door of the shop.

"Miss Dobbins." Silence.

"Well, then, such a surprise for you, I suppose. I did not

know I would be seeing you here. I came with my father who is delivering some lumber."

Am I prattling on?

Looking up and meeting her eyes, he answered formally. "Mr. Lowe, at your service, miss. I must say you are certainly the last person I envisioned seeing here today. Not…" He seemed to be stumbling for words. "Not that I was envisioning you." He licked his lips again.

"My father is too busy to take me on a tour and Mr. Ames could not find a sentinel to do so. I hope you do not mind the intrusion into your work day." She bit her lower lip.

For the first time, he smiled. "Not at all, miss. It is a relief to get out of the shop to accompany a lady. Let me show you around a bit."

Pointing at the two identical buildings across from each other, he explained that these were the filing shops where he generally worked. It was difficult to take in all the information about the process of refining the muskets. Susannah was completely distracted by the physical appearance of the man as he extended his muscular forearms while explaining the functions of each shop. Although covered with soot and sweat, there was an attraction to the strength of the man that overcame any squeamishness about his rough appearance—as well as his earthy scent. She was almost instinctively drawn to him. Her thoughts lured her to forbidden desires, envisioning those hands holding her closely with a passion that sent chills to her inmost being.

What am I thinking? Stop this sinful nonsense.

"Are you all right, Miss Dobbins?"

He was staring at her with narrowed eyes.

"Yes, I am quite well. Perhaps we can walk for a bit while you show me the rest of the grounds."

Dan looked down at her delicate shoes. "Are you certain you can manage the walk, miss?"

"Yes…of course."

Standing a few feet apart, the two strolled down the dirt path toward a smaller building facing south. "This is one of the stores where we keep supplies. Nothing special."

She smiled, suddenly feeling shy. "Perhaps not. But it is

a lovely day for a walk." She twirled her parasol.

"'Twill not be so lovely later when the heat bears down. I will make every endeavor to lead you under the shade trees on our walk."

"That is most considerate of you."

Dan cleared his throat. "So, your friend Elias has gone back to Boston, eh?"

He cares about Elias! Does that mean he was jealous? Her heart raced at the possibility.

"Yes. I am afraid I realized that I had made a mistake in thinking so highly of him. Sometimes we can judge a person too quickly. Do you not agree?" Susannah met his eyes in what she hoped was a meaningful gaze.

Covering a mocking laugh somewhat unsuccessfully, Dan grinned. "I suppose that is true. But in this case, I feel I judged Elias both quickly and accurately. He is a priggish fribble."

Susannah covered her mouth, attempting to smother her laughter. "Yes, I suppose he is rather conceited and frivolous. But I enjoyed his company for a time." She smiled flirtatiously. He appeared not to notice.

"This very long building over here is the forging shop." The closer they got to this shop, the louder the voices became from inside as the workers yelled over the sharp clanging of the hammers.

"So did he kiss you?" Dan kept looking straight ahead.

Susannah's mouth opened in surprise. Had she heard him correctly?

"What?"

"Did he kiss you?"

They were moving away from the loud sounds of the forge so they both lowered their voices.

"And what if he did kiss me?"

Dan smiled. "Ah, so he did." He gave a self-satisfied grin. "But, undoubtedly, 'twas not a *real* kiss. Most prigs cannot see past their own faces to give a woman a decent kiss."

Susannah huffed. "And I suppose *you* know how to give

a decent kiss?"

She was shocked when she realized what she had said. Her throat squeezed tightly as her pulse raced. *What did I just say? Am I daring him?*

He grinned, stopped walking, and led her to the side of the forging shop where they were unseen by anyone that might walk by.

"If you want a *real* kiss, you have to find a real *man*."

Susannah could not breathe as he stepped closer to her.

He spoke in a low tone. "A real man will treat you as if you were the most prized partner he could ever find. He would take you in his arms and press his lips against yours with a passion that would set you afire, body and soul. *That* is a real kiss by a real man." Impulses of desire flowed throughout Susannah's entire being. Her knees felt weak.

She could barely speak as she swallowed dryly. "Are you going to kiss me?"

Susannah thought a look of regret passed across his eyes.

He stroked her cheek with a soot-encrusted finger, then stood back.

"No. No, I am not. I will never kiss anyone again."

"Again?" Her heart still beat furiously and her thoughts jumbled with confusing signals. "So you *did* kiss someone then."

Dan's face filled with pain.

"Was it a long time ago?" Susannah's curiosity overcame her manners.

"Yes, some years ago."

"So what happened to her?" She needed to know.

Dan gave her a stare that melted her heart. "She died."

He gently took her elbow and walked her back to the pathway.

"Over here is the old air furnace."

Susannah could barely walk but this time she could not blame her too-tight shoes. She spoke few words the rest of the tour.

By the time Dan Lowe brought her back to the wagon, her strength had completely ebbed.

Her father looked at her inquisitively.

"What's this on your cheek, my dear?" He wiped off the streak of soot that Dan Lowe had smeared with his finger. "Did you get too close to the fire?"

She swallowed.

"Yes. Entirely too close."

Chapter 11
Alarm

Danny slept poorly that night after the tour.

Recalling the welcoming look in Susannah's eyes and the lure of her soft lips, he was alarmed by the temptation he had barely resisted.

Get a grip on your senses, man. He was going to have to avoid such close encounters at all costs. He could not risk his family's curse — it might endanger Susannah. The thought of an untimely end for this woman, who was battling to steal his heart, filled him with an ache that rivaled any illness he had known.

I would rather live without her, knowing she was alive...somewhere.

Tucking his clean work shirt into his breeches, he grabbed his cap from the wall hook and headed for the barracks kitchen. Passing by Ansel's room, he noted the neatly folded bed linens.

He must have worked early today.

Danny was grateful to be back in the finishing shop again. He had been recalled to the water shops for a couple of months to help fill a large order for muskets. An illness among the workers had left the ranks hurting. Since Danny could work both areas of production, he and a few others were drafted back to the shops. He preferred the more refined task in the filing shops. It took more skill and, in this heat, less sweat.

Poor Ansel. Hope he advances soon.

He sat wearily at the long table and Cook brought him a bowl. She plopped a wad of semi-dry gruel into it.

It did not whet his appetite, but he politely said, "Thanks."

The plumpish woman, who was holding the pot in the

crook of one arm and a wooden spoon in her other hand, eyed him carefully.

"Looks like someone slept poorly last night."

"Is it that obvious?" He rubbed his aching eyes.

"Aye, lad. Best to be rested up for work. You've a long day ahead." She stared at him with motherly concern.

Lazily lifting his eyes toward hers, he attempted a vague smile. "Thanks, Missus Parker. I'll be fine."

Pointing the spoon at him, she gave him a knowing look. "Ya know what ya need, lad? A missus of your own — some womanly affection. Help ya sleep better." Winking at Danny, she swept her long skirts across the wooden floor to the hearth.

Danny inwardly groaned as he rubbed his hand through his thick curls.

Will no one leave my affections alone?

He swallowed several bites of the gritty mixture and drank down the entire tankard of cider Missus Parker had brought to him.

Pushing himself away from the table, he forced himself to stand tall, take in a deep breath, and walk outdoors where the sun was beginning to cast its early morning glow.

He felt more at peace at this time of morning than any other. The relative quiet of early day always made him think of Deer Run. It seemed as if memories of his home village were invading his thoughts more frequently of late.

Trudging toward the filing shop, his pulse suddenly raced when he heard the sharp clanging of an alarm bell. It was incessant and made everyone on the grounds stand still, as if frozen. The persistent, rapid clangs of the bell seemed to increase in intensity, causing his rapid heartbeat to surge as well.

Where was it coming from? Danny's ears strained to fix the location.

Shock turned to fear that prompted an overwhelming alertness.

"Water shops!" Danny bellowed. As if they were soldiers in a finely trained regiment, dozens of workers set in motion at the same instant.

No one knew what the need was, but everyone knew it was a dire emergency. Bodies of men raced up the hill toward the mill, driven by concern for their fellow armorers.

Danny's throat constricted with fear. He had only heard that alarm bell one time before and he knew the consequences: Men were injured and perhaps dying.

Dear God, no.

He did not even know what to pray, so overwhelmed were his anxious thoughts.

Barely noticing a rider galloping past him on the road toward the mill, Danny's dry mouth grew dryer yet with each intake of air. A two-wheeled cart drawn by a man moved toward the armory grounds from the direction of the water shops. Their paths were converging.

"Stand back!" the worker shouted. He was covered with soot and blood. "Move away." He was hauling two bloodied workers in the cart. Danny stepped out of his way but not before he saw the faces of the injured. His chest gripped so tightly, he could not catch his breath.

Ansel!

He spun around and followed the cart carrying his friend and another mill worker. Draped limply across each other, their limbs flopped mercilessly over the cart's edge as it was hauled down the bumpy road.

Dear God, let him be all right.

He occasionally glimpsed his friend's eyes open, then fall closed again.

Arriving at the closest barracks, the mill worker stopped at the door and Danny helped lift the injured men out. Ansel was first and Danny grabbed his friend's legs and helped ease him onto the first bed they could find.

"Get the doctor." Danny yelled at the men crowding around the doorway. Fighting back tears, Danny carefully removed Ansel's work apron and nearly gasped at the sight of his bloodied waistcoat. Gently unbuttoning the garment and then his friend's shirt, he nearly vomited at the bright red liquid that oozed incessantly from a chest covered with open wounds and bruises. He struggled to keep his voice steady.

"Ansel. It's me, Danny." He swallowed back the bitter

acid in his throat.

His friend slowly opened his eyes and gave a weak smile. "So why aren't ya at work, my friend." The effort of speaking caused Ansel's face to twist in pain. He appeared to be having difficulty breathing. But he forced his eyes open and clenched Danny's shirt, drawing his face near so Danny could hear him. His voice was coarse and raspy.

"I found...a hammer and chisel...at the mill...on the floor." He inhaled with obvious pain. "...hidden behind a barrel."

Danny's thoughts ran wild.

What is he saying? Has he lost his senses?

Ansel seemed determined to continue, despite the torment of his condition. "I checked the grindstone...evening last. It was sound."

The young man's face was turning grey and Danny's face contorted with emotion.

This cannot be happening! God, please...

Ansel continued more slowly. "The grindstone...flew apart....Someone..."

His voice caught and his eyes looked up. A slight smile appeared.

"I see Him..."

A gurgling sound followed Ansel's next breath. Then, he breathed no more.

Danny's face contorted as tears meandered down his cheeks. His voice choked.

"Ansel."

He could not speak as he slowly unclenched Ansel's fingers from his waistcoat. Placing his friend's hands across his chest, he noticed a figure standing next to the bed. Ezra was crying unashamedly. Rubbing his eyes, Ezra asked with a muffled voice, "Who did he see?"

"God."

After a moment, Danny reluctantly stood up from his friend's bedside, rising on unsteady legs. It took him awhile to realize other injured workers were being brought into the barracks. Danny felt numb as he stumbled from bed to bed, taking in the sight of bloodied co-workers, some silent, some crying in pain. His gaze was drawn to a uniformed man—an Army officer—laying on one of the cots.

Jerking his head as if to clear it, he nearly stumbled backwards a step.

Lieutenant Dobbins. Why was he in the water shop?

Strange sensations of unreality filled his mind, as if he were in a dream. Staring like a drunken man, he was alerted into a sobered state by the shout of a sentinel who had appeared at the door. "Dr. Pynchon's here."

The arrival of the physician caused everyone to cast hopeful glances. Perhaps he could save some. Even one.

The doctor went first to the uniformed man. Stephen Dobbins was alert but in obvious pain and his left arm appeared badly damaged. A quick examination by Dr. Pynchon drew an initial diagnosis.

"This arm appears to be broken."

Danny suddenly focused on Susannah's brother, who was bravely trying to withstand the agony of his injury.

"Should I fetch his father?"

Dr. Pynchon looked at Danny inquisitively. "Is this man's family nearby?"

"Yes. Just down the hill. I know where his shop is."

"By all means, get the man. Perhaps we can move him home after his arm is set."

"Yes, sir."

Grateful to get his mind off the horror of his friend's death, Danny flew out the door and ran down the hill toward Boston Road, where Mr. Dobbins's shop was situated. Danny could not even allow himself to recall what had just happened. He was on a mission to help Susannah's brother. At least there was something that could be done to help Stephen Dobbins. That thought kept his mind from going mad with grief.

The sunrise glared into Danny's swollen eyes and he grabbed his head in pain. Stopping for a moment in the roadway, he stumbled along looking downward, until he reached the store. Mr. Dobbins was standing in front of his store gazing toward the armory. His look of concern deepened when he saw Danny.

"What has happened, Mr. Lowe? I heard the alarm."

Danny was out of breath but swallowed with difficulty in between pants.

"The mill…a grindstone." He gasped for more air. "There's been a terrible accident. Your son is alive, but he is injured."

Mr. Dobbins's face blanched. "Injured, you say?"

"Yes. A broken arm, the doctor says. But he indicated that Lieutenant Dobbins will likely recover."

The storeowner untied his apron and threw it inside the shop. "I'll close up the shop immediately." He looked more closely at Danny. "Mr. Lowe, are you injured?"

Danny followed his gaze to his waistcoat and work shirt. They were covered with blood. Ansel's blood. Danny's eyes welled with tears.

"No, sir. It is Ansel's blood." Mouth trembling with emotion, he met Mr. Dobbins's eyes. "He is gone."

Mr. Dobbins appeared to struggle to hold back his own tears. His voice whispered. "I am sorry." Grabbing Danny's arm, he patted it for a moment. "Dangerous work you do."

"Yes, sir."

"Please. Can you tell Susannah what has happened? She needs to know. But do not let her come to the armory. I do not want her to see all that has occurred. Tell her to fix up a room forthwith so that Stephen can come home to recover."

"Yes, sir."

Mr. Dobbins followed Danny outside. "Thank you, Mr. Lowe. I regret the loss of your friend. He was a fine Christian man."

Danny looked at the ground. "Yes. Yes, he was."

Turning around before the tears began again, Danny wiped his face off with his sleeve and sniffed sharply. His thoughts were so numb, he had difficulty recalling Mr. Dobbins's instructions for Susannah. He forced himself to concentrate.

Tell her about Stephen. Tell her not to come to the armory. Have her fix a room for her brother.

Without even remembering how he got to her two-story home, he suddenly found himself in front of the large portal.

He had to knock on the door twice before it was answered. Sleepy-eyed, Modesty opened the door and started to smile, but her face fell when she saw Danny's blood-covered clothes.

"Mr. Lowe. Are you all right?" Her face grew whiter than its normal shade.

"I am fine. Please, is Miss Dobbins here? I must speak with her."

Danny's urgent voice seemed to prompt her to action. "I'll get her right away, sir. She is just getting up." Flying up the stairs, she forgot to escort Danny into the parlor. He strode toward the doorway that held embarrassing memories of the party—and Elias. Those thoughts faded momentarily as the reason for his visit flooded to the forefront of his mind.

Standing there holding his hat, he closed his eyes, trying to forget the nightmare of this morning.

"Mr. Lowe." Turning around to face Susannah, his appearance caused her to gasp and thrust her hand over her mouth.

"What has happened? Are you hurt?"

He stared at his fingers fidgeting with his hat.

"No, miss. 'Tis not my blood."

Still seeming to be in shock, she blurted out, "Why are you here?" She clutched her throat.

He moved closer to her, imagining that she feared the worst for her family.

"Your brother has been injured. But he will likely recover."

Her face turned pale. "Injured? Likely recover? How serious are his injuries?" Her lips were starting to tremble and she moved backward toward the two-seater chaise and sat down. She seemed to be breathing too rapidly.

Without thinking, he moved toward the chaise and sat next to her. "Please do not fret. He likely broke his arm but he should recover. The doctor wants him returned home and your father wishes for you to prepare a room for him."

Danny tried to focus on the message but he was taking in the silken robe that covered her night chemise. It was tied at the top but her feminine form was obvious through the thin layers. Her long light brown tresses flowed like a glittering shawl about her shoulders and back. He had never seen her hair undone before — at least not up close. The uncovering of such arresting beauty captured his senses. Suddenly remembering where he was, he looked down at his hands. Blood-encrusted hands.

"Mr. Lowe." Susannah placed her fingers over the red stains on his skin. "Are you certain this is not your blood? You may be hurt."

"No. I am not injured."

She squeezed his hand with the warmth of hers. "May I ask whose blood this is?"

He struggled to hold back his sobs but soon lost the battle. "Ansel's."

Danny gripped his hair with one hand and then wiped his dampened face. "I must go now." He tried to stand but Susannah grabbed his hands with hers and drew him back onto the chaise.

Her eyes brimmed with tears as she searched his. "I am so sorry, Dan." She tenderly kissed his bloodied hands with moist lips and the blood on his fingers mingled with her tears. He tried to wipe off the blood smeared on her face. With each stroke of his fingers, he saw her eyes close. Wisps of her long hair teased the skin on the back of his hand.

God help me.

He did not remember when his lips met hers but the sensation was one that he desired to go on for eternity, were that possible. Longing encompassed every part of him as he drew her rounded shoulders and stroked the smooth silk material in circles of desire.

Danny felt her fingers pulling his face toward hers as she returned the moist kisses that were wooing him to consume her with his passions. Warmth and yearning overwhelmed him as her irresistible kisses begged him for more.

Pausing to breathe, he gently grabbed her hands, and swallowed with difficulty.

"We must stop."

The look in her eyes was beguiling. Instead of stopping,

her lips sought his for more torturous pleasure that threatened to overcome all that he knew was right.

"Susannah." Her lips left little room for conversation. "Please stop."

She paused and with gasps of breath, stroked his face. "I am so sorry. It was so pleasant..." Turning redder than she already was, Susannah turned away.

Danny squeezed her hands. "Yes. Most pleasant." His voice quivered.

He stood up on unsteady legs and drew her up from the chair. "I must go."

He turned to leave but spun and drew her once more into his arms, holding her silken covered body close to his. Wild desire raced through his mind, as he pulled away, breathing in fits and starts. "I must leave."

This time he did not turn back but hurried out the doorway.

* * *

"Are you all right, miss?"

Susannah had not noticed Modesty coming into the room. The maid had a peculiar look on her face and appeared to be smothering a slight smile. The smile quickly faded.

"I know something terrible has happened, miss."

Susannah attempted to recover herself. "Yes. Something happened at the armory—I know not what. I do know that Mr. Lowe's good friend has died. And Stephen is injured."

Modesty's hand flew to her mouth. "No! Mr. Stephen? And Mr. Lowe's friend killed?" Tears filled her eyes.

Susannah's lips trembled. "Yes. We must fix a room for Stephen so he can come home to recover."

Modesty curtsied. "Yes, miss." She started to leave but then paused. "Miss Susannah, may I help you get cleaned up a bit?"

Susannah looked down at her robe. There were smears of blood and dirt all over her clothing and her hands as well. She felt her cheeks grow hot.

"Modesty, please do not say anything about this to my father." She bit her lower lip.

Modesty walked closer to her. "Miss Susannah, I'll not mention a word. Sometimes love that was just waitin' to grow in the sunshine, blooms in the midst of darkness instead." The maid gently patted her arm and went to the kitchen. Without turning around, she called back. "I'll fetch some water to your room."

Susannah pulled the edges of her robe together and wrapped the cloth tightly around herself. In the midst of this terrible tragedy, she touched her lips, still perceiving the passion of Dan Lowe's kiss.

Perhaps Modesty is right. I pray she is right.

Chapter 12
Conspiracy

There were six new graves dug in Springfield that day. But only one filled Danny's heart with emptiness.

Danny stood among the armory workers, surrounded by upheaved dirt. He stared, his face devoid of emotion, as the hastily crafted pine boxes were lowered by ropes into the ground.

My shrouded friend. I shall never see him again 'til eternity.

He watched as the sealed coffin concealing Ansel's remains was lowered last.

I shall never stand beside him again.

Looking around, Danny observed a piteous scene, as the long line of men each scooped the dry, warm earth and sifted it through trembling fingers over each box resting in its hole.

Danny took his turn, but felt as if he watched his movements from afar, a cold observer of the scene. His benumbed manner made his movements stilted, like an old man who has seen too much death.

He barely noticed an approaching figure until the man stood in front of Danny.

"Lowe. Come with me."

Mr. Ames.

Danny was too preoccupied with his misery to be alarmed, but he noticed a few workers glance their way.

"I need a few words with you." Danny was startled by the loud, angry tone of Mr. Ames. They walked silently the rest of the way, traversing the mile-long path up to his office on the hill.

Confusion interrupted his grief.

What is going on?

Mr. Ames plodded his way to his office, his mouth

frowning while his gaze appeared to be locked on his dirt-covered leather boots. He removed his formal, wide-collared coat and wiped his glistening forehead with the sleeve of his shirt. Danny noticed the deepening furrows on the man's sun-browned face. He looked like he had aged ten years in ten days.

Approaching the office door, the two men waited for the sentinel to step stiffly aside so the pair could enter.

"I wish to discuss some things with you, Lowe, not the least of which is this ruptured musket I have on my desk."

Danny's eyes widened at the loudness of the superintendent's voice.

Is he trying to humiliate me in front of everyone?

Fear mixed with outrage flamed in Danny's heart.

After they were inside the office, Mr. Ames slammed the door shut.

Danny's throat clenched as he waited for the superintendent to start his reprimand. Instead, Mr. Ames slowly turned toward him with a look of apology and sympathy.

"Please forgive me, Mr. Lowe." He kept his voice in a quiet tone so as not be heard anywhere except in his office. Walking toward his sole window, he glanced outdoors and closed the casement. "I know it is warm but this should only take a moment. And it is imperative that I not be heard by anyone but you."

Danny's eyes narrowed. "Mr. Ames, I do not understand."

"Nor do I—at least, not the full measure of the situation. But this day's events convince me that we have spies in our midst. And they know that you reported to me that an employee—nay two men—were heard speaking in French. They may think you have identified them and could testify against them in a military court. That puts you in danger."

Danny was already warm but this piece of news caused new beads of sweat to form on his face. He felt dizzy.

"Please, Mr. Lowe, sit here." Mr. Ames pulled a chair over and pushed it behind Danny's legs. He crumpled back onto the seat. Mr. Ames went to a pitcher and poured him a tankard of ale. "Here drink this."

Danny guzzled several swigs of the warm liquid before feeling well enough to speak. "I am sorry, Mr. Ames. This day..." He shook his head slowly and stared with dull eyes at the floor.

"You need say no more." Mr. Ames walked toward the closed window and stared in the distance with his hands clasped behind his back. He turned back toward Danny. "I deeply regret the loss of your friend. He was a faithful worker these many years and he will be missed. As will the others."

Words choked in Danny's throat and all he could manage was a muffled, unintelligible reply.

"Mr. Lowe, I believe someone overheard us speaking at the common after Sabbath service a week ago. At the time, I was suspicious that we were being watched by someone. And then *this* happened, confirming my fears."

Mr. Ames turned to his desk and picked up the ruptured musket that had been lying there. Danny remembered that mass of iron all too well.

"This," he said holding up the musket, "is why I know that someone is trying to get rid of you. I know this is not yours."

Danny turned his eyes toward those of Mr. Ames. "No sir, it is not. But how did you know that? It bears my initials, sir."

"You think I do not know my workers or their skills? When the proof master tossed this mess onto my desk, I inspected it myself. I saw it bore your initials. But not the mark that you always chisel near your letters."

Eyes wide, Danny dropped his jaw. "You know my mark?"

"Aye. But apparently our proof master does not. But I said nothing, because until everything is uncovered, there are few I can trust. I also looked closely at your initials and noted the slight depression in the iron. Whichever letters it bore, it was filed down and then yours were stamped—by someone else. And until we know who did this, you are safer if we pretend that you have left the armory. At least for now."

Mr. Ames looked at the floor and scowled. Looking directly at Danny, he drew in a deep breath and said, "After today's so-called accident, the stakes are getting higher. We must get to the bottom of this but I want you out of here."

Danny swallowed with difficulty. "Where am I to go, sir?"

"I will spread the word around the grounds that I am unhappy with your carelessness and that you decided to leave. You said something about heading for New York to find employment. I do want you to head west—at first. But then proceed north to your village. I will send you a note by post rider when it is safe to return. It is imperative that no one knows where you are. Not even…close friends." He gave Danny a sympathetic smile.

An unfamiliar ache in Danny's heart deepened the pain of this day.

Will Susannah understand that I care about her? Leaving without telling her where I've gone?

"Yes, sir."

"I know this is difficult. But after today, I am certain you understand. Perhaps our spy will grow more careless with you out of the way. Perhaps it will make it easier to catch him."

Danny suddenly remembered Ansel's words on his deathbed.

"Mr. Ames, before Ansel died, he told me he had found a hammer and chisel hidden in the water shop. He said the stone was sound evening last. But someone may have damaged the grindstone. He was trying to say that when he died." Tears welled in Danny's eyes at the memory.

"Aye. I'm afraid 'tis true." Mr. Ames went to a drawer in his desk and removed a small packet. "Here is a month's wages. Please accept this to tide you over 'til I can send for you. And please remember, no one from Springfield must know where you go—that knowledge could put others in danger, as well."

The sober warning sent chills through Danny.

"Yes, sir." Standing up on wobbly legs, Danny looked at Mr. Ames. "Sir, there is someone I must say farewell to."

"I understand." The superintendent smiled sadly. "But you must not tell her where or why you are going. Nor will you be able to write while you are away. I am sorry, lad."

Danny's nostrils flared as he fought for control. "Yes, sir."

* * *

"Going away? Where? Why?" Susannah could barely contain her distress at the news. She could see that leaving Springfield was not pleasing to Dan either, but she was at a loss to understand any of it.

"I cannot tell you." Dan stared at the floor in her parlor. Dusk was fast approaching and the dimness of light in the room reflected their waning joy. It was a joy that just a few hours before in this very room had held so much hope for them. But in these last few moments, gloom filled every chamber of her heart. First, Stephen upstairs and injured, and now Dan leaving. Her arms ached for him already.

"Do you not know that you take my heart with you when you leave?" Sobs erupted from her swollen throat.

Dan walked toward her and slowly embraced her. She leaned on him for strength, her legs weak from the sadness of his announcement. He gently stroked her back with his large, calloused hands that trembled with each move of his fingers.

Pulling her away slightly, he put his forehead against hers and looked down. "Susannah, there is something that I must tell you before I leave. It may change your mind about me, but I must tell you lest you discover on your own. You may never want to see me again, but I must tell you." He drew in a shaky breath. "It is about my father."

Susannah looked him in the eye. "I know about your father. I know he was a King's soldier in the war."

Danny's brows furrowed and he held her a few inches away. "How…?"

"Ansel told my father and me—at the picnic that Sabbath day." She stared at her feet for a few seconds then met his gaze. "I am so sorry for what I said. My tongue is full of evil at times. I pray you can forgive me. It does not matter to me who your father is...or was."

Danny held her arms with fingers that massaged her linen sleeves. "Are you certain it does not matter?" His countenance filled with pain.

Susannah longed to alleviate his fears. She touched his face with both hands. "I am certain," she whispered. Then her lips trembled against her will. "Please, do not go."

He kissed her quivering lips with his own, which trembled with every hungry encounter. Pulling away, he looked at her with earnest eyes.

"Please, Susannah...some may say things while I'm gone...they are untrue. Have faith in me. Please—please wait for me."

He turned and left without looking back.

Chapter 13
Refuge

Welcoming warbles of the blue-crowned vireos were a balm to Danny's exhausted soul.

Home.

Although fatigued from walking twenty miles through the night, that familiar birdsong — an echo from his childhood — refreshed him. Approaching the home of his Grandmother Eaton, he decided to stop there first. He had little strength left to go the additional mile to his parents' cabin.

A young boy with blond hair carried a bucket of milk from the barn. The sight of his eight-year-old cousin elicited a wide smile.

"Joseph!"

The startled boy nearly splashed the contents all over the ground. Seeing who had called him, a grin as wide as a ship's hull alighted on his face.

"Cousin Danny!"

He placed the bucket on the ground and ran toward his older cousin, throwing himself full force into Danny's arms. The young boy nearly knocked the sleepy traveler off his feet. Smothered in Danny's waistcoat, Joseph said, somewhat muffled, "'Tis so good to see you." Pulling away, he squeezed his cousin's arm with small hands. "Why are you here? I'm so happy to see you."

Hugging him again, Danny wearily patted the boy's shoulders. "I am delighted to see you, little cousin. Where is your mother?"

"Inside." Joseph whipped around and yelled, "Mother! Come quickly!"

Danny's Aunt Sarah opened the door. Seeing who had arrived, her countenance lifted.

"Danny!" She ran toward him, a wooden spoon in one hand, and embraced him.

"You do not intend to use that upon me for showing up unannounced, I pray."

"Well, I just may!" She gently touched his sleeve with the gruel-covered spoon. "But perhaps I will feed you first. Come inside—you look done in. Nathaniel is out in the sty feeding the pigs. He'll return forthwith. Mother is attending a birthing. And little Rachel is asleep in the cradle, so keep your voice hushed."

All three strode toward the house, Sarah's arm nestled around Danny's. She gave him a sideways hug. "I shall inquire later as to why you are here."

"Thank you—for giving me time to refresh." Danny looked fondly at his aunt. Sarah was only seven years old when Danny and his twin were born and Sarah always seemed more like an older sister. They had always been close.

Entering the doorway was like a return to his younger days, with small children filling up the long tableboard. Besides Joseph, there were three younger boys, all blond-haired, and all with gruel surrounding their mouths.

The six-year-old grinned. "Hi, Danny!"

Danny stroked his hair. "Hello, Myles. Benjamin. And this little fellow must be Ethan."

Sarah held a look of pride. "Yes. All my little men." She tousled the youngest boy's hair. He was barely old enough to sit at the table. "And, of course, now we have a little lady to join our troops—Rachel, James's daughter. Your niece, Uncle Danny." She pointed to a small cradle a few feet away.

Danny propped his musket against a wall and silently walked over to the cradle and carefully stroked the sleeping girl's cheek. "She looks like Anne." The realization brought tears to his eyes, stirring his already fragile emotions.

Sarah walked toward him and placed her hand on his

arm. "Come, break your fast with us."

Following her gentle prod, he sat next to the four-year-old who was holding his spoon in his mouth sideways and laughing mischievously.

"Benjamin, enough foolishness. Finish your gruel." Sarah rolled her eyes and grinned secretly at Danny. She whispered, "It is humbling when you see your children act as you did as a child."

Danny smiled sleepily then yawned. He swallowed several bites of the warm gruel, but then placed his spoon on the table. "Aunt Sarah, please forgive me but I must lie down."

Narrowing her eyes, Sarah placed her hands on his forehead. "Are you ill, Danny?"

"No. Just so tired I could slumber right here."

"Come. Let me show you a bed. You can sleep in the boys' room."

He followed her on legs that barely seemed to function. Seeing the soft quilts on the boys' mattress, he fell onto them and closed his eyes. The last thing he heard was Sarah's voice.

"Rest well, dear Danny."

* * *

Upon opening his heavy eyes, he finally focused on the woman sitting in the chair by the window. She was sewing and did not notice that he was awake.

"Mother."

Beaming with obvious joy, Mary Lowe hastily stood up and placed her project on the chair.

"Sarah sent Joseph to tell me you were here." She leaned over him and squeezed his hand. "I wanted to see you right away. Are you ill?"

Concern filled her eyes as she inspected every inch of his face.

"No, mother. I am not ill." He sat up, feeling stiffness in all his joints. "I was fair exhausted from walking all night."

Her eyes narrowed. "Why were you walking here in the

darkness? What has happened?"

What can I tell her?

He rubbed his hair with one hand. "Something happened at the armory. I am not free to share all the details, but it was deemed safer for me to leave there for a bit."

Her eyebrows furrowed. "Safer? Perhaps you should not return. Perhaps you need to stay home." Her voice rose with anxiety.

Danny took his mother's hand and squeezed it. "They will let me know when I may return—but not until it is safe. Please do not fear." He gave her an encouraging smile to alleviate her concern. "In the meantime, I shall enjoy some time with my family."

She kissed him tenderly on his cheek. "Sarah has supper nearly ready. Come, gather some strength from some well-needed food. By the looks of you, you could use some sustenance."

"You always think I am too skinny."

"Perhaps that is because you are." She grinned at him and opened the door to the main room. "Mother, look who has awakened."

Danny viewed his Grandmother from across the room, but even in the dimness of late afternoon, he could see she was aging rapidly. Although grinning at her oldest grandson, she got up from her chair somewhat slowly and reached out to him. "Give your grandmother a kiss, fine lad."

He swept her into a warm embrace. "You are still as beautiful as ever, Grandmother."

She looked at him sideways. "Lying will get you on the road to hell, my dear boy." Grinning, she hugged him again, then slowly returned to her chair. "I was up half the night with a birthing."

Danny scowled. "So you are still working hard as midwife in Deer Run?"

"Of course. But I have an assistant now—your Aunt Hannah. She is my keen right hand." She smiled with pride.

"Well, I am not surprised, Grandmother. She always did like going on calls with you."

"And just think, Danny, you were her first birthing!"

"'Tis true." Mary helped Sarah set out plates on the long tableboard. "I asked for her to come to my birthing. Little did we know there would be *two* lads birthed that day!"

"I am certain that James and I caused quite the stir." Danny sniffed the air. "Aunt Sarah, your supper is making me hungry enough to eat an ox."

"Well then, if you promise not to tell the boys that I have served you first, I will feed my hungry nephew forthwith."

Sarah picked up a plate and filled it full with stewed beef and vegetables.

Staring at the plate, a feeling of warmth flooded his heart.

"Thank you, Aunt Sarah. 'Tis so good to be home."

Chapter 14
Freedom

Danny had forgotten that it was nearly the Fourth of July, but the residents of Deer Run had not. Their annual celebration of the birth of the United States was one of the town's largest festivities all year. And on this twenty-fourth birthday of America, nearly everyone's spirits were soaring — all except Danny's.

He could not shake the events of the last week that felt like a heavy, dark fog. The pain over losing his friend Ansel was now coupled with a new, unfamiliar ache: A longing to be with Susannah. It was a deep yearning that he found both pleasant and frightening at the same time.

Thoughts of his first love when he was only seventeen filled him with melancholy. They had only been sweethearts for a few months when she was taken abruptly from him, the victim of influenza. He decided back then he would not give his affections away ever again. Watching his brother, James, lose his wife in childbirth only strengthened that resolve. It was safer for his heart to remain unattached.

The words of Missus Endicott at Anne's funeral back in April had planted the idea of a family curse in his mind. He had always felt different — he, the son of an enemy soldier while all his friends were the progeny of heroic patriots. Perhaps this was God's way of dealing with the situation.

But now his heart had leapt headlong into the affections of another. What was he thinking? Of course — he was *not* thinking. He was merely swept up by her beauty, her tenderness at his loss, her amusing banter, the way she walked, the way she kissed…

He sighed. *I am hopeless.*

"Danny? Good day. Is anyone there?"

His brother, James, waved a hand in front of Danny's

face, which snapped him out of his thoughts and back to the present. Sitting on the lawn of the town green, Danny was suddenly aware of activity swirling everywhere around him.

"You look deep in thought. So tell me about Springfield." James laughingly pulled on Danny's short hair. "I see the city dwellers no longer believe a queue to be fashionable." James plopped on the dry grass next to him.

Danny smirked. "I finally gave in to ridicule. Besides, my long tail was in danger of catching fire from the forge. That would not be a pleasant way to lose one's hair."

"No. I suppose not." James's expression grew serious. "I am sorry about Ansel. He was a fine man."

"Yes, he was." He paused, not certain how much to reveal. "James, I do not want Mother or Father to know this, but the accident at the mill — it was no accident. Someone chiseled a weak spot near the mortise of the grindstone. It flew apart when it was spinning, sending huge chunks of granite everywhere."

"No!" James rubbed his hands across his forehead. "Do they know who?"

"No. That is why I have been sent away. The superintendent is concerned for my safety because of other events. If they discover the spy's identity, then I can return. They will send me a note by post rider."

James stared earnestly at his twin. "I shall say nothing to the family. But be careful. I shall pray that God protects you." Looking off in the distance at the racing events, James shook his head. "'Tis not surprising that spies would target the armory. What better way to steal our weapons and disrupt our defenses?"

"Yes." They were both silent for a long moment.

James looked back at his brother. "So, let us not dwell on such things on the Fourth of July. Let us celebrate this happy anniversary of our country. And perhaps you can tell me if there is a young lady in your life? You somehow seem a bit...different." He grinned.

Danny squirmed in discomfort. "Yes, but I am not certain what to do."

James made a face of mock horror. "Not certain what to do? Why, if you love her, then marry the lass." He elbowed him teasingly.

"It's not that simple."

"Why not? Is she not a Christian?"

"Yes. 'Tis not her. 'Tis…you know. This curse…"

James looked completely dumfounded. "Of what do you speak? Has living in the city turned you into a madman? Listen to yourself."

"No, you listen. Look what happened to Deborah when I was seventeen. Then Anne. I overheard Missus Endicott at the graveside. She said we were cursed. It makes sense to me."

"Missus Endicott? That gossipmonger? Danny, listen to yourself. No, better yet, listen to God's Holy Scripture. It says in Proverbs 3 that 'The curse of the Lord is in the house of the wicked: but He blesseth the habitation of the just.' Was our family a 'house of the wicked'?"

Danny stared at the ground between his crossed legs. "No."

James spoke passionately. "Death will befall us all. Life on this earth is limited and no one knows when God will call us to eternity. Does that mean that we do not love whilst we inhabit this temporary body?" James blinked his moist eyes. "I miss Anne so very much. But would I have missed out on the joy of her arms because it was such a short time that I was able to love her? I would never give it up, for all the riches of this earth." He pointed toward the baby several feet away being rocked in the arms of their Aunt Sarah. "Would I give up the gift of my daughter — the very evidence of Anne's and my love? Never."

Pondering James's words, Danny met his brother's eyes. "Have you never felt different? Because of our father?"

James shook his head slowly. "Not as different as you always felt. You have been carrying that 'guilt' your whole life. You must let it go. Father is a loyal American, not the enemy soldier he once was. Would you hold that against him his whole life?"

"I love Father."

"I know you do. But can you forgive him his past?"

Danny was silent for a moment. "Yes." Wiping the sweat from his face with his sleeve, he drank ale from the tankard he had set on the ground. "I am quite the fool, am I not?"

"Most lads in love feel like fools. So tell me about her. I want to know all about this fair lass that has won my brother's stubborn heart."

"She is...how do I describe her? So lovely...so tender yet amusing. She is so..." Danny was at a loss for words.

James smirked. "So tempting? Is that the word you were fumbling for?" He laughed loudly. "Oh, I can see on your face what you are thinking about this young lady. So tell me, what is her name?"

Inhaling deeply as if afraid to speak it, he softly breathed her name: "Susannah. Her name is Susannah."

* * *

The festivities of the day were complete at dusk following the reading of the Declaration of Independence. To this day, the words of this document stirred the heart of Daniel Lowe, Sr., and reminded him of that Fourth of July twenty-two years before when he had decided to become an American. That resolution in his mind had completely changed his future.

Seeing his wife and children watch the glowing bonfire, he thanked God for the gifts that his decision had birthed. His wife, Mary, and each of his children: the twins who were now grown men; his four older daughters on the brink of womanhood; Ephraim on the verge of manhood; and little Betsey, the apple of her father's eye. Scanning the faces of these blessings, he noticed for the first time that Polly was not with them. He turned to look around and still did not see his oldest daughter. Concern gripped his heart.

She'd best not be with Jonathan.

Tapping Mary on her shoulder, he whispered, "Where's Polly?"

Looking around the crowd, her eyes widened. "I know

not."

At that moment, Daniel noticed Jonathan approaching from behind the crowd. He slowly walked toward him. "Sir, may I speak with you?"

Daniel's eyes narrowed. "Yes, and you may tell me where is my daughter, Polly, if you please."

Tilting his head toward the other side, he said, "She is over there."

Polly was staring at the bonfire, blending in as though she had been there a long time. He saw her pull a piece of dried grass out of her cap then straighten out her gown.

Daniel's jaw clenched as Jonathan started to speak.

"Sir, if you would be so kind, my father wishes desperately to see you. His health is getting quite poor. Dr. Burk was out yesterday and said that my father has little time left." Jonathan paused. His dark eyes glittered in the firelight. "He asks for you every day—says that he must speak with you."

Eyes narrowing, Daniel looked pointedly at the man. "If he is so ill, why are you not with him?"

Jonathan looked at the ground. "I only came near the very end of the festivities. My father wanted me to come for at least part of the celebration. Said he was sorry that I was spending so much time tending to a dying parent."

Guilt swallowed Daniel's heart.

"I am sorry about your father. Tell him...I shall visit him tomorrow."

Jonathan grabbed his hand and shook it tightly. "Thank you, sir. I shall tell him."

Watching the young man turn and race toward home, Daniel's thoughts vacillated between intense hatred and deep regret. He closed his eyes tightly.

God, help me do the right thing.

Chapter 15
Repentance

Daniel dreaded this visit.

The last time he had approached the Grant cabin was over twenty years before. Treading down the hill toward the nearly dilapidated, one-room shack brought back painful memories that he would prefer to forget once and for all. For whatever reason, he was forced to face the demons that plagued his past. He hoped it would be over quickly.

Glancing to the far side of the small abode, Daniel's heart lurched at the view of the headstone he and several others had carried to mark the grave of Jonathan Grant—Josiah's father.

Jonathan had been the only bright light on that mission of mercy.

Daniel recalled his dreaded encounter with Josiah who was, at the time, under the scourge of smallpox. Josiah's hatred for Daniel, who Josiah believed had stolen Mary's affection, consumed the stricken patient. In a jealous rage, he'd even thrown a basin filled with vomit onto Daniel's shirt. It had been the smock that Mary had sewn for him and Daniel had been livid.

But that visit led Daniel to a friendship with Josiah's father, a man of honor and integrity. Their friendship was cut short, however, when Jonathan caught the smallpox. Within days, he had died.

Why couldn't it have been Josiah who died instead of Jonathan?

Daniel stopped short before knocking on the door. Was his heart so unforgiving that he could think such a thing?

God forgive me.

Gently tapping on the splintered door, a weary-looking young man opened it. Although there were deep circles under Jonathan's eyes, he smiled.

"Please, come inside."

Daniel walked across the threshold and was immediately assaulted by a foul odor. He fought back the sickening feeling that threatened to overtake him. Bravely walking toward the man lying in the bed, he was even more horrified by the now sagging, pockmarked skin. It gave the man's face a bizarre, other-worldly look. The sight repulsed him.

Dear God, do not let the man see it in my eyes.

"Here is a chair for you, sir." Daniel looked back at Jonathan holding a small stool — one of the few places to sit in the entire room. "May I get you a refreshment?"

Daniel swallowed with great difficulty. "No, but thank you, sir."

Jonathan leaned over his father and looked at him with concern. "Father, I will leave you to visit with your guest. I shall be outside if you need me."

Josiah nodded and smiled weakly. "Thank you, son."

Watching the young man walk out the door, tears brimmed in Josiah's eyes. "I do not deserve such a fine son."

Daniel looked down at his folded hands. "I suppose none of us does, Josiah."

"I, least of all." Josiah's gaze held Daniel's. "I want to thank you for coming, Daniel. I know that you did not want to." His words were spoken slowly and he began a heartrending cough that lasted a full minute. He began to gag and Daniel automatically grabbed a basin nearby. As Josiah vomited meager contents into the bowl, Daniel's thoughts returned to the last time this had happened. He held his breath.

This time, Josiah said a weak, "Thank you."

Daniel set the basin aside and began to say that, of course, he had wanted to come. But he knew full well that was a lie. "You are right, Josiah. I did not want to come." He took in a deep breath. "But I am glad I did."

"Are you?" Josiah's eyes were glazed and in pain.

"Yes. And I am truly sorry you are so ill. I would not wish this on anyone."

Josiah smiled weakly. "Not even on your worst enemy?"

More coughing.

When the spasm was over, Josiah grabbed Daniel's arm with what little strength he had.

"Daniel, please forgive me — for the way I treated Mary, the way I treated you, for everything."

For the first time, Daniel not only felt compelled to forgive him, he was desperate to do so. "Yes, I forgive you. I have kept this bitterness in my heart far too long." Looking down again, he folded his hands. "Please forgive me."

Josiah's fingers gripped his arm tighter yet.

"I know this is not what you had wanted — my son and your daughter — together. But I beg you…do not make him suffer because of my sins. You can see what a good man he is. Nothing like his father." At these words, tears rolled down his sunken, leathery face. Another round of coughing ensued. Daniel felt helpless.

"Can I get you anything?"

Jonathan hurried into the house.

"Father!" He poured a small amount of a pungent-smelling medicine into a vial. "Here, drink this." Jonathan's hands trembled as he held his father up high enough to sip the laudanum. Josiah fell back onto the pillow. After a few seconds, Josiah closed his eyes and rested from the narcotic.

The son looked up at Daniel. "I think he cannot visit any further today. But I thank you for coming."

Once again, Daniel was startled by the resemblance between Jonathan and a young Josiah before he had been stricken with smallpox. But this time he noted the look in Jonathan's eyes.

What was it Mary always said? You can see a man's soul in his eyes?

If that was the case, then Jonathan's soul was nothing like his father's had been as a youth. Instead, Jonathan's eyes looked like his grandfather's — his namesake.

Standing up from the chair, Daniel was filled with so many turbulent emotions, he could not even begin to sort through them. Acutely aware of his need to pray, his broken spirit sought solitude.

"Thank you for inviting me to come. I shall return

tomorrow."

Chapter 16
Mourning

The next morning, the bell at the meetinghouse tolled nine times, indicating the death of a man. Josiah Grant had passed into eternity. After a pause, it began to ring again, this time forty-four tolls for Josiah's age. Daniel stood in front of his cabin and counted the clangs.

"He lived a year less than I have." He spoke to no one in particular.

Polly came running out of the house when she heard the bell. Tears poured down her anguished face. "I must find Jonathan." She threw her apron on the ground and ran toward the Grant home.

"Polly, wait!" She ignored her father's command.

"Polly!" His military voice did not cause his daughter to slow her pace. If anything, she ran away even faster.

"Polly…" His voice whispered in defeat.

Mary walked outside, her eyes downcast. Closing the door behind herself, she strode toward Daniel and placed her arm through his. "Such a sad day. We must rejoice in that we know where he is for eternity." She smiled up at him through moist eyes.

Daniel stared blankly into the distance, numbness overshadowing his thoughts. "I did not have a chance to tell him I was sorry — sorry for interfering with Polly and Jonathan."

Mary squeezed his arm. "Thank you, Daniel." Her voice was a whisper.

As if coming out of a trance, his voice held new resolve. "After I feed the stock, I will hasten to help with the burial. It's the least I can do."

Leaning down to kiss Mary tenderly, he moved quickly toward the barn. "I will feed the animals right away. Do not hold breakfast for me."

Filling the troughs of the pigs and cow as fast as he could, he wiped the alfalfa from his hands and off his linen shirt. Hurrying down the road toward the Grant home, his mind filled with regret.

Dear Lord, I am a stubborn fool — an old, bitter fool. Please help Polly and Jonathan find it in their hearts to forgive me.

He felt the urge to move faster, but it was made more difficult by the limp he still bore from his war injury. Although it took just fifteen minutes to traverse the path, the only person he could find at the Grant home was Dr. Robert Burk.

The sullen look on Robert's face emphasized the fatigue in the man's eyes. "Already got him buried, Daniel. I was with him most of the night."

Daniel's eyes fixed upon the fresh mound of earth.

"I...I was hoping to help with the burial."

Robert gave a grateful smile. "Kind of you to offer. Jonathan and I managed, along with the reverend. Already had the coffin ready. We all knew it wouldn't be long." The doctor placed his tricorne hat upon his head. Looking up at the bright sky, he sighed. "Should be another blazing day."

"Yes." Daniel licked his dry lips. "Do you know where I might find Jonathan? I must speak with him."

"He left already. The young lad was so heartsick he just wanted his father buried and a few words spoken by the reverend. He seemed most anxious to leave — said there was nothing left for him here in Deer Run."

Daniel's heart lurched. "Was he alone?"

"Aye. He was alone. Polly came looking for him and I told her he'd gone. I think she went to find him."

Daniel's ears were pulsating with his rapid heartbeat. "Do you know which way they went?"

"Down toward the main road south. Along the river."

"Thank you." Daniel barely recognized his own voice, the constriction in his throat tightening each word.

Hurrying toward the river road, the ache in his left leg soon seized into a pain that cut short his quest. With great difficulty, he turned around and leaned against a tree, waiting for the agony to subside. Gasping for breath, he was overcome by sadness and worry.

Dear Lord, please bring them home.

A gentle breeze stirred the damp hair near his forehead. His breathing slowed as he carefully limped toward his cabin.

* * *

Daniel sat on the woodpile all morning, waiting for his daughter's return. Waiting and praying.

Mary brought out a tankard of cider to refresh him. Worry had forged deeper lines on her thin face. She silently went back inside.

He heard the other girls arguing inside about something and Mary's sharp voice snapped a reprimand. Silence followed.

Staring down the path, he thought he saw a slight movement of white amidst the greenery. Focusing as well as he could on that image of hope in the distance, he soon drew in a sharp sob. "Polly."

He limped as if in a dream toward the young woman, who was walking alone toward home.

Polly glanced sideways at her father but did not speak. Her face was smudged with dried tears and her linen gown slightly rumpled. Flecks of weeds dotted the length of her clothing. She tucked in several strands of loose blond hair under her mob cap.

"Polly…"

"I do not wish to speak, Papa."

"I must speak with you…and Jonathan."

"'Tis too late. He has gone." Her voice was terse.

Daniel stood dumbstruck. When he found his voice again, he begged a question. "Where has he gone?"

Polly turned toward him with ferocity in her eyes. "I know not."

Spinning on her heels she raced into the barn. After a moment, he could hear great sobs coming from the hayloft.

His lead feet refused to move his legs. Dizzying thoughts filled his troubled mind.

What have I done?

Chapter 17
Homesick

Early morning sun shone through the open doorway of the barn. Lowing oxen in the stall nearby interrupted Danny's slumber but he quickly nestled back into a dreamy state. He wanted to make up for the sleep deprived him by the intense, late August heat. He was in no hurry to start his day.

Rolling on his back in the hay, he stared up at the trusses. A swallow flew across from one beam to another. He imagined the bird sought its mate.

"I hope you find her." His voice was a whisper.

"You hope who finds who?" A small voice was nearby.

Danny rolled toward the voice and saw his cousin Joseph scratching his head and holding a bucket.

He smiled sleepily. "I hope that swallow up there finds his wife."

"Why?"

"You'll know when you're older." Danny grinned.

Joseph scowled. "That's what Father always says. 'You'll understand when you're grown up.' Well I wish someone would just tell me now."

Danny playfully threw a pile of hay at the boy. "Oh, so you want me to tell you about lads and lassies kissing, do you?"

A look of horror emerged on Joseph's face. "That is disgustin', Danny."

Danny rolled onto his back again and laughed. "I suppose I thought that when I was your age as well, Joseph."

He watched the boy walk to the milk cow and set to work.

James appeared in the doorway, partially blocking the sunlight. "Get up, brother. 'Tis Sabbath, you know."

Danny lay without getting up. "I hated to awaken. I was

having a dream."

James walked over to him and stood with his hands on his hips. "Guess I don't need to ask who you were dreaming about." He smiled. "I'm sure you miss her."

"'Tis made all the worse because I cannot write to her. Nor she to me." He rolled onto his side and sat up, brushing the hay from his sleeves and out of his hair. "She must be wondering by now if I am staying away for good. I know it feels like forever to me." He picked up a long piece of the hay and chewed on it.

James crouched down next to him. "I've been praying they would find the criminal at the armory and arrest him. I've been praying for Susannah as well—that she would not despair about your feelings toward her."

"Thanks, brother. If anything, my feelings for her have only grown stronger. At times…it feels like a physical ache— like I'm only a piece of a person without her." He shook his head. "I wish I could see her. I miss her more than I ever thought possible."

Standing to his feet, James reached down for Danny's hand and pulled him up. "Come on. Let us share breakfast with Aunt Sarah and the family. I'm glad we spent the night last night. Gives us more of a chance to visit with them. Besides I think Mother and Father could use a break from so many bodies about. Things seem a bit…tense, of late."

Danny looked at his brother. "I thought it was just me who noticed. Things are not right. I don't know if Polly will ever forgive Father for what happened with Jonathan. Does anyone know where he is? Where we can find him? Father even says that he will give them his blessing, but no one seems to know his whereabouts."

James looked at the ground and put his hands in his pockets. "It is troubling. And Polly does not look well. I wish there were something I could do."

"I suppose you can add them to your list of prayers. Let's go inside. I'm starving."

They crossed the threshold into Grandmother Eaton's home. She was just on her way out the door.

"My, there are enough babies arriving this year. Deer Run seems to be doing its best to become a city, judging by the numbers of birthings I've attended. You men..." Shaking her head and pointing her finger at Danny and James, she had a scolding look on her face.

Danny raised his hands in surrender. "I am innocent, Grandmother."

She patted his cheek and grinned. "Good lad."

"Come inside, now." Sarah called Danny and James to the tableboard. Serving up gruel and eggs to her little troops, she made more room for her two nephews. "Sit here and eat."

Nathaniel was just finishing his meal and still drinking cider. "Sleep well, Danny?"

"Yes, thank you, Uncle. 'Twas restful and cool."

James gave a mischievous grin. "And full of dreams." He arched his eyebrows up and down.

Nathaniel sat up straight and gave a facetious look of shock. "Say 'tis not so? This handsome single man has fallen under the spell of a fair maiden? Do tell us about her?"

Six-year-old Myles grinned with cider dripping down his chin. "Cousin Danny's in love!"

"Hush now, Myles." Sarah caught Danny's eye with a mischievous look. "Do tell, Danny. Who is she?"

Sarah sat down and propped her hands under her chin and stared at him. "I await your reply." She fluttered her eyelashes and grinned.

Danny felt his cheeks turning warm and began to stammer. "She is...from Springfield. She is a lovely Christian woman of whom I am very fond."

Sarah, Nathaniel and James burst out laughing.

"Fond? Danny you are a treasure! We can see on your face that you are far more than 'fond' of her. So when might we expect to meet her? When will you get married?" Sarah stared at her nephew with anticipation in her countenance.

"Well, I have not asked her yet."

Nathaniel gave a teasing scowl. "Well why not? 'Tis better to marry than to burn, as the Apostle Paul says." He grinned at Sarah.

Danny looked down at his hands resting on the table. "I am afraid I've not much in the way of worldly goods to offer her."

Sarah looked confused. "Well, you have good employment. If she loves you, what more is there to need?"

Danny shifted uncomfortably. "Aunt Sarah, you've no idea what she is used to in the way of comforts. Her father is a merchant. They have a large home. She owns fine clothing — the most fashionable styles. I...I can offer her none of these fineries."

She reached across the table and grasped his hand. "You can offer her the affection and security of one of the finest young men I know. That is sufficient wealth for any woman. And if that is not enough for her, than she does not deserve you, my dear nephew." She kissed his hand and squeezed it.

He squeezed hers back. "Thank you, Aunt Sarah. I pray you are right."

Standing up, she gave a self-satisfied nod. "Of course, I am right. Am I not always right, Nathaniel?"

"Of course, Sarah." He rolled his eyes so comically that both Danny and James burst out laughing. She threw a rag at him and he grabbed her and pulled her on his lap. "I will make you pay for such abuse, dear wife." He pressed his lips against hers for so long, that Danny cleared his throat, embarrassed by the display of passion.

"So Uncle, is it not Sabbath day? Time to refrain from pleasure?"

Nathaniel paused with moist lips and grinned. "This would just make the tithingman jealous. I am quite certain that no one checks *his* marriage bed on the Sabbath."

Sarah wiggled out of his arms and pulled her bodice up higher. "Well, lads, you can see that your uncle takes the Apostle Paul quite seriously." She leaned over her husband and kissed him on the lips. "We can continue later. Time to get ready for the meetinghouse."

* * *

The bell at the meetinghouse was still tolling when the twins approached, followed by Sarah and Nathaniel and their family. James carried his young daughter on his shoulder. At four months of age, little Rachel was full of smiles and drool. A river of saliva was slowly making its way down James's back when a young woman hurried up with her kerchief.

"Let me catch that drool for you, James." She dabbed at the moistness on his heavy linen waistcoat.

"Thank you, Esther." Turning toward his brother he introduced them. "Danny, this is Esther. She and her family moved here two years ago."

She curtsied and smiled shyly. "So pleased to meet James's brother. I've heard so much about you."

"Well, I hope he didn't tell you all the mischief from growing up." Danny looked inquisitively at James. His twin was turning red in the face.

Esther laughed. "Only good things, I assure you."

"Well, good. Then you will not think too ill of me. Shall we go inside?"

Danny imperceptibly nudged James while walking up the steps.

"What?" James whispered. "She is just a friend. Nothing more."

"I see." Danny grinned. He enjoyed teasing his brother back. He had taken enough jokes this visit about his affections for Susannah. It was nice to jest back, even if Esther were only a friend.

I suppose time will tell.

Before walking into the meetinghouse, he glanced over at the church graveyard and noticed Dr. Burk placing flowers on a grave.

"Whose grave is Dr. Burk visiting?"

James's eyebrows furrowed. "You did not know? His wife died over a year ago. She was with child after all those years of being barren. Then during the birthing she and the infant both died." James looked at Rachel propped on his lap. He kissed her downy hair and looked at Danny. "Makes me even more grateful to have my Rachel."

"Yes. Sad indeed, about the doctor."

Doctor Burk came into the meetinghouse and took off his hat. Sitting down next to Rebekah Bannister and her large family, Danny noticed the doctor smiling.

Danny nudged James. "What happened to Mr. Bannister?"

"Got in a tavern fight. Someone stabbed him. Missus Bannister and Dr. Burk will be wed next month."

Danny raised his eyebrows. "I have missed much news since I've been gone."

The service began. Danny glanced over at his parents and siblings sitting to the side. His view was not clear, but the whole family seemed exceptionally sober this morning. Glancing at Polly, he was startled anew by her paleness. Deep circles under her eyes likely resulted from another sleepless night. He knew from his mother that Polly had slept little since Jonathan left.

It broke his heart that Polly would not confide in him. They had always been able to share personal things together while growing up. Lately, she was distant and withdrawn.

Lord, where is Jonathan? Please help my sister.

The reverend was preaching about purity and the importance of avoiding fornication. Recalling his passionate kiss with Susannah, Danny had a new understanding of this powerful temptation. He shifted in his seat.

I wonder if someone spoke to the reverend about Susannah and me?

As he pondered his intense desire for the woman he loved, his attention was drawn to his family. Polly had slipped out of the pew and run outside.

Danny glanced at James who looked troubled.

Leaning toward his twin, Danny whispered, "I'll return forthwith."

Exiting as quietly as possible, Danny went out the heavy wooden door and squinted in the bright sunlight. Descending the steps, he looked around for his sister. It took him a few moments before he saw her on the edge of the wooded area behind the meetinghouse. She was heaving onto the ground while leaning on a tree.

Danny ran toward her and held her up until she was

finished. Handing her a kerchief, he led her to a rock underneath a shade tree.

"Polly." His eyes moistened. "Is this...is this what I think it is?"

She covered her eyes with her hands and sobbed. "Yes." Her voice was small and tight.

Danny stood up and placed his hands on his hips.

Lord, what do I say?

"Polly, you must let me find Jonathan."

She glared at him through her tears. "No!"

"But why not?"

"Because...this is my fault, not his."

Danny shook his head slowly. "How can you say that? That makes no sense..."

She grabbed Danny's hand and gripped it. "I was the one who desired this. I...was the one who would not stop." Her voice pinched. "It was not his fault. He was grieving for his father. Do you not see?" Deep sobs burst from her throat.

Danny put his arm around her and held her for a moment.

"Have you told Mother?"

"No. But I know she suspects. It will be obvious before long." She stared off into the distance with a vacant look.

"How can I help you, Polly? It pains me to see you go through this."

She looked up at him with anguish. "Pray for me."

He gripped her shoulder. "That I will do."

After several moments of silence, Polly wiped the tears from her face. "I am ready to go back inside."

"Are you certain?"

"Yes." She boldly stood up and strode toward the meetinghouse to resume worship.

Lord, please help us all.

Danny took a deep breath and followed her back up the steps.

Chapter 18
Changes

It was not until the leaves on the maples started turning red that the letter finally arrived from the armory:

> To Mr. Daniel Lowe. Jr.,
>
> Requesting your return to the Springfield Armory.
> All should be well.
>
> We are grateful for your service.
>
> I am, Sir,
>
> Your most Humble Servant,
>
> David Ames,
> Superintendent

After reading the short note, Danny closed his eyes.
Finally, I can see Susannah.

He wanted to send her a note telling her of his imminent arrival, but he could probably get there faster himself than the post rider would deliver the news.

After months of working on his parents' farm, Danny was grateful that the harvest was nearly complete.

At least I could help them for a time.

Hurrying into his parents' cabin, he saw only his mother working on her spinning wheel. Seeing him carrying the letter, she stopped the large wooden wheel and her eyes moistened.

"I see they have sent for you." She swallowed back her tears and smiled. "I know you are anxious to return. But I shall dearly miss you."

Danny had not realized until this moment how much he would miss his family as well.

"It seems I am always saying farewell to those I love. Whether here or in Springfield." He looked down at the letter in his hands. "They have told me it is safe to return. I do not wish for you to worry about me."

She stood up slowly. "I shall always worry about you. But when I do, I will remember to pray for you." She kissed him tenderly on his cheek. "I'll pack some food for your journey."

He impulsively hugged her and kissed the top of her cap. "I love you, Mother."

Her face twisted in pain. "You know you always carry part of my heart with you, Danny. Please, fare well, my son."

"I shall." He looked around the room. "Where is everyone?"

"Most of them left for the field to finish the corn harvest." She dried her face with her linen sleeve. "They just left. But I do not know where Polly is."

Mary walked to the table and began to slice some bread for his knapsack.

"I'll find them and tell them I am leaving."

Hurrying out the door, he started for the field but was stopped by a voice coming from the barn. "Danny."

Polly was leaning against the edge of the barn door, looking thin and pale. Walking toward his sister, he followed her into the wooden structure where she sat on a mound of hay. "You're leaving." Her voice was sullen and weak.

"Yes, I must." He plopped down on the hay next to her. "Have you told mother yet?"

Picking up a piece of alfalfa, she drew with it on the dirt floor. "No. But I have decided to go see Aunt Hannah today. I cannot face Grandmother."

Danny stared at his hands. "I understand."

"Perhaps Aunt Hannah will come with me and speak to Mother. I am afraid to tell her alone. I know how hurt she will be." Polly's lips quivered.

Danny squeezed her arm. "She will be more hurt if you

do not confide in her. She loves you."

"I know." Tears dripped onto the hay as she stared at the floor.

"Polly, the post rider gave me this as well." He handed her a note.

"Jonathan!" She tucked the folded parchment inside her bodice.

Danny's voice was impatient. "You must tell me where he is!"

Polly sought her brother's eyes. "I do not know." Her voice was vehement. "And even if I did, I would not tell him about the child. He deserves better than me."

"Better than you?" Danny shook his head, bewildered.

"Yes…better than a woman who would take advantage of a man's grief."

She pushed herself onto her feet and wiped the hay off of her skirts. "I must go see Aunt Hannah."

"Polly, wait!" Danny stood up and reached for her arm. "You know I have to return to Springfield. But I beg of you — if there is anything I can do for you — you must write to me immediately. I love you, dear sister." He held her close, tears dripping onto the top of her linen cap.

She held him for a moment. "Thank you, dear brother. I love you, too."

Crying rivers of tears, she trod down the road toward their Aunt Hannah's house.

Dear God, please help her — and her child.

* * *

Glancing out the window in hopes of seeing the field workers, Mary was surprised to see Polly and Hannah instead.

The door creaked on its hinges when she opened it. "Come in. Such a surprise to see you, Hannah."

Her sister-in-law smiled but Mary knew that there was something wrong. Very wrong. She and Hannah had been best friends since childhood. They had always been like sisters growing up, making Hannah's marriage to Mary's brother, James, a mere formality of their already-close relationship. Hannah could never hide distress from Mary.

"Mary, Polly came to see me this morning." Hannah put her arm around Polly's shoulder. Polly stared at the floor with her arms folded tightly across her chest. "Polly needs to tell you something — quite important." Hannah squeezed Polly's shoulder encouragingly.

Polly opened her mouth, but only sobs came forth.

Dear Lord, is it true? I tried to believe it was impossible!

Mary met Hannah's face and tears brimmed in both sets of eyes.

"I think...I think I know what you need to say, Polly." Mary's lips trembled uncontrollably. Polly walked toward her mother's arms and they clasped each other tightly, sobbing.

My daughter? She has always been so obedient. Am I dreaming?

After a few moments, Hannah gave her kerchief to Mary. Mary dabbed at her cheeks and then blotted the moisture from Polly's.

"Sit down, Polly." The young woman did as her mother directed. Mary smoothed her ruffled gown and sniffed.

I must get control over my pain — over my disappointment.

Hannah spoke before Mary could get any words out. "Polly is over two months with child. Her little one's birthing should be in April."

Her little one.

Just hearing those words sent Mary's thoughts reeling. She started to feel dizzy and sat on a bench.

"Where...where is Jonathan, Polly?"

Her voice thick from crying, Polly wiped the tears from her face again. "I do not know."

Suddenly enraged, Mary glared at her oldest daughter. "You do not know? How can this be? He needs to be responsible for the welfare of your child."

Polly visibly wilted. "It is my fault that there is a child. I am responsible."

Mary rose up from her chair, energized by her anger. "He is just as responsible — more so — than you are. And he will support this child whether he is trying to run away from his responsibility or not!"

"He is not running away from his responsibility. He does not know!"

This was too much for Mary to think about. Heart racing, she did not know whether to cry or scream. Maybe both. She sat down with shaking legs.

"Whether or not he knows of the child, he knows what he did to you."

Polly glared at her mother. "He did not 'do' this to me. I was the one who wanted him to. I did not want him to stop. I was afraid I would never see him again because of Papa. I could not bear the pain. I wanted to love him — to be one with him."

Benumbed, Mary stared at her daughter. "Polly," she whispered in anguish.

"I am sorry, Mother. I know this has hurt you. But I cannot have you or Papa blame Jonathan. This is my fault."

Flinging the door wide open, Polly ran off.

Hannah looked with sympathy at Mary. "Let me go after her. Perhaps I should bring her home with me for the night. It will give you and Daniel a chance to speak." Hannah hugged her shoulder.

Mary watched Hannah leave. She was unaware how long she sat there but she was startled to hear the voices of the other children coming in from the fields.

Daniel! What will I say to him?

James, Ephraim, and the girls came in the door and stopped short when they saw their mother.

"Mother?" Prissy stared with concern.

"Where is your papa?"

"He's out in the field." James narrowed his eyes. "What has happened?"

Without answering Mary slowly got up. "Prissy, please serve up the meal. I need to speak with your father."

Stumbling more than walking, Mary hugged her arms around herself. The cooler air should have prompted her to grab her shawl, but her thoughts were too troubled to notice the need. Shivering slightly, she finally saw Daniel near the wagon loaded to the brim with freshly-harvested corn.

Her husband turned and reached out to her. "I know. Danny told me he had to leave. I shall miss him as well."

She stared at him, too distressed to speak.

"Mary?" Daniel enveloped her in his dirt-covered arms. "What weighs on your heart?"

"Hold me, Daniel."

"Gladly."

His comforting warmth flooded her with strength.

After a moment she leaned back, tears brimming again in her swollen eyes. "I must tell you something."

She started with Hannah's visit and then, bit by bit, relayed everything that her sister-in-law and Polly told her.

Daniel sunk to the ground. "He did this to her. I shall kill him." His jaw clenched.

"No, Daniel—you will not. And Polly was quite clear." She took a deep breath, drawing courage from the depths of her shattered being. "Jonathan did not do this to Polly. She asked him to. She encouraged him."

Daniel looked up at her in complete disbelief.

"Polly?"

"She said that she knew she would never see him again because of your feelings toward Jonathan. She said that it was *her* desire that led to this."

Daniel turned white and covered his face with his hands. He did not move.

"Daniel?" She put her hand on his shoulder. "Daniel, please come to the house. You need victuals."

He spoke with a voice she did not recognize. "Please, leave me to myself."

She breathed in sharply and struggled to speak in a whisper.

"Yes, Daniel."

Turning, she walked with plodding steps back to their cabin. When she was a dozen yards away from him, gut-wrenching sobs burst forth. She looked back and saw him on his knees, prostrate. All she could hear him cry was, "God forgive me."

Chapter 19
Springfield

The streetlights were being illuminated one by one as the dusk set in far too early.

Where did the summer go?

But then a more painful question forced its way into Susannah's thoughts.

Where did Dan go?

She had given up waiting for a message from the post rider. Dan had said he could not tell her where he was going.

Could he not at least have written to me? At least one time?

She blinked back tears and looked at the diary that lay by her bed.

It had been over a week since she had poured out her thoughts on paper. It was becoming too repetitious...too painful. She had tried to keep track of the numbers of days that he had been away until, reaching day ninety, she had forced herself to stop. Somehow, the thought of being without him for a hundred days would mark a turning point in her hope. She was afraid that she would despair of ever seeing him again.

Walking toward her window, she could barely make out the color change in the trees. Shadows were elongated along each building and the dry leaves rustling in the autumn wind sounded eerie and unsettling. She shivered.

Perhaps I should close the window for the night.

She hated to do it. It seemed as if that would signify surrender to the change of seasons that lurked over her spirits. She had resisted autumn since she was a child, clinging to the long days of summer sunlight as long as her senses could. Fall always carried sadness for Susannah. This one was the bleakest of all, with her mother now gone a full year.

And Dan gone – perhaps for good?

She shivered again and finally succumbed to the season. Pulling down on the double hung casement, Susannah's eyes widened as a shadow approached on the street. At first the solitary traveler frightened her until she noted the familiar gait of the man she had waited for since summer.

"Dan!" She whispered under her breath, then shouted. "Dan!"

She was greeted by a smile that made the lack of sunlight unimportant. The glow of his expression was light enough for Susannah.

She flew to her bedroom door and flung it open. Nearly tripping on the stairs, she clung to the railing for support, her shaking legs fumbling their way down each step.

Before he could knock, she jerked open the front door and stood with her mouth agape, smiling and breathing rapidly from her quick descent.

"Dan." Her voice a breathless whisper, she realized she was barefoot but did not care.

"May I come in?" The look on his face enraptured her with delight.

"Yes." She stood back so he could enter. She heard Modesty behind her but kept her eyes fixed on Dan. "Modesty, please set another place at table."

She heard Modesty giggle. "Yes, miss." The padding of the maid's feet was followed by her closing the door to the kitchen.

Silence ensued while the two stared at each other.

"Susannah, I missed you so much." His voice caught in his throat.

"Where were you?" She searched his eyes.

"I was told to go home. There were strange goings-on at the armory and Mr. Ames said I was in danger – that I must leave. I was not to tell anyone else lest they be in danger as well."

"Danger?" Her eyebrows furrowed.

He pulled out the note from Mr. Ames. "Here."

She scanned its contents and her eyes widened. "You

were in danger?"

"Apparently. But he said it is now safe."

"Thank God." As she handed the note back to him, he grabbed her hand, holding it.

"Susannah...I never thought it would be so long. I dreamt of you so often. I...I hope you know how desperately I wanted to see you."

"No more desperately than I longed to see you." Her lips quivered and her eyes grew moist. Her voice became a whisper. "I thought you were not coming back." Tears escaped despite her efforts to hold them back.

He pulled her toward him and held her. She laid her head against his chest and heard the thump of his heartbeat. It was a soothing sound that lulled her anxious thoughts. The smell of his deerskin jacket blended with wood smoke and sweat. She relished the intensity of his scent. Pulling away slightly, she looked up at him—taller this time because she was barefoot—and whispered.

"You must be starving."

"I am. I am starved for your affection."

His full lips pressed against hers with an intensity that curled her feet. Tasting him was more delightful than a meal of sweetened apples and she hungrily responded to his flavor. His hands wrapped themselves around her upswept hair and then surrounded her waist with an embrace that made her gasp.

"Dan. I missed you so."

"No more than I missed you. Susannah..."

The door opened behind them and her father walked in.

Susannah hurried to push loose strands of hair behind her ear and smoothed down her dimity gown. "Father."

I hope I am not as red as I feel.

By his peculiar stare, she knew she must be.

"Well, Mr. Lowe. Good to see you back in Springfield. It has been some time." His look was inquisitive.

"Yes, sir, I am greatly pleased to be back. I was following Mr. Ames's instructions to stay away until he sent for me."

Susannah grabbed her father's arm. "Father, Dan's life was in danger! He has a note from Mr. Ames, saying it was safe to return."

Her father scowled. "Yes, I know there was some ugly business going on there. They arrested someone who was responsible for the terrible disaster at the water shop."

"May I enquire about the well-being of your son, Lieutenant Dobbins?"

"Certainly, Mr. Lowe. He has recovered well and is now back at work. We are grateful he was not injured further." Smiling at Dan, he grabbed his arm. "Please stay for supper with us."

"I would be honored, sir."

Susannah's face illuminated with joy. "Supper with my two favorite gentlemen."

Grabbing Dan's arm, she led him down the hallway toward the dining area.

* * *

"That was an amazing meal. Please tell Modesty how much I appreciate it."

Dan grinned at Susannah and she used her bare foot to play with his calf under the table. He tried not to laugh and at one point, he jumped and bumped his knee on the table.

"Please excuse my clumsiness." He gave a warning look to Susannah but could not help but grin at her innocent-appearing face.

Mr. Dobbins took a sip of his wine. "She has been a most helpful cook since we arrived in Springfield. I am grateful that her father could spare her, with so many brothers underfoot." Mr. Dobbins wiped his face with his napkin.

"Her younger sister is taking care of the household now." Susannah laughed. "I cannot imagine having seven brothers and sisters."

Danny raised his eyebrows. "Well, I can. And I do."

Susannah and her father both looked at him in surprise.

"Eight children?" Susannah looked from Danny to her father then back again.

"Yes. Beside my twin brother, James, I have five sisters

and a ten-year-old brother named Ephraim."

Mr. Dobbins raised his wine glass in a toast. "To large families. May they be a blessing to all." He took a sip and glanced at Susannah over the lip of his goblet.

Danny raised his glass and took a sip. Meeting Susannah's eyes, he noticed she was blushing a deep red. This time, he gently nudged her foot with his boot. She squirmed in pleasure.

"You have both been most kind, but I must return to the armory. I will meet with Mr. Ames in the morning and resume my schedule as soon as possible."

"'Tis Wednesday. Will I not see you then until Sabbath?" A shadow had fallen across her face for the first time since he had arrived.

"I suppose not." He felt her foot caressing his leg again. "But I pray the time goes quickly."

"I pray it, as well." She lowered her eyes then looked up. "Have you heard that Ezra now attends Sabbath services? Along with your other friend…the one who used to come with you and Ansel…"

"Oh, you mean Cyrus Graves. The large fellow with the light hair."

"That's the one. Since that terrible day at the armory, Ezra's been coming quite regular. He seems quite taken in with the reverend's preaching."

Danny's eyes moistened at the last time he had seen Ezra. It was at Ansel's deathbed. "I am so pleased that he is coming. I'll have to speak to him when I return up the hill." Danny yawned. "Forgive me. I have walked twenty miles today and I fear I am quite tired."

"Forgive us, Mr. Lowe. We have kept you far too long." Mr. Dobbins stood. "Can I drive you in my wagon?"

"No, sir, but I am indebted to you for the offer. Thank you."

Danny walked toward the door accompanied by Susannah. He looked back and saw that Mr. Dobbins was not following them. He smiled.

Standing at the front door, Danny gently gripped her

arms and touched his forehead against hers. "Until Sabbath, then."

"Until Sabbath." She grabbed his face and planted a moist kiss upon him before racing barefoot back up the stairs.

Turning around near the top step, she looked back at him and smiled. "Welcome home, Daniel Lowe."

"'Tis good to be home, Susannah Dobbins." He grinned and doffed his cap before stepping out the door.

Chapter 20
Caution

It seemed longer than three months since Danny had eaten breakfast with his co-workers.

The kitchen in the barracks felt different. Several familiar faces were missing now and a few new men had been hired. All hungrily attacked the generous offerings of the cook. With the colder weather, Missus Parker added extra helpings to get the workers through the morning shift. Besides gruel, plates of salt pork, eggs and biscuits were piled high in the center of the long table. The plates quickly emptied.

"So Danny, where'd ya go?" Ezra washed down a biscuit with a large gulp of cider.

"I was told to go home—'til things settled down a bit."

"So did ya hear about Lieutenant Morris being arrested?" Ezra leaned in toward his friend.

"Morris? That new officer with the fanciful ways?" Danny listened intently.

"Get this." Ezra stared at him intently. "His real name was 'Maurice.' A frog, no less!"

Cyrus interrupted. "He wasn't a Frenchman. His father was. He was born right here." The worker pointed his fork to emphasize his words. "Seems his father died in the French Revolution. Morris—or Maurice—always blamed this country for his father's death…for not helping with their cause. He decided to get back at us by destroying our weapons. Right where they're made." He huffed and continued eating.

Danny sat straight on the bench. "Born an American…and still loyal to France? I don't get it." He shook his head in disbelief.

"Seems he still had connections to the Frenchies. We're not exactly on good terms now, are we?" Ezra scooped up the last mouthful from his plate and stood up. "Long day ahead."

"So, ya back in the filing shop today?" Cyrus looked at Danny as he guzzled the last of his cider.

"Don't know. I'm supposed to report to Mr. Ames when I return. Guess he'll tell me where I need to go."

"Not bein' promoted to his secretary now, are ya?" Cyrus grinned.

"I doubt that. I'm just anxious to return to my old job. Just want life to be as it was." He paused. "As much as it can be."

"Not quite the same without Ansel, is it?"

"No. Not quite." Danny took his last sip and left.

Although not much had changed physically on the hill, it still seemed different. Danny stared at the ground, lost in thought.

Morris. Maurice. A French sympathizer in our midst – right in the United States Army!

Shaking his head in disbelief, he suddenly stopped.

How could an army officer have changed my initials on the barrel of the gun?

A shiver ran through his spine and it was not from the early October breeze.

Then he recalled the night he had heard an officer and a worker speaking in French. No one had said one of the workers was apprehended. Is it possible the conspirator was killed in the disaster at the water shop?

I pray that is so.

Forcing his feet to move faster, he hurried the last hundred yards toward the superintendent's office.

Approaching the sentinel guarding the door, he noted the high woolen collar on the private's neck.

Must be a bit more comfortable now in this cooler season.

"May I see Mr. Ames, please? I was told to report."

The sentinel was apparently informed as well, and did not question Danny's request. He moved stiffly aside to allow entrance.

Danny carefully opened the door with the loudest creaking hinge he had ever heard. Danny winced at the sound.

"Blasted door! It takes a government requisition just to get a door oiled around here." Meeting Danny's eye he attempted a smile. "Come in, Mr. Lowe. Good to see you back at the armory."

"'Tis good to be back, sir."

The superintendent threw a pile of papers on his desk. "Have a seat, sir." His voice was friendly but cautious. "I want to apprise you of the current situation here. I imagine you have heard about the arrest of Morris—or Maurice, as we now know was his surname."

"Yes, sir. The workers informed me at breakfast. I was quite surprised by that revelation."

"Yes." Mr. Ames sat wearily on the chair behind his desk and exhaled slowly. "Sorry it took so long to send you the letter to return. We were investigating all the men who were injured or died in the explosion—their backgrounds, possible sympathies with the French. We came up with nothing after all this time."

Danny swallowed. "So what you are saying sir is, we still do not know who may have conspired with Maurice."

Ames scowled and met Danny's eyes. "You are correct. We are hoping that we missed something—anything—that might mean one of those killed was involved in the disaster. We certainly cannot find any reason amongst our other workers who are still alive. The upshot is, we are not certain of anything. And I beg you to still be cautious, just in case..."

Danny narrowed his eyes. "I will, sir." He tried to calm his racing heart.

"I could not do without you here at the armory any longer. The destruction inside that one water shop, along with the loss of so many workers, has set us back weeks in production. We need your skill and must make up time." He met Danny's eyes squarely. "Are you game for returning to work with an eye over your shoulder? Can you concentrate on your duties and still be cautious?"

Danny set his jaw. "I know I can, sir. My father always taught me to work hard and look sharp—at the same time." He gave him a reassuring smile.

Ames smiled with relief. "Good. I felt it only fair to inform you completely before taking you back on. And by the way, the paymaster will pay your wages for the time you were gone."

Danny widened his eyes. "Thank you, sir."

"I am certain you can use some extra dollars — in case you have any plans for your future." Mr. Ames winked.

Danny could feel his cheeks warm. "Thank you, sir."

"Well then, back to the filing shop for you. I think you will find a large stack of barrels to refine." He held out his hand. "Good day, Mr. Lowe."

Danny shook the man's hand. "Good day, sir."

Turning to leave, he took in a deep breath and did not exhale until he had left the building.

I must not tell anyone of this concern. Certainly not mother — or Susannah. Especially not Susannah.

Focusing on the filing shop in the distance, he resolved to get back to work — *and* look sharp at all times.

Easier planned than accomplished.

Chapter 21
Apples

It was the end of another Sabbath day in West Springfield and Danny walked Susannah back to the dock to wait for the ferry. It was time to return to Springfield — and another week apart.

Staring at the wide Connecticut River, the distance seemed to reflect the chasm separating the two.

Another six days without seeing her.

That realization always left a deep emptiness in his heart.

He had been back in Springfield for four weeks now without any further incidents at the armory. The greatest danger he seemed to be facing was succumbing to despair at not being able to ask for Susannah's hand in marriage.

Despite the wages he had tucked away, he still lacked sufficient funds to provide a home worthy of her. The best he could offer her right now was a rented room in a boarding house on Boston Road. The occasional swishes of her fine woolen gown against his leg as they strode toward the ferry, made him ache for the day they could be together always. As if she were reading his mind, she squeezed his arm.

"Dan, I always dread the end of Sabbath day. The long days in between seem to draw out further each week." Her eyes did not meet his but he could see her blinking as she stared at the path ahead.

"I know. I am preparing for when I can ask your father for your hand. But — this is not yet the time."

Blinking back tears, she looked up at him intently. "My father would not mind letting us live in his house. He would readily offer."

Danny paused and stared at the curls around her face stirring in the chilly breeze.

"Susannah, I need to be able to provide for you. Not lean

upon your father's generosity. A husband must take care of his wife." He smiled with more reassurance than he felt. "As soon as I can provide a home for you, I will gladly ask your father for your hand. And your heart."

Her lips upturned. "You already have my heart."

Danny wished they were alone so he could taste those lips with his own. Susannah grinned even wider.

"I have a surprise for you, Dan."

"What sort of a surprise." He swallowed, swayed as always by her arresting charm.

"When you were gone, I made a promise to myself. That as soon as you returned, I would learn how to bake for you." She gave a conspiring look. "So, Modesty has been teaching me and tonight I will make you a dessert from apples and cranberries. My father has invited you to come so you can taste my creation." Susannah gave a self-satisfied nod.

Leaning close to her ear, he whispered. "Will it be as sweet as your lips?"

"I pray it will be sweeter." She blushed a rosy red.

"That could not be possible."

As the ferry approached to bring the group of church-goers back to Springfield, Mr. Dobbins walked a few steps toward Danny and Susannah.

"Have you invited Dan for pie?"

"Yes, just now." Susannah pulled her Indian shawl more tightly around her shoulders.

Turning toward Ezra and Cyrus standing a few feet back, Mr. Dobbins shouted a friendly greeting. "Gentlemen, would you enjoy some dessert at our home before you return to the armory this evening?"

Danny immediately felt Susannah flinch and lean closer toward him. Her smile had faded.

His eyes drawn to his two friends, Danny saw them glance at the Dobbins family, including Susannah's brother, Stephen, in his Army uniform. Ezra spoke first. "I thank you kindly, Mr. Dobbins. I think I shall get some rest before the long week starts."

Cyrus doffed his hat at Mr. Dobbins. "Aye, 'tis a long

week ahead. But I thank ya as well, Mr. Dobbins."

Danny felt Susannah's grip on his arm relax.

"Is everything well?" He whispered close to her ear.

"Yes, quite well." Her fleeting glance did not reassure him.

The ferry worker announced that all could board and Danny wrapped his arm around Susannah's shoulders when she shivered.

"You need a woolen shawl. This one is lovely but not very warm."

She nestled next to him while holding the handrail tightly with one hand. "You are keeping me warm."

"Are you certain all is well. You seem a bit…troubled."

"Everything is well. I am with you — how could anything not be fine?"

The early November weather sent collective chills across the ferry passengers. Women drew their cloaks closer around their necks. Men pulled their collars up higher. And Danny wrapped willing hands around Susannah's waist as he drew her next to his heart. She leaned against his chest, sending warmth throughout him and increasing the tempo of his heartbeat.

Lord, help me be patient for the day we can be together — every day.

He sighed and held her closer.

At last, the ferry docked on the Springfield side of the river. Passengers scurried down the ramp and up the bank. The chilled air appeared as smoke when everyone breathed, and the ladies giggled through chattering teeth as they walked quickly to their homes.

"See you on the morrow, Danny." Ezra waved, stuck his hands in his pockets and ran up the hill toward the barracks.

Cyrus tipped his hat and followed Ezra.

Susannah took in a deep breath and exhaled chilled vapor. "Well, then, let us have some pie." Smiling at Danny, she led the way to their entrance.

When they entered, Mr. Dobbins took Danny's wool coat and hung it on a hook. Lieutenant Dobbins removed his tall hat with the bear fur trim and set his uniform cover on a table. The three men walked into the parlor and Mr. Dobbins pointed to a settee for Danny to sit. Stephen flipped up the tails of his uniform and collapsed into a chair rubbing his hands together.

"Lovely evening — to stay indoors near a fire." Stephen blew warm breath into his cupped hands.

Although Mr. Dobbins and Stephen always made Danny feel welcome, he still felt somewhat awkward in the formal parlor. He shifted in his seat and cleared his throat.

"You seem to be well-recovered from your injury, Lieutenant Dobbins."

Stephen smiled. "You can be formal at the armory. But here, you can call me Stephen."

"Very well — Stephen. That will take a bit of getting used to."

"And yes, I am quite recovered. Thank you." His face sobered. "That was — an unforgettable day."

"Yes."

"I am so sorry about your friend, Ansel. He was a good man — an honest worker."

"Other than my brother, he was my best friend."

Stephen scowled. "Lieutenant Morris was supposed to be inspecting the water shops that day. He suddenly came down with a 'tormenting pain in the pit of his stomach' — or so he claimed. They sent me instead. That was how they began to suspect Morris — Maurice as we now know." He shook his head angrily. "The effrontery of it all — a sworn officer of the United States Army."

Modesty came to the parlor doorway. "Miss Susannah says that tea is being served in the dining room. Soon to be followed by her apple-cranberry pie." She giggled and went back to the kitchen.

All three men stood up, ambled to the next room, and found seats at the table. A linen cloth had been placed along the length of the wood, and formal dishes and cups set out. Teapots oozed vapor of deliciously-scented brews of bohea and hyson through the delicate china spouts. Bowls of sugar nested nearby as well as sticks of cinnamon with a grater.

Danny's mouth watered at the aromas, especially the scent of pie wafting in from the kitchen.

Mr. Dobbins grinned at Danny. "Smells more enticing than the kitchens at the armory, I daresay."

"There is no comparison, sir." Danny licked his lips. "Those apples smell sweeter than any dessert we are served in the barracks."

Stephen, sitting on Danny's right, leaned toward him, whispering. "I would not get my hopes up too high, if I were you. My sister lacks, shall we say, the finer womanly skills in the kitchen that one might hope for." He rolled his eyes.

Danny raised his eyebrows amusedly. "Spoken like a true older brother." He muffled a laugh.

Mr. Dobbins scowled at his son. "Let us be encouraging, now. She has been practicing for days with this receipt."

Stephen sat up with a straight face. "I shall do my best, Father, to promote my sister's fine cooking endeavors — however it tastes to my unsuspecting senses." He squelched a grin.

Susannah appeared in the doorway, a look of panic on her face, and then disappeared quickly back into the kitchen.

A moment later, Modesty, peeked into the dining room. "It will not be too much longer, gentleman." She hurried away.

Several more moments went by. Mr. Dobbins cleared his throat. "Perhaps, gentleman, you would like some tea? Black or green, Mr. Lowe."

"I shall take black, sir." Danny pushed his cup closer to the steaming pot. Rich, red liquid filled his china cup. Danny carefully added a teaspoon of sugar, and very gingerly, picked up the teacup.

After they had all been drinking tea for several more minutes, Susannah finally appeared carrying plates of the dessert. Edges of the pie were as black as a smithy's anvil while the middle still had moist dough floating on a pond of chopped fruit.

Mr. Dobbins let his jaw drop before he appeared to catch himself. "It looks…delicious, my dear."

Susannah plunked the dessert plates in front of her father and Danny, and raced back into the kitchen. Danny heard her crying.

"Excuse me, gentlemen." Danny boldly stood up from the table and hurried into the kitchen area where Modesty was comforting Susannah.

"May I speak with Susannah a moment, Modesty?"

She winked at him. "Of course, Mr. Lowe."

When they were alone, Danny wrapped his arms around her quivering shoulders.

"I love that you worked so hard to make this for me."

"You must think I am a pathetic cook. I cannot even make a simple pie." She burst into tears.

"You are not a pathetic anything. You mean the world to me. Anything new takes practice. Do you think I could make a musket at the armory the first week I worked there? It took me a long while to perfect the skill. I love that you worked so hard to please me by making a pie. But more importantly, I love you."

She stopped crying and looked up at him. "I love you, Dan. I am so sorry about dessert."

He stroked her curls along her cheek. "Of what do you speak, miss?" He grinned mischievously. "I am having dessert right here."

Leaning into her face, he kissed her lips with a tenderness that moved quickly into a thrill that sent his heart racing. Pausing and out of breath, he smiled. "Your lips are the sweetest fruit I could ever desire. May I have another serving, miss?"

Smiling, she wove her arms around his waist and snuggled closer. "If you must, sir."

"I must. I am starving."

Elaine Marie Cooper

Chapter 22
Thanksgiving

It was Susannah's first Thanksgiving in Springfield that November 27, 1800. Preparations had been underway for three weeks for today's dinner celebrating the Lord's blessings. The greatest source of her thanks was that she could spend all day with Dan and her family.

Rewinding the string that suspended one of the two chickens roasting over the fire, she smiled in spite of her nervousness about making her first holiday meal.

"I see ya smilin' over there, miss. I doubt you're thrillin' about those two fowl cookin' in the hearth." Modesty loved to tease her about Dan.

Susannah broke into a full grin. "Hardly. You know me too well, Modesty." She stood up from her task, wiping her greasy hands onto her duck cloth apron. "Modesty, I want to thank you for all your help these last months. I...I've not always been the kindest to you. I pray — can you forgive me?"

Modesty's eyes moistened. Dropping her wooden spoon into a large bowl, she strode over to Susannah and hugged her. "Of course, miss. I know I was a bit of a handful at first." She lowered her eyes in embarrassment. "I think, while I've been teachin' you to cook, you've been helpin' me be more — ladylike. I thank ya for that."

Susannah gave her a quick hug and then scanned the room nervously. "What am I forgetting?"

"I think you're forgettin' to breathe, miss." Modesty threw her head back and gave a hearty laugh as she returned to beat the egg whites for the green corn pudding.

"I am frightfully nervous. My last cooking endeavor was a disaster." Susannah rolled her eyes at the memory.

"Well, you've learned much in these last weeks, miss.

And I must say, I appreciate your help in the kitchen. It has made the time go faster."

Susannah perused the pies sitting off to the side. Sniffing them, she closed her eyes in pleasure. "I hope these taste as good as they look—and smell!"

"Once the fowl are done, and this corn pudding is baked, we shall be ready to serve."

"I pray everyone will feel thankful, after they've eaten my cooking."

* * *

The gentlemen were called to table and Danny's empty stomach growled the whole distance to the dining room. After celebrating Thanksgiving and God's blessings at the meetinghouse all morning, Danny was more than ready to indulge in the meal— Susannah's first Thanksgiving meal.

I pray it goes well—for her as well as us.

Sitting in the same seat he had in his prior visit, Danny's taste buds swelled at the tantalizing plates set out by Susannah and Modesty.

"This looks incredibly tasty, Susannah."

She blushed while Modesty brought in the platter of roasted chicken.

"I hope everyone enjoys it." Susannah nervously bit her lower lip.

Danny's appetite for food was temporarily forgotten as he took in the soft muslin dress that swathed her form in numerous layers. Her lean arms were covered with a single layer of the material, revealing her creamy skin underneath. Her bodice was not revealing, but her curves were such that, even completely covered, her femininity wrapped around his senses, sending warmth up and down his spine. Attempting to recover himself, he cleared his throat.

"I am certain I will enjoy you...I mean enjoy the food."

Mr. Dobbins raised his eyebrows. Lifting his newly filled wine goblet, he raised a toast. "To feminine beauty, as well as delicious food."

Danny's cheeks burned as he held up his goblet. "Yes."

Stephen took a swallow and set his glass down. "This looks most delectable, Susannah…and Modesty. I must say, dear sister, your cooking skills have improved immensely."

Susannah blushed. "With Modesty's help. I could not have improved without her."

Modesty gave her an appreciative tap on the shoulder as she brought out the last dish.

Mr. Dobbins reached out his hand toward the maid. "Modesty, please join us for Thanksgiving meal. This is a holiday, after all and you have worked so hard."

"Thank ya kindly, Mr. Dobbins, but my sister made up our family meal and I'm lookin' to be with my family for the day."

"Well then, have a blessed Thanksgiving, Modesty, and enjoy your meal with your family."

"Thank you, sir." Modesty curtsied politely and untied her apron as she went back into the kitchen.

Mr. Dobbins cleared his throat. "Well then, let us bless this fine meal."

They all bowed their heads.

"Our Heavenly Father, we so appreciate this abundant meal so evident of the numerous blessings you have bestowed upon us this last year. Let us not forget the wonderful message from the pulpit this morning, that 'You will not forsake your people.' Help us to be worthy of the callings you have laid upon our hearts, to do good, to work hard, and to always give you thanks. We are especially grateful that you spared my son, Stephen, in the tragic incident last summer." Mr. Dobbins's lips trembled. "We are eternally grateful that You had Your wings of protection over him. And we pray for those who have lost loved ones this year, that You would comfort them in the knowledge that, one day, we shall all be together again. Amen."

"Amen." Danny appreciated the extra squeeze from Susannah's hand. He looked up from prayer to meet her tender look.

"How is your brother James faring, Dan?" Looking at her father, she explained. "His twin lost his wife several months ago. She left behind an infant."

"He is doing well. As well as one can expect." Danny put a brave smile on his face. Besides concern for James, he was deeply worried about Polly. Letters from home had indicated much sadness and distress. The last letter from her indicated that she had moved in with Aunt Hannah and Uncle James. She was still refusing to let anyone know the whereabouts of Jonathan. Danny sighed but looked up with a forced smile. He did not wish to concern Susannah or her family with his family's scandal.

"The victuals look hearty and delicious, Susannah. Thank you, all, for inviting me."

Mr. Dobbins began to pass the plate of corn bread. "I would have hosted Ezra and Cyrus as well, but it seems they had family nearby to celebrate with."

Danny noticed Susannah look down briefly but then she hurried to pick up a bowl of roasted sweet potatoes. "Please, have some. The potatoes the farmer brought in to your store were excellent, Father. I am so grateful the local farmers exchange goods for such delicious fare."

"'Tis almost like being on the farm at home." Danny chewed his food with vigor. "I thought when I moved to the city, I would lack the fruit of the land I was used to. But with the farms so close by, there is much available to enjoy."

"Much more here, than in Boston. Everything is closer." Mr. Dobbins swallowed a helping of the chicken. "This is so tender and sweet. You and Modesty picked out the perfect fowl."

"Modesty's cook book says the fowl with yellow legs are sweetest. I suppose the book was right, because those are the ones she chose. I must say, it was quite the sight watching her single them out at market. They did their best to evade her efforts to corner them—such squawking and feathers flying. Every time she would grab one, Modesty would get a feather up her nose and start sneezing. Then the fowl escaped and the hunt was on again. But Modesty was undaunted. She finally grabbed her apron and wrapped them in a ball as soon as they were caught. You should have heard her! 'You'll not escape this cook again, nor send feathers up my nose, ya foul fowl.'"

All three men laughed. Danny could easily picture the feisty Modesty refusing to surrender to the obstinate birds.

Stephen took a sip of wine and his face turned sober.

"So what do you think of the election next month, Father?"

Mr. Dobbins scowled. "I think our country is in for another precarious attack upon our freedoms. With that extremist Jefferson in the running, no telling where our country is headed."

Stephen nodded. "The newspapers are filled with attacks on President Adams—accusing him of being a monarchist, senile, vain and having an 'ungovernable temper.' 'Tis getting fractious and ugly. And that beastly Burr running with Jefferson." Stephen shook his head and took another sip of wine.

"Well, when the Electoral College meets December 3, let us pray they remember Jefferson's zealous support of the French, despite their attacking our naval vessels. I think Jefferson was in France far too long. His arrogance smacks of sedition."

The room became very quiet.

Danny noticed Susannah had grown very pale and she rested both hands on the table. She gripped the tablecloth. Eyes narrowing, her voice trembled when she spoke.

"Do you think we will have another war, Father?"

Mr. Dobbins reached toward his daughter's hand and gently squeezed it. "Please do not fret, my dear. And forgive me for such unseemly, political talk on Thanksgiving Day. No, I do not think we are headed to war. Our most recent conflict is too fresh in everyone's minds for anyone to desire such unpleasantness again."

Although Susannah's lips seemed to attempt a smile, Danny's heart ached at the worry he saw in her eyes. He lifted his wine goblet for a toast. "To peace. And to God's guidance in our elections."

"Here, here." Stephen lifted his glass, as did Mr.

Dobbins.

"Well, now. Let us eat some of that mincemeat pie I've been hearing about. I understand from Modesty that it is the receipt that Missus Washington made for her husband, our venerable and late President George Washington. May his soul rest in peace."

Susannah smiled weakly. "Yes. I shall serve it forthwith."

Exiting the room, Susannah slipped into the kitchen while the three men watched her.

"I should never speak of political concerns in front of Susannah. It always causes her distress." Mr. Dobbins wiped his cheek with his napkin.

Stephen smoothed his napkin on his lap. "'Tis best women cannot participate in these ugly dealings. Or vote."

"Here, here." The three men lifted their glasses in agreement.

* * *

Thanksgiving ended all too quickly and the early darkness signaled it was time for Danny to return to the armory.

"Thank you, all, for this holiday meal. You made me feel quite at home."

"'Twas our pleasure, Mr. Lowe." Mr. Dobbins bowed at his waist to Danny who returned the gesture. Slipping away, Susannah's father left them alone to bid farewell.

Taking her hands in his, Danny looked apologetically at Susannah. "I regret the conversation at supper upset you. I hope these political concerns did not dampen your holiday." He stroked the backs of her hands with his fingers.

Susannah stared at his hands. "When I was small, Mother used to tell me about how worried she was when we were infants. Stephen was just a year or so older than I—we were both born during the war."

"As were James and I." He picked up her hands and kissed them.

"She spoke of the terrible nightmares she would have

because of her concern the British would return to Boston. She fretted over our safety, keeping us both close at all times, in case we had to evacuate. Mother said she would never forget the utter relief she experienced when the treaty was signed. She said…it was not for herself that she feared. It was for my father and for us." Susannah lifted her eyes to meet his and continued.

"When my father and Stephen were discussing the election, for the first time, I understood my mother's fears. Because I feared for you. What would happen if we had another war?" She stroked his hair near his cheek and he kissed her palm while closing his eyes. His voice whispered.

"We will not have a war. And I will be safe. Even if there were a war, I would stay here, helping make the necessary weapons." He kissed her hands and she stroked his face. Her touch mesmerized him.

Seeking her lips, he hungrily sealed his to hers. Out of breath, he stopped and felt her warm breath against his cheek.

Susannah continued kissing his cheek with lips that sent pleasure with their every touch. "I love you, Dan. I could not bear to lose you."

"You will not lose me. I am helplessly in love with you, Susannah. Please wait for me whilst I save for the day I can provide you a home."

"You know I will wait. My heart is already your home."

Feeling dangerously lost in his passion, he kissed her briefly and pulled away.

"I must go. Goodnight, my love."

"Goodnight. I love you always."

Chapter 23
Gift

Walking toward the Dobbins's front door at the end of Sabbath, Danny reluctantly faced another week separated from Susannah.

But besides her usual regret at his leaving, she had seemed extraordinarily somber. He shot her a concerned glance.

"Is anything wrong? You appear to be in the sulks." He took her hand and stroked it slowly.

Avoiding his gaze, Susannah squeezed his hand gently and stared at the floor. "This time of year…'tis always difficult since Mother died." She bit her lip and looked warily at him. "Did I ever tell you that my mother was a papist?" Her face flushed.

"A papist? You mean a Roman Catholic?"

Susannah appeared to cringe. "Yes. Perhaps I should have told you before."

"Why?" Danny drew her into his arms. "Did you think that would matter to me?"

Her eyes darted toward his, then away again. "I was not certain. My mother's family always celebrated Christmas as the birth of Jesus. I know that most of the churches feel it is unscriptural, but Mother always said it was her favorite holiday growing up. Although we did not celebrate it in our home, each Christmas Eve she would leave a tiny gift for Stephen and me on our pillows so we would find it in the morning. She said that it was just a reminder of Christ's birth—and a reminder of how much she loved us." Susannah's lips trembled and she blinked rapidly.

Danny held her closely and stroked her back slowly. She quivered in his arms. After a few moments, he pulled away so he could look at her face.

"I wish I had known your mother—I am certain she was a wonderful woman since she had such a lovely daughter. I am sorry that December is so difficult for you. It has so many happy memories, yet now is so sad."

She drew in a shuddering breath. "Yes. I am so relieved you do not feel appalled by my family background."

Danny threw his head back in laughter. "That does seem ironic, Susannah, considering the concerns about *my* family." He looked at her moist cheeks and dried them off with his fingers. "But pray, tell me. Perhaps I have taken leave of my senses, but I have noticed some discomfort when you are near my friends at the meetinghouse. Am I correct or am I merely imagining?"

Susannah blushed and looked at the floor. "I am certain it is nothing."

Danny's eyes narrowed. "What is nothing? Tell me. Did Ezra do something to you?" He gripped her arms, anger surging through his veins.

"No, not Ezra. Cyrus."

Danny reeled at her words.

Cyrus? My friend these many years. How could this be?

"Cyrus? What happened? Did he put his hands upon you?" His heartbeat began to surge and his temples throbbed.

Susannah placed her hands on his chest and caught his gaze with an earnest stare. "No, nothing like that." She gripped his woolen lapel.

"Then what?" His throat parched and he tried to swallow.

Leaning against him, she clung to his coat. "At first I just thought he was concerned about your whereabouts when you were gone. He would ask me at Sabbath service if I knew where you were. He just seemed to be interested as your friend. I thought nothing of it." She paused and gripped the fabric of his coat tighter.

"And then?" It was all Danny could do to keep his voice calm.

"Then, after you returned, he would give me the strangest looks. And one time, when you had gone for a moment, he walked over to me and said, 'So Danny's back—

your hero. I guess the hero always get the lass.' But it was the look in his eye that made me shiver. Although he smiled, his eyes were cold, empty, brooding. I quickly excused myself from his presence and then you were back a moment later."

"Why did you never tell me this?" Danny's voice trembled in his anger but he desperately wanted to keep it steady and calm. Inwardly, he raged.

"I do not know. I did not want to come between you and your friend." Tears rolled down her cheeks.

Danny pulled her away from his chest and looked into her eyes. "No one is more important than you, Susannah. I never want you to fear coming to me if you are concerned. It does not matter who it is. Please promise me you will tell me if you are ever afraid again." He touched her lips with his finger.

She kissed the tip of his thumb. "I promise." Her voice whispered.

Planting a tender kiss on her lips, he held her in his arms, fearing to release her from the safety of his embrace.

After a moment, he knew it was time to bid farewell. Reluctantly he let her go, knowing it would be another week before he would see her again. It was also a few days before Christmas. He vowed to somehow make it special for her. And he vowed to confront Cyrus.

* * *

Returning to the barracks, he went to Cyrus's room but his friend was already asleep. He almost shook the man awake but thought better of it.

I'll see him in the morning.

Angrily thudding back to his own sleeping quarters, Danny prepared for bed, but his heart still lurched with unresolved conflict.

He sorted through the conversation with Susannah.

None of this makes sense.

Cyrus had been his longtime friend at the armory as they worked side-by-side in the water shops. When Danny was promoted to the filing shop, they remained friends, enjoying meals together and a camaraderie that had developed and grown in the past four years. Cyrus was one of the few workers who attended the meetinghouse every Sabbath day with Danny — and Ansel.

Why would he have called me a "hero" and said those things to Susannah?

He had no reason to question her words or her very real fear. He could feel it in the way she clung to him.

Lord, give me wisdom.

Sitting on the edge of his bed, he was too agitated to sleep.

I need to walk.

Thrusting himself to his feet, he grabbed his wool coat and slipped past his sleeping roommates. He quietly shut the door and breathed in the sharp, frigid air that stung the inside of his nostrils.

Throwing his scarf around his neck and pulling his woolen cap over his ears, he plodded through the few inches of snow, trying to sort through the distress eating at his soul. The frozen white scrunched beneath his leather boots as he looked up into the clear, star-strewn sky. He found solace in the knowledge that there was a Creator Who had cast the nightlights into the universe. He prayed the same God would cast away his fears.

Heading toward a grove of birches at the far end of the armory grounds, Danny leaned against one of the tree trunks, lost in thought.

God, help me. Give me wisdom.

He did not have a sudden rush of inspiration. But gazing at the white trunks standing like soldiers at attention, he noticed that one of the trees had fallen over.

Must have been the recent wind.

He focused his eyes on the mass of tangled branches and narrowed his vision to one particular branch. Pushing away from the birch that he leaned upon, he walked closer for a better view.

A cross!

Reaching toward the oddly shaped branches, he saw not a haphazard display of wood, but a clearly outlined, naturally occurring cross in the web of twigs. Pulling out his pocketknife, he sliced through the far tip of each end of the cross-shaped intersection of thin branches. Holding it up, he held it against the sky for a backdrop.

It is a perfect shape!

Closing his knife blade, Danny returned the tool to his pocket and raced back to the barracks. Quietly walking toward his cot and past his snoring comrades, Danny blew warm breath onto his fingertips and withdrew the knife again. This time, he carefully whittled off the thin white bark, exposing the soft wood below. When he had it to the shape he desired, he put away his knife, tucked the cross under his pillow, and fell down on his bedding fully clothed.

I really must get up and change.

He closed his eyes and was lulled by the sound of his sleeping roommates.

* * *

At breakfast the next morning, Danny eyed Cyrus from across the table. His friend was jabbering away as usual, grinning with food in his mouth and guzzling warm cider in between bites. Danny eyed him suspiciously, barely finishing off one plate of eggs and pork, his appetite diminished by the angst in his gut.

As Cyrus swallowed his last swig and stood, Danny pushed up from his seat. "Cyrus, I need to speak with you." He used a low, measured tone.

Cyrus's face sobered. "Of course, Danny. Outside all right?"

Danny followed his friend to the door and they both flinched at the cold temperatures.

Sticking his hands in his coat pockets, Danny faced Cyrus with a penetrating stare.

"What have you been saying to Susannah?"

"Whad'ya mean? I barely speak to your lass. What's she tellin' ya?"

"She says you were anxious to know where I was when I left. And after I came back, you said something strange about me being a 'hero' and 'getting the lass.'"

"Of course I was anxious to know where ya were. We all were. Did'na know what had happened to ya. And blast, man, you were a hero that day trying to save Ansel. Helpin' out. What's the problem?" Cyrus scratched his head and met Danny's eyes with a confused look.

This sounds ridiculous. He must think I'm a fool.

"No problem, Cyrus. Just wanted to make sure there wasn't one. It's been a strange time."

"I'll say, lad." Slapping Danny on the shoulder, Cyrus headed toward the path to the water shops. "No harm done." Smiling, Cyrus doffed his hat and left.

I must be taking leave of my senses.

Shaking his head, he strode toward the filing shop to start his day.

* * *

Danny carefully wrapped the whittled cross inside a piece of muslin cloth that he had begged from Missus Parker. He stuck the note inside, explaining that the walnut dye covered all except the top of the cross. The white, bare wood at the very top signified God's light shining down from heaven. He had signed the note, "So you know how much I love you, Dan."

Kissing the cross and tying the small package with twine, he placed it carefully into his coat pocket and slipped out the barracks door.

It was still mid-afternoon and the workers were at their job posts. He was not finished with his workday either, but breaks were allowed, and this Wednesday required a trip down the hill to Stratford and Dobbins Mercantile. Today was Christmas Eve.

Half walking, half slipping, he quickly made his way down the hill toward Main Street.

I hope I do not run into Susannah.

Occasionally glancing over his shoulder, he was relieved to see the mercantile was open.

Carefully opening the glass door so as not to rattle it, he

closed it and turned toward Mr. Dobbins who was unloading boxes of newly arrived tins of tea.

"Mr. Lowe. What an unexpected surprise!"

Mr. Dobbins's smile was genuine and he stuck his hand forward to shake Danny's.

"My hands are a bit smudged from work, sir." Danny doffed his cap instead.

"Well, since I am unpacking tea, I will accept your excuse. What can I do for you?"

"I do believe that today is Christmas Eve, sir. Not that I celebrate it. But Susannah explained that her mother did…and I wanted to do something for her. Could you put this on her pillow tonight so she can find it in the morning?"

Mr. Dobbins's eyes brimmed. He was quiet for a moment then took the small package from Danny's hand. "I'd be pleased to do so for you—and for my daughter." Looking up at Danny with sad yet grateful eyes, Mr. Dobbins smiled bravely. "I thank you, sir."

Danny's nostrils flared and he fought back the emotion that surged inside his heart.

"You are most welcome, sir." Danny turned to leave, then spun on his snow-covered heels. "And…a Happy Christmas to you, sir."

Mr. Dobbins grinned. "A Happy Christmas to you as well, Mr. Lowe."

Chapter 24
Terror

"Running out of coal? What are we supposed to do, lay twigs on the forge?" Ezra shook his head angrily and stabbed his fork into his eggs.

"I don't know what they'll have us do." Danny sipped his tankard of warm cider. "Seems as if we're far enough behind on production as it is. But Mr. Ames apparently refused the shipment. Said it was full of foreign matter — bad quality."

Ezra narrowed his eyes. "But Mr. Williams approved that coal."

"There's the rub. Ames says that Williams's local connections in Springfield made him choose a local merchant. Ames says its bad coal and he'll not accept it." Danny finished off his breakfast.

"Seems those two never can agree." Ezra put his woolen cap on. "Well, time to go make some musket barrels. Maybe I should look for some dry leaves to fuel the fires."

Danny smirked. "Might not be a bad plan." Looking over toward Cyrus's half-filled plate, Danny furrowed his brows. "You're awful quiet this morning. Feeling ill?"

"A bit." Cyrus took a small sip. "Maybe I best see the doctor and get a pass today."

Suspicion edged Danny's every encounter with Cyrus these last weeks. He attempted to be casual in his reply.

"Well then, get some rest." Danny pulled his hat over his ears and headed for the door. Turning back he saw Cyrus picking at his food. "Can I get you anything?"

Without meeting his friend's eye, Cyrus said, "No. Thanks."

Danny wheeled around and opened the door to the frigid January cold. It cut through his clothing like a knife.

165

Pulling his collar higher, he raced for the filing shop to start his day, looking forward to the warmth from the forge.

Wonder how long we can keep the fire going?

* * *

"Time to shut down the fires!" The bellowing voice of the foreman rose above the clanging hammers.

Danny looked up from his work, filing and smoothing the exterior of a Charleville musket barrel. He reluctantly put it aside for the night.

This is getting troublesome.

He still had enough energy to put in a few hours of work, yet here they were shutting down early.

His feet were numb from the cold and, despite wearing his coat under his work apron, he still shivered from the extremely low temperature.

I hope spring gets here soon. He shook his head with a wry expression. *What a pathetic thought in January.*

Removing his apron, he hung it on the hook next to the others.

"So, we're off early." One of his co-workers grinned and blew warm breath on his hands. "Might spend some time with my wife. How about you? Hear you have a lass in town."

"Word does travel." Danny grinned. "That sounds like a plan. Wouldn't mind seeing her at all."

A dozen workmen poured out the door, followed by exclamations of pain at the biting cold. Their voices echoed through the stark stillness of the dark landscape, their footsteps cushioned by a couple of inches of fresh snowfall.

Danny was half way back to the barracks when he stopped short.

Blast! Forgot to lock up the musket.

Taking in a painfully cold breath, he reluctantly returned to the filing shop, annoyed with himself. He was so anxious to see Susannah, he had been completely distracted.

Entering the darkened shop, he let his eyes adjust to the dimness. Even when it was dark the forges usually lit the interior sufficiently but it was pitch black right now. Leaving the door open for the scant light it afforded, he felt his way to his workbench and clenched the barrel of the Charleville. It was nearing completion, necessitating tighter security. He half-stumbled toward the locked cabinet, pulled out the key from his pocket, and flung the creaking door open. He thrust the half-finished musket into the opening and slammed the cabinet closed, locking it in a swift motion.

Got to get going.

He turned to leave but stopped and drew in a sharp breath. His hair stood up on his neck.

"Is someone there?"

He had heard nothing, but someone's presence was palpable. And then he smelled it.

Smoke!

The forges were out for the night. Why did he smell something burning?

"Who's there?" His throat tightened in fear, every muscle in his body taut with tension.

A voice sent cold shivers up his spine.

"Well, Danny, this is perfect. Now I can kill you *and* blame the fire on you as well. Nothin' like killing two birds with one stone." The voice was familiar but the tone was not. It was purely evil.

Cyrus?

Glancing quickly around, it was too dark to see the source.

Where is he?

Danny fought rising panic. The voice seemed to echo from anywhere and nowhere in the empty shop.

"Thought you were safe with Morris outta the way? Well, wrong, my friend. He and I had lots of plans. I just do them on my own now."

"Cyrus." Danny did not recognize his own voice. "Why? Why are you doing this?" He tried to swallow but the increasing smoke dried his mouth further.

"Did ya know my mother was French, Danny? Thought not. I've been waitin' a long time to get back at you. America's hero, trying to report plots against the armory.

Always gettin' promoted. Even gettin' the beautiful lass in town. Well, Danny, your days as the handsome, brave American are over."

Cyrus seemed to come out of nowhere. Danny saw the glint of the steel knife just in time to avoid a slash across his face, but not quickly enough to evade it piercing his left arm.

Danny leaped away from him, grabbing at the searing pain in his arm. Warmth trickled down his sleeve. He did not look at his wound since he could now see Cyrus in the dimness. He was not about to let him out of his sight.

Grabbing an iron barrel from a box, Danny flung it at the enraged man, temporarily knocking him off balance. Looking for anything else he could find as a weapon, he lurched aside just before Cyrus lunged at him again. Danny picked up a hammer and tried to throw it at Cyrus, but the enraged man evaded the swing.

The fire surged with energy, burning Danny's eyes and gagging him.

The light reflected off of Cyrus's sweat-covered face and Danny was chilled by the sinister look in the man's eye. It was filled with hatred.

He heard voices in the distance through the open door.
I've got to get to the door!
Someone far away yelled, "Fire!" The clanging of the bell could be heard above the increasing roar of the blaze.

Cyrus appeared determined to finish the job and, with fury, leaped toward Danny again. Danny tried to maneuver away from his attack, but felt a burning sensation below his ribs. Grabbing his side that seared with pain, he looked up at the blade that now hung like a French guillotine over his head. He heard the loud report of musket fire. Cyrus flew backward toward the far wall and slumped with his head downward. He was propped against the wall, unmoving.

A strange feeling of numbness coupled with weakness drew Danny to his knees. He fell on to the wooden floor, weak as his sister's rag doll.

He felt hands opening his coat and heard someone —
Stephen? — yell for the doctor.

Danny tried to open his mouth but he couldn't think

clearly enough to form words.

Why is my shirt so wet?

He heard others approach and voices but they all seemed so far away. Hands picked him up and intense pain surged through his torso and arm as he was laid on a tarp. He wanted to cry but he did not have the strength. Harsh movements—like riding on a wild horse. Freezing air.

Why am I riding a horse?

In the distance he heard a voice. "Hang on, Danny."

Ezra?

He tried to open his eyes but they would not obey him.

Sleep. I need to sleep.

* * *

Susannah flung open the door of the barracks where they had placed Dan. Dr. Pynchon was working on his still form.

"Dan?" Her voice was small, choking from the smoke outside as well as her fear from within.

Walking in a daze through the makeshift infirmary, she wondered if her wobbly legs could carry her. Looking at Dan lying on the cot covered in blood, she could not hold back a groan.

Dear Lord. Help him!

She felt someone gently grab her arms and was grateful for the support.

"You should not be here, miss." Ezra stared at her with wide eyes and a pale face. He was covered in blood.

Dan's blood?

An inner reserve of determination rose within her. "I will stay."

Walking toward the group working on him, she saw Dr. Pynchon, worry creasing into every wrinkle on his face. "Miss Dobbins, you must stand back."

"I will not, sir. I want him to know I am here."

He relented but said, "Do not be in my way, then."

Missus Parker, the barracks cook, was in tears, carrying an armload of bloodied linen bandages. "You'd best sit near him. Speak to him."

Susannah boldly drew near Dan's head and knelt on the cold floor beside him. She winced when she saw the open wounds on his upper arm and below his ribs. He shivered and she removed her red cardinal cape. Draping it across his legs and stomach, she tenderly tucked it around him.

Returning to the head of his bed, she knelt down near him again and stroked his still cheeks. She struggled to control despairing thoughts as he lay still, with no response to her touch. Leaning in closer, she whispered into his ear. "Dan. I am here. Dan, I love you."

She gripped his right hand and desperately tried to avoid looking at the surgeon and his assistant as they cleaned the wounds with rum and prepared the needles with strands of catgut and silk. She saw him flinch when the rum flowed across his open wounds.

"He is in pain." Her eyes pled with the doctor for help.

"Here. Dip your fingers in this laudanum and place one finger at a time into his mouth. That way, he will not choke on it."

Susannah grabbed the vial he handed her, dipping her smallest finger into the liquid, and stroking inside his cheek with the medicine. His face winced and she again dipped into the narcotic, allowing minute portions to absorb into his mouth. After doing that several times, he appeared to relax.

The door suddenly burst open, allowing swirls of ash and snowflakes to enter the already cold and smoky barracks. A soot-covered sentinel filled the doorway. "Everyone must evacuate this building. It is in danger of catching fire. Hurry!"

An expletive burst from the doctor's mouth. "Like being back at war." Angrily picking up his suturing equipment, he barked orders. "I need several hands to carry this patient. Now!"

Everyone scrambled to help lay Dan back on a stretcher. Susannah hurried to stand, pulling her wool cardinal over Dan's torso. The man assisting the physician grabbed a blanket from one of the beds and draped it across her shoulders. They braved the frigid weather once again. The air was filled with choking plumes of smoke and gagging coughs were heard from the crowd fighting the blaze.

Susannah glanced toward the building that was on fire —
what was left of it — and saw a long line of workers handing
buckets of water down the line from a well. One fire hose was
in use from the other well. Staring with horror at the raging
flames, she saw the roof collapse, sending an eruption of
sparks everywhere.

Pulling the blanket tightly about her shoulders, she raced
toward the building where the group was transporting Dan.
She felt like her legs were not connected to her body.

This is a nightmare from hell.

Gasping for breath, she opened the door of the building
and followed the medical group assisting her friend — her
love.

Several men laid Dan onto another bed and Dr. Pynchon
prepared to suture the wounds.

Taking her place by his head again, her trembling,
freezing hands stroked his face. "I am here, Dan. Please…
please do not leave me. Please come back."

Lord, please do not take my Dan.

Weeping uncontrollably, she laid her head next to his,
grasping the cross he had made for her in her hand.

Chapter 25
Strength

His eyes struggled to open but heavy weights kept them closed. It took every ounce of determination in Danny's will to force the lids from their sealed state. His strong resolve finally won.

Where am I?

His fogged vision barely made out light blue walls decorated with paintings of flowers.

Am I dead?

He knew he was not in the barracks but this was unlike any room he had ever been in. Perhaps he was in heaven. But if he was, why did his body feel so cumbersome and his stomach so nauseated?

Turning his head to the side, he winced at the pain even the slightest movement seem to elicit.

"Mr. Lowe!" The voice belonged to Mr. Dobbins.

The most that Danny could force from his dry throat was a raspy, "Sir."

Mr. Dobbins leaped from his seat and stood over the patient. "Please do not move, Dan. Dr. Pynchon says you must stay as still as possible for two weeks. To let your wounds heal."

Dr. Pynchon? Wounds?

As if in response to his questioning look, Mr. Dobbins put a hand carefully on his uninjured arm. "You've been injured, Dan. You are in our home but you are recovering. You must rest." He poured amber liquid into a small vial. "Dr. Pynchon said to give you some ale the moment you could swallow."

Mr. Dobbins held the vial near Dan's parched lips while he lifted his head slightly from the pillow. Dan swallowed the contents eagerly but then fell back onto the soft muslin mound. He winced in anguish.

"Let me give you some rum for that pain." He picked up a tall bottle sitting on the bedside table and poured the dark brown liquid into the same vial.

"Ale? Rum? I must be…in sad shape." His voice was a hoarse whisper. Dan drank the rum and then his eyes opened wide. "The fire. Cyrus." His mouth trembled as he fought back tears from the memory. "I never saw it coming."

"None of us did, Dan. He fooled us all." Mr. Dobbins shook his head sadly as he placed the empty vial back near the bottles. "We're just so relieved you are alive. I must go tell Susannah you are finally awake. The only way I could get her to leave your side was to assure her that I would awaken her the moment you came 'round."

He gently placed his hand on Dan's uninjured arm. "We've been praying for you, Dan. Thank God, He answered our pleas. We have sent word to your parents by post rider."

"Thank you, sir. I am grateful for your prayers…and your care."

Mr. Dobbins smiled, his eyes moist, and left the room.

How long have I been unconscious?

He wanted to move but he remembered the words of caution from Mr. Dobbins.

Wonder how much longer 'til the two weeks are up? Suppose it doesn't matter since I feel too weak to do much of anything.

The alcohol from the ale and rum burned in his empty stomach. Everything seemed to burn—his head, his side, his arm. But the worst pain was realizing he had been betrayed by Cyrus—a friend who had tried to kill him.

He closed his eyes only to force them open again when he heard the door.

Susannah's hair was undone and disheveled and her eyes deep set and dark with worry. But her appearance was a most healing medicinal, filling him with renewed strength.

"Dan!" Tying her muslin robe, she hurried to his side.

He lifted his right arm slowly toward her. She grabbed his hand and squeezed it with fervor.

"Thank the good Lord, you are awake. Dr. Pynchon said the sooner you awoke, the better your recovery would be."

Her relieved face suddenly melted into a contortion of anguish. "I was so worried." Stroking his right arm with trembling hands, her eyes overflowed with tears.

He forced himself to smile although it took great effort. "I'm still here, Susannah. How long…was I unconscious?" It was so difficult to speak.

"Two days." She wiped the moisture from her cheeks and sniffed. "Father told Dr. Pynchon it would be warmer here in our home for you. Ezra and several others transported you in a wagon. We covered you with blankets to keep you warm."

Danny's eyes narrowed. Confusing images swirled through his mind.

"I saw you."

"You saw me?"

"Yes. I saw you lay your head next to mine on the stretcher. You had covered me with your red cloak."

Susannah looked perplexed. "But Dan, your eyes were closed."

"I'm not sure why I saw you, but I saw myself as well. Like I was above everyone. I could see you holding the cross and I saw you crying." He reached up to touch her face. "I…I wanted to speak to you but I could not."

She pulled his fingers to her lips and kissed his palm slowly. "I love you so much."

He smiled weakly. "You are my love."

Danny's eyes grew heavy.

He heard her sing softly, with a sweet melodious sound.

When I survey the wondrous cross
On which the Prince of glory died,
My richest gain I count but loss
And pour contempt on all my pride.

Susannah continued humming the melody while slowly stroking his arm. It was so soothing. He yawned and dreamed of being enfolded in her arms.

Chapter 26
Visitors

The bowed head of a man with long, dark, silver-streaked hair came into Danny's view as he opened his eyes. The man appeared to be in prayer, with his chin resting on folded hands and his shoulders hunched forward.

Danny opened his mouth with difficulty.

"Father?"

Daniel Lowe Sr. jerked his head upward. With anxious eyes, he cried, "Danny!"

Pulling himself awkwardly from his sitting position, Daniel reached toward his son's right arm and gripped it with a fervency that told Danny how worried he'd been. The older man appeared to work frantically at calming his tense jaw. The fear in his voice was clearly audible.

"Danny. Thank God you are all right."

"Father, why are you here?" Danny could not fathom that his parent had traveled twenty miles in winter—a season known for increasing the residual pain from his father's war wound—just to see if his son was well. "It is winter."

Daniel rubbed his face with the palm of one hand. "I would have come if I'd had to cross through hell to get here."

Danny stared at his parent, overwhelmed by feelings that he could not describe. Surprise, vulnerability, gratitude, love. They all blended together like a sea of emotion that poured out in waves of audible sobs from deep within Danny's spirit.

Daniel Sr. carefully set his face on the pillow next to his firstborn's head. Avoiding his son's wounded arm and torso, he grasped Danny as closely as he could and struggled mightily for composure. After a moment, he lifted his contorted countenance.

"When I heard you'd been wounded, all I could think was that I might never see you again. I could not bear it—I had to come. It was all I could do to keep your mother from coming with me but I insisted she remain home." Daniel wiped his nose with a kerchief. "I have sent a message to her by post rider that you are recovering. She was beside herself when I left."

"Father, how did you get here?"

Daniel gave a wry smile. "How else? Richard Beal came through once again for our family, driving me here in his sleigh. We made the journey in a day's time."

For the first time since being wounded, Danny started to laugh, then winced. "Guess I'd best wait on the jesting for a bit." He grabbed at the wound that pulled painfully every time he moved. The feeling of flesh being tugged from within was sickening.

"Yes. You need to rest. Mr. Dobbins says the doctor will be here to check you soon."

Despite his pain, Danny's curiosity piqued. "So…did you meet her?" He could feel his heartbeat quicken.

Daniel winked at his son. "Oh, you mean the maid, Modesty. Lovely lady. I think you will make a fine couple." His grin threatened to excavate numerous new wrinkles into his cheeks.

Danny closed his eyes in exasperation. "Father…"

"Oh, you must mean the lovely Miss Dobbins — the lass who has been fussing over you ever since I got here late last evening, coming in to check upon your condition every few moments. Might that be 'her' you referred to?"

Although still weak from his blood loss, Danny could feel his cheeks getting warm. "You know it is, Father." He grinned despite himself.

Daniel's face sobered as he patted his son's arm lightly. "She is a fine lass, Danny. Your mother and I are so grateful that you have found someone to love — who obviously loves you just as much."

A knock on the door caught their attention.

"Dr. Pynchon to see you, sir." Modesty's voice whispered softly as she escorted the physician into Danny's recovery room.

The grey-haired man held his hat in his hand as he walked toward the bed, scanning the patient with his eyes.

"Dr. Pynchon, this is my father, Daniel Lowe, Sr."

"So pleased to meet you, sir." The physician held out a hand in greeting. "You have quite a strong son here, sir. We are grateful to God he has survived."

"As are we, doctor. We are eternally grateful to you for taking care of him."

Modesty turned toward Danny's father. "Sir, I have some breakfast ready for you downstairs. Please join us so you can sustain your strength as well, sir."

Daniel looked at his son. "I'll be up later after I've eaten. Listen to the doctor and abide by his rules." Nodding to accompany his admonition, he left with Modesty.

Dr. Pynchon sat on the chair beside the bed. "So how are you, Mr. Lowe? You gave us quite a fright there, I don't mind telling you." The physician's woolen pants were rumpled and they appeared to have been worn for quite some time without benefit of cleaning. "So, are the ladies of the house taking fine care of their favorite patient?" He did not bother hiding a grin.

Dan shook his head. "Not just the ladies of the house—I think every woman from West Springfield *and* Springfield has been dropping by with food and blankets. The Deacon's wife has arraigned for a steady stream of soups and broths to be sent by the church members. I am well souped."

Dr. Pynchon threw his head back and laughed. "Nice to see you can still jest." His face sobered. "Your body took quite a blow, lad. You lost a great deal of blood. Fortunately your stomach and bowels escaped the knife—but not by much. Let me look at those stitches."

The doctor got up and lifted the quilts. Danny winced as the muslin bandages were removed. "Are the fair ladies changing the dressing every day?"

"Yes." He tensed as the physician probed the skin nearby the reddened, vicious gash under his rib.

"Still quite tender. We need to watch for infection but, otherwise, it seems to be healing well. Soon we should be able to remove the silk." He put a fresh wrapping of gauze around Dan's torso to keep the injury covered. Dan winced whenever he moved. "It will take some time for the muscles to heal. But soon we should be able to get you up and about."

"I feel weak as a kitten." Danny wondered if he'd ever get his strength back.

The doctor patted his arm. "Your blood loss makes you feel this way. Good victuals, good rest..." He looked up as Susannah walked in the open door. "Good female companionship," the doctor whispered then smiled, meeting Susannah's gaze. "Good day, Miss Dobbins."

Susannah curtsied. "Good day, Doctor. How is Dan?"

"Getting better all the time. I can see you have been giving him expert nursing care. He will be up and about before you know it."

Her face beamed. "That is fine news, indeed."

"We can take these stitches out in a matter of days. In the meantime, keep the dressing clean. And your patient happy."

"I shall." She stared at Dan with unabashed affection.

Dr. Pynchon raised his eyebrows and smirked. "Just remember he must not move too much. Or get too — stimulated." He gathered the bandages and put them back in his bag. "Good day, Mr. Lowe. Miss Dobbins."

"Good day, doctor." Susannah's cheeks were bright red as she looked back at Dan. "Well, that was certainly embarrassing." She bit her lip.

Dan grinned at her reaction. "Speaking of such matters, can you tell me who exactly removed my breeches? I discovered they were missing but I do not remember taking them off." He could not help but tease her.

She huffed in indignation. "Daniel Lowe, it was not I, I assure you. I would have, of course, if there was a need, but Missus Parker managed, along with the good doctor." By now Dan was laughing and holding his side in pain. "You deserve that pain, sir, accusing me of such impropriety."

"I am sorry, Susannah. It's the first time I've laughed in over a week." He clenched his jaw in pain and held his ribs.

"Dan!" She rushed to his side. "Please stop. I cannot bear

to see you in pain." She poured him a vial of rum. "Please drink this."

"Trying to get me drunk, are you?"

She rolled her eyes. "Drink." He did not argue with her.

Handing her back the vial, he grabbed her arm gently. "Kiss me, Susannah."

Her eyes glanced around furtively. "Dan, you are in bed."

He smiled playfully. "Would you deny your affectionate care to a suffering patient?"

She grinned. "Well, it *is* what the doctor recommended— to keep you happy." She leaned over his face and whispered. "I shall do my best to relieve your suffering."

Planting a warm kiss on his rum-tinged lips, she moved her shoulders flirtatiously. "Is that sufficient medicine for you, sir?"

"Never." He pulled her down again to his face and covered her mouth with his trembling lips. He hungrily tasted her sweetness, delighting in her flavor, her warmth, her passion.

Someone cleared his throat from the doorway.

Susannah leaped up and threw her hands over her mouth. "Mr. Ames!"

David Ames stood in the doorway, his face filled with amusement. "I see that your nurse is attending to your every need."

"Yes, sir. I mean no, sir, this is Miss Dobbins…this is all my fault, sir." Danny's face burned.

"Do not worry. I'll not inform the fathers eating their breakfast downstairs. Your secret is safe with me."

"Sir, there is no secret. We were merely kissing."

Mr. Ames threw his head back, chuckling. "I know that, lad. From what I understand, you are likely too weak to get into any serious trouble."

At these words, Susannah blushed deeply. "Please forgive me, sir. I shall hasten to finish my breakfast now." Staring at the floor, she slipped quickly out the door and closed it behind her.

Mr. Ames raised his eyebrows and chuckled. "Well now, that is the most color I've seen in your cheeks since you were injured."

"I deeply apologize, sir."

"Why? For having normal affections for a beautiful young lady? Naught to apologize for, lad." He gently tapped Danny's right shoulder in a fatherly manner. His face grew serious. "The Filing and Stocking Shop is a complete loss. It is an abomination that we had a traitor in our midst these many years."

Danny met his gaze. "He certainly was the proverbial wolf in sheep's clothing, was he not?"

"Tares among the wheat." Mr. Ames sighed. "We have to move some of our operations at the armory into one of the barracks. We are farther behind than ever on production."

Danny swallowed with difficulty. "How much did we lose?"

"Five hundred muskets, plus other equipment." Mr. Ames stared up at the ceiling and exhaled slowly. Meeting Danny's eye he attempted a weak smile. "At least you are alive. I never could have forgiven myself if Graves had done you in. I'm sorry I took you back before we knew his true colors."

"Please do not blame yourself, sir. The fire would have happened whether I was there or not. Just bad timing that I returned to the shop. At least, now we know who to blame."

Mr. Ames met his gaze. "Very gracious of you, lad." He sat down in the chair next to Danny. "I've come to tell you — the United States Government has a reward for you, for your service and your wounds. There'll be a compensation for you when you come back to the hill. Perhaps you might find some use for it — perhaps a home for your lass." He winked at Danny.

Danny's mouth opened and he licked his lips. "Compensation?"

"Aye. I'm certain you're looking forward to getting your strength back, so you can start your lives together. Better than kissing from an infirmary bed." Mr. Ames grinned as he pushed up from the chair.

A huge smile erupted on Danny's face. "Yes, sir. I shall work on getting my strength back forthwith."

"Good day, lad." He paused. "'Tis truly a blessed one, seeing you doing so well." He bowed to the patient and exited quietly.

Compensation. A home for Susannah.

He sighed with relief and gratitude.

Thank you, Heavenly Father.

Chapter 27
Spring

As the strength of winter ebbed, Danny's vitality returned.

Tucking his new linen smock into the woolen pants that the ladies in Springfield had fashioned for him, Danny was careful to avoid the scarred area on his torso. His muscles still felt shrunken from weeks of healing, but he knew they would fill out again soon. Swinging a hammer at the armory would bring his sinews back to their usual firm dimensions.

Staring at his hand opening and closing, Danny determined to renew his hardiness as soon as possible. It was not just for the sake of making muskets that he craved his former vigor. It was the thought of holding Susannah in these weakened arms that spurred him to resolve. Now that there was a reward waiting for him from the government, he anxiously sought to redeem it for a home — for a future with Susannah as his wife.

Staring out the window at the rivulets of snowmelt stirred excitement within him. The tracks of liquid sliding down the casement seemed as eager to find the earth below as he was desirous to begin his new life. Coming so close to death gave him an even greater appreciation to treasure each day.

Picking up the woolen waistcoat that matched the pants, Danny heard a knock at the door. "Come in."

Susannah saw that his waistcoat was still unbuttoned and she turned her back to him while he completed donning his attire.

Walking toward her, he wrapped his arms around her from behind and held his cheek next to hers. "Soon, I shall not have to leave you, even for one night." He kissed her cheek slowly.

As she turned around in his arms, her eyes sought his.

She breathed in an unsteady breath. "I am so relieved you are well…but I am so accustomed to you being here every day. The thought of you moving back to the hill fills me with sadness."

He tipped his forehead against hers. "I shall find out the details of the reward forthwith, then begin to make arrangements to purchase some land. It will not be long." His voice had lowered to a whisper and his mouth swept across her forehead and down her cheek, resting comfortably over her waiting lips. Waves of desire flooded him as he sought her mouth, then her bare neck.

He could hear her catch her breath and pull away. "I hope it is soon. Waiting for you becomes more difficult each time I am in your arms."

Grinning, he nuzzled her cheek and spoke near her ear. "Are you trying to tell me that you desire me, Miss Dobbins?"

Gasping, she pushed him away. "Far more than I should, Mr. Lowe." Stepping back from him, her cheeks flushed. "Yes, I desire you. But we must wait."

"Yes. Yes, we must — as difficult as it is." Clearing his throat, he picked up his wool coat. "Nearly spring, but the air outside still bites. Winter is an unfriendly dog." He bent over for a slow, tender kiss. "But you are a tender lamb. Soon to be in my fold."

"And happily so." Susannah grinned and looked at the floor for a moment, then grew pensive. "'Tis difficult to believe that a year ago we had just moved here. I was…so different. I am embarrassed by the pompous person that I was." She shifted her feet.

"We have all changed much in a year." Staring at her, he stroked her cheek with one hand. "You…you are more beautiful than ever. I thought you were lovely when I first saw you, but now…"

Her cheeks grew red. "'Tis your love that glows from within me. As Shakespeare wrote, 'When I saw you I fell in love, and you smiled because you knew.'"

Danny tilted his head. "When you saw me you fell in love? But you despised me."

"Not so, Dan." Her voice whispered and her mouth trembled. "I fell in love with you from the start but I tried to tell myself 'twas not so. I tried to convince myself that your eyes did not make me weak at the knees and your strong arms did not fill me with a desire to feel them wrapped around me. I even told myself that I could forget your soothing voice and tender lips that I longed to feel on mine. I was a fool to argue with myself. I knew that I loved you from the start. And knew I always would."

Danny drew her close and kissed her tear-stained cheeks. "I was a fool as well, Susannah. Thoughts of you kept me awake at night. But I thought there was no way you would ever pay a poor amorer any mind. You deserved better."

Placing her hands on his cheeks, her gaze pierced through to his heart. "'Tis I who does not deserve you. I love you and will always feel grateful to be loved by you."

He kissed her long and deeply, before forcing himself to push away. "I must go." His breathing was erratic and his heart raced. Walking toward the door he paused and looked back. "I shall hasten to make arrangements. And I will be with you on Sabbath."

"Yes." She smiled amidst her tears.

Walking carefully down the stairs carrying his bag, he left the home that had been his infirmary for well over a month. Opening the front door, he inhaled the fresh, chilled air deeply through his nose.

The scent was unmistakable.

Spring

Chapter 28
Unexpected

The wagon carrying a man and woman slowly approached the temporary barracks. Dan had just risen from a rest—a common practice since returning to work two days prior—and he stretched his arms carefully as he worked out the kinks from his taut muscles.

Something about the young woman on the wagon seat looked familiar but he was too far away to see her features. What was obvious was her enlarged belly that indicated a birth not far in the future.

Why does she look so familiar?

Drawing closer he caught a better view of the woman's blond hair falling in strands from under her straw bonnet. He heard her thank the driver.

Polly!

He paused in his steps then hurried out to his sister. "Polly. Why are you here?" He grabbed the bag that the driver handed down to him before placing his arm around her shoulders. The moment he embraced her, she crumpled into his arms, sobbing.

"Forgive me. I had nowhere else to go."

She clung to him with such desperation that tears welled in his own eyes.

What has happened?

Before he could comfort her sufficiently to hear her story, another young woman caught his eye, approaching the barracks.

Susannah!

She stood with her mouth agape, holding a package. Danny and Susannah's eyes met as he stared over Polly's shuddering shoulders. The look in Susannah's eyes screamed betrayal. Dropping the package, Susannah covered her mouth and bolted across the muddy grounds.

"Susannah!"

Polly pulled her head up from his shoulder. "Danny?"

Danny's heart raced. "'Tis all right. Please come inside. I shall speak with her after you are settled." Guiding Polly toward the barracks, he led her indoors to the relative privacy of his single room. Pulling up a chair, he indicated for her to sit. She awkwardly set her hips onto the wooden seat while holding her belly. He could not help but stare at his sister's altered appearance.

She smiled sadly. "Quite the changed sister, am I not?" Fresh tears rolled down her cheeks and her eyes stared with an emptiness that he had never seen before. She stroked her large belly and shifted uncomfortably. "Danny, I am so sorry that I came without sending word. I felt I had no choice."

He reached for her hand. "Do Mother and Father know you are here?"

"I left them a note with Uncle James and Aunt Hannah so they would not worry. But I could not bear to stay any longer."

"Why? What has happened?"

Polly swallowed with difficulty. "May I have a drink please? I am parched."

"Of course, forgive me." He hurried to the building that housed the kitchen and found a clean tankard. Filling it with cider, he hastened back to his room in the barracks and handed it carefully to Polly.

Guzzling it quickly, Polly handed it back to her brother. "Thank you, Danny. You've always been so kind."

Danny did not know where to begin so he waited for her to explain. After a moment, she inhaled a quivering breath. "The reverend sent me a writ. He insists I make a public confession—in front of the entire meetinghouse."

Stunned, Danny's mouth dropped. He blinked quickly. "I suppose it had not occurred to me what they would ask of you. But it does not surprise me."

Polly slowly raised her darkened eyes to meet his. "So you agree, this must be done?"

He stuttered. "I...I am not saying I want this to happen, Polly. This breaks my heart. But this is the manner of dealing with fornication—you know 'tis so. At least...at least they no longer use the whipping post." His heart beat erratically at the thought of his sister being stripped to the waist and publicly whipped.

Her demeanor melted into heart-rending sobs. "I know 'tis so. But that does not make this easier."

Wrapping his arms around his sister, her tears soaked into his linen sleeve. When her crying subsided, he took her hands.

"Polly, listen. I know this weighs on your heart. But you must consider what you have done. What if all the unmarried women had children with no fathers to raise them? How can the church stand back and give its approval? You know 'tis sin."

"I know." Her face was red and contorted. "But I will not say that my child is wicked."

He stroked her hair back. "No one will ask you to say this child is wicked, Polly. 'Tis the sin that is evil, not the child."

She leaned her head wearily against his arm. "I am so very tired, Danny."

He held her face toward his. "I will speak with Missus Parker. She will fix you some supper and find a place for you to rest. We will speak more later." Giving her a sideways hug, he left to find the cook who had become his nurse and friend.

After Polly ate some bread and cheese, he made sure that she was safely settled into a room where no one would disturb her. While he waited for her to go to sleep, his mind returned to the scenario in the armory square when he had seen Susannah watching him hug his sister.

I must go find Susannah.

* * *

She heard Danny speaking earnestly to her father in the foyer of their home, but Susannah was too heartsick to get up from her bed.

So that's where he was last summer. Spending time in the arms of that other woman.

Hot tears melted across her scorched cheeks. She had been crying for hours but she felt as if fresh floods of moisture were still imminent. It was the only apparent sign of life on her countenance since her features were unmoving in their grief. Numbness enveloped her in the brutal pain of betrayal.

There was a slight knock on the door. When Susannah did not—or could not—answer, the hinge creaked slightly as Modesty peered around the door.

"Miss, please come forthwith. Someone to see you."

"No." Her nose was so plugged up that Susannah did not recognize her own reply.

Modesty boldly scurried toward the bed. "Miss, 'tis important. Please, come."

Her head lifted with an unfamiliar weight of heaviness. Blinking, she looked distractedly at Modesty and her eyes narrowed. "I am not prepared to greet anyone."

Modesty appeared determined. "You will want to greet this someone." The maid poured some water from the pitcher into the basin and took a cloth out. Dipping it into the water, she wrung it out and bustled back to Susannah. "Here, miss."

The cool cloth was soothing as Susannah closed her eyes, relishing the temperature on her blazing forehead. "Thank you, Modesty." She started to lie back down but the maid caught her arm. "No, ya don't, miss. Come with me."

Susannah did not have the energy to resist. She followed Modesty to the door on unsteady legs and headed downstairs at the urging of a giggling Modesty.

When she saw Dan standing in the parlor, she stopped abruptly.

"Why are you here?" Her voice delivered accusation and anger. "'Tis quite obvious where you were last summer, sir. And all that time I waited for you—believing you were waiting for me. But no! You were with that…that woman!"

Danny stood there, fingering his hat nervously.

He started to speak but Susannah interrupted. "How could you tell me you loved me when you loved another. You loved another woman!"

Danny blurted out in a panicked voice. "Polly is not a woman. She is my sister!"

Susannah stood there in stunned silence. She could hear her father and Modesty giggling in the other room.

Then the absurdity of Dan's statement made her start to laugh, as well.

Dan stood there, looking uncomfortable, turning red. "Susannah, I did wait for you. I was with no other."

Susannah approached him slowly, feeling the heat of embarrassment flush her cheeks. Taking his hands she spoke sheepishly, "Please forgive me."

Mr. Dobbins came in from the other room and looked at his daughter with his arms folded. "I told you there likely was an explanation." Smirking, he bowed at his waist to Dan. "I did not realize that you had a married sister, Dan."

Susannah saw him swallow with difficulty. "That is just it, sir. My sister, Polly, is not married." He looked down at the floor. "I understand, sir, should you wish to keep your family from scandal." Dan did not look up.

Mr. Dobbins walked slowly toward Dan. "Dan, let he who is without sin cast the first stone." He patted his right arm in a fatherly manner.

Dan looked up with a hesitant gaze. "Are you certain, sir?"

"I am certain."

Dan breathed a sigh of relief. "Sir, then I implore you. May I ask your daughter's hand in marriage? I was going to wait until Sabbath day, but – under the circumstances – I feel I must assure Susannah of my great love and affection for her." The whole time he stared at Mr. Dobbins.

"Well then, Dan, I suggest you assure Susannah of your great love and affection, rather than me." Mr. Dobbins smiled with amusement.

Dan jerked his head in Susannah's direction. "Yes." He swallowed visibly and moved uncertainly toward her. "Susannah, please…do me the honor of becoming my wife." His voice was low and impassioned. He licked his lips several times.

She reached her hands out toward him. "Yes. A thousand times, yes!"

His countenance beamed as he held her. "I love you, Susannah. I will do all I can to make you happy."

Pulling away she sought his eyes. "You've already made me happy."

Mr. Dobbins cleared his throat. "About your sister, Dan. She needs somewhere to lodge. Why do you not arrange for her to stay here in our guestroom?"

Dan looked baffled. "That is most generous of you, sir. Are you certain?"

"Yes, quite certain. Please bring her as soon as you are able. My daughter's future sister-in-law is in need." Mr. Dobbins had a faraway look in his gaze.

"I thank you kindly, sir. Susannah, I will arrange for Polly to arrive as soon as she has rested in the barracks." He squeezed her hands in his and kissed her fingertips. "I love you so."

"I love you." Grinning from ear-to-ear, she waved farewell as he returned to the armory.

Closing the door, she turned around and leaned against the wooden frame. "I'm to be married." She closed her eyes, relishing the thought.

When she opened them, she saw her father standing there, hands on his hips, staring into the distance.

"What is it, father?"

He jerked his head up in surprise. "What, dear?"

"You seemed lost in thought." She slipped her arm through his. "Pray, what are you thinking?"

"I was just thinking about your mother. How much she would have loved to see you become a bride."

Susannah's eyes misted. "I miss her so." Laying her head against her father's shoulder, she was quiet for a moment. "That is so kind of you to allow Dan's sister to stay with us in her time of need."

Her father did not speak for a moment. "What is it, Father?"

"'Tis not just kindness, Susannah, that prompts me to

open up our home." He paused. "Your mother was once in Polly's shoes."

Susannah's mouth dried. "Mother?"

"Yes." He sat down in the settee. "Your mother and I were so in love, but your grandfather would not hear of us getting married. You know, I was not of their class."

Susannah nodded without speaking.

"One day, we were all alone. One thing led to another. Before long, we knew that she was with child — she was carrying your brother." He stared into the burning hearth for a long while. "So how can I not open up our home?" He looked at his daughter with moist eyes. "I am sorry to tell you of my failures."

Susannah hurried to his side. "You are not a failure, Father. This could happen to anyone. Please do not drown in your own condemnation." She put her arms around his shoulders and hugged him.

After a moment, he sighed and squeezed her arm. "I am a flawed man who has known God's grace, although I do not deserve it."

Susannah looked into his eyes earnestly. "Who among us *does* deserve it, Father?"

"Thank you, Susannah." They both stood looking into the flames. "I love you, daughter."

She swallowed with difficulty. "I love you too, Father."

Chapter 29
Sisters

Watching Polly finish eating the last of her breakfast, Susannah smiled warmly at her, hoping the Dobbins' guest would feel at home.

Polly looked shyly at her host and hostess.

"I cannot thank you enough for your kindness, Mr. Dobbins. Susannah." She smoothed the linen material across her large belly. "I was planning on finding a job at the barracks…cooking for the workers or something. I never intended to take advantage of your hospitality." She glanced down at her hand.

Mr. Dobbins swallowed the last of his coffee. "Think nothing more of it, Miss Lowe. It would not be the best of circumstances being surrounded by the men at the barracks. Some of them are gentlemen, like your brother, but some are rather—coarse. 'Tis best you remain here." Standing up, he wiped his face with his napkin. "Time to open the shop. I pray you ladies have a pleasant day."

Susannah smiled. "We shall, Father." Reaching over to squeeze Polly's hand, she finished her own cup of coffee. "I look forward to getting to know my future sister-in-law. I am so pleased I will finally have sisters!"

Polly gave a weak smile that did not reach her eyes. "Yes, there are certainly many sisters at our home in Deer Run."

Susannah noticed a look of sadness in Polly's eyes that touched her heart. "I am so happy to have you here, Polly. Let us sit in the parlor a bit…get to know one another better."

The women stood up from their chairs and Polly awkwardly shifted away from the edge of the table. The material on her homespun petticoat caught against the tablecloth, threatening to pull the pewter spoons off onto the floor. "'Tis cumbersome." After pulling the tablecloth away from the gown that covered her large belly, Polly managed to extricate herself from the chair completely.

Susannah walked around the table, placed her arm through Polly's, and walked toward the parlor. "Here, please sit, Polly. And should you get too tired, please let me know."

"You are so kind, Susannah." Polly eased herself onto the settee and crossed her legs at the ankles. Smoothing her hand across the furniture fabric, she etched her fingers along a line of raised embroidery. "Your furniture is so fine."

"I suppose so. But I have learned that 'tis far more important who is sitting on the furniture rather than the worth of the design." Susannah gave an embarrassed smile. "And I am certain your brother can assure you that I have not always been so kind."

Polly raised her head with a surprised expression. "Nothing of the sort. He always has the highest regard for you."

"Well, I have changed some. God has wrought His work in my heart and I pray that He is more pleased with who I have become."

Polly stared at her folded hands. "God has much work to do in my heart, I fear." She bit her trembling lip. "I have sinned greatly…and I know not what to do."

Susannah did not know what to say.

Please, dear Lord, give me wisdom.

She breathed in deeply. "I do not know what you should do, Polly. But I am here to listen if you want to talk with me about it. Until yesterday, I knew naught of your situation. I do not know the circumstances…or even who your child's father is. But I do wish to help."

Polly met her gaze with moist eyes. Taking in a shuddering breath, she opened up to Susannah.

"My child's father was the son of someone my father despised. I am not certain of all the reasons, but my father loathed the very ground the man walked upon. When Jonathan—that is my child's sire—and I met, we were so attracted to one another. It was as if the sun seemed to rise with his smile and when he left my presence, the clouds overcame the day. He was my joy—my love." Polly looked at her hands and wept.

Susannah sat next to her on the settee and gripped Polly's fingers. Pulling out a kerchief from her pocket, Susannah handed it to the weeping mother. When Dan's sister began to calm down, Susannah encouraged her to continue. "So what happened, Polly?"

"Jonathan's father, Josiah, was dying. Papa went to see him and Jonathan told me that his father begged Papa to give grace to Jonathan — that he was a different man than Josiah. It took some time for Papa to repent. But when he did, he was going to give Jonathan permission to ask for my hand. But — by the time Papa had changed his mind, it was too late. Jonathan had left Deer Run. And I was already carrying his child."

Susannah's heart ached at this revelation. "Well, surely if Jonathan loves you, he would be willing to return to marry you and care for his child."

Polly's face contorted in pain. "He does not know about the baby."

Susannah's heart skipped a beat. "What? Why ever not? You must tell him at once!"

"No!" Polly bit her lip. "I am sorry. I did not mean to raise my voice. But this is my fault and I cannot hold Jonathan accountable for my sinful behavior."

"What do you mean? How can this be only your doing?" Susannah shook her head in confusion.

Polly turned a deep red. "This is most embarrassing, Susannah. You will think quite ill of me."

"I assure you, Polly, I will not. I am just trying to understand. I want to help you." She gently squeezed Polly's fingers.

Taking in an uneven breath, Polly exhaled slowly. Her voice was low and filled with pain. "I wanted to comfort him in his grief — to show him how much I loved him. In the heat of our passion, I gave myself to him."

Susannah could not speak. *What do I say, Lord?*

Polly looked up slowly. "I told you this was embarrassing. I would not blame you if you sent me out upon the street now."

Shaking her head, Susannah gripped the young woman's hand even tighter. "No. I do not judge you, Polly." She swallowed with difficulty. "I can understand — losing yourself in passion." She thought of all the times she had embraced Dan and nearly lost herself in his love, wishing it could go on until…she breathed in sharply. "I understand such feelings. What I do not understand is, why you have not told him about this child?"

Polly looked up with an impassioned stare. "Because this is not his fault. He deserves better than being trapped with a woman who seduced him. I took advantage of his grief when his father died. I had no right." At this, Polly melted into tears and covered her face with both hands.

Susannah wrapped her arms tenderly around Polly's shoulders and let her cry. At length, the tears subsided. Handing Polly another kerchief to wipe her eyes, Susannah looked straight at Polly and said, "We must find Jonathan and let him know."

Polly's voice sounded lifeless. "'Tis too late."

"What do you mean?" Susannah's eyes searched Polly's.

"I have already sent Jonathan a letter. I lied, telling him that I found another man to love. I have not heard from him in months now."

Susannah's heart wrenched. "Polly, no."

Polly sat unmoving, staring toward the small flame flickering in the hearth. "My one sin has turned into many."

Biting her lip, Susannah's thoughts tumbled through her mind.

Help me, Lord. Help Polly. What do I say?

After a few moments, Susannah's thinking cleared. She knew she did not have every answer. But she knew she could help Polly understand that she would be there for her as a friend. And she could pray for her.

"Polly, you look tired. Perhaps a rest would help you and your little one. You had a long journey yesterday and I am certain that you are exhausted."

Polly smiled gratefully. "Yes." Pushing herself awkwardly up from the settee, she rubbed her lower back.

"Thank you, Susannah."

"For what, Polly?"

"For not judging me. For being my friend." Tears rolled down her cheeks and Susannah stood up and hugged her.

"Let he who is without sin..."

"I feel as if there are many in Deer Run who wish to cast stones at me. And in truth? I deserve it."

Susannah looked pointedly at her future sister-in-law. "Then in truth? We all deserve it. For we all have sinned. Come — let me help you up the stairs."

Arm-in-arm, the two young women slowly climbed the steps to the second floor.

After Polly laid down to rest, Susannah leaned with her back against the door she had just closed to the guest room.

Lord, give me wisdom.

Chapter 30
Decisions

Polly had been in Springfield for over two weeks when she made an announcement.

"'Tis time I returned to Deer Run—I wish to have my child at home. And I know I need to make my public confession at church, no matter how difficult this will be." While they sat at the table at the Dobbins home, she met Danny's eyes. "I was wrong to run away and I must face my sin. And…I miss Mother. I need her." Tears threatened to overflow her lower eyelids but Polly maintained her composure.

Danny grasped her hand. "I know this is a difficult decision for you but it is the right one. I will contact my supervisor and make arrangements to take a few days off so I can take you home."

Mr. Dobbins interjected. "Let us all go. Susannah has desired to meet your family, Dan. Why do we not all travel there and become acquainted? Mr. Stratford's nephew is quite capable of watching the shop for a few days. And I would not mind a refreshing trip to the hill country. What say you?"

Susannah beamed. "A trip to your home! That sounds lovely! And I so wish to meet the rest of your family, Dan."

Danny scratched his head. "Susannah, I do not know…"

What will she think of my humble home? Not to mention my huge family?

Polly spoke up. "That is a wonderful idea, Danny. The whole family can get acquainted with Susannah."

Everyone seemed enthused except Danny. He took in a deep breath.

I suppose 'tis inevitable they must meet…

"Very well, then. But Susannah, please understand my

family's humble circumstances..."

She grabbed his hand. "Are you still worried about this? What will your family do? Make me kill a pig?" She giggled.

"Oh, no." Danny jested. "'Tis spring after all. Pig killing only happens in the fall. Perhaps Father will just have you lead the oxen to the field for plowing."

Susannah's face fell.

Mr. Dobbins and Polly burst out laughing.

"Susannah, no one will ask you to kill a pig. Or lead the oxen to the field." Danny took her hand and kissed it. "They know you have never lived in the country. You only need to do what you feel comfortable doing. They will not set you to mucking out a pigpen."

"Whatever that is." Susannah blew out a relieved breath then scowled. "They may think I am quite an incapable wife for you, Dan. What if your mother does not approve?"

Polly spoke up. "You will win her over with your kindness and your faith, Susannah. That is far more important than slaughtering animals."

Danny leaned over to Susannah and kissed her tenderly. "Besides, you can manage the pigs later."

She threw her napkin at him and he ducked, laughing, from the linen's assault.

* * *

Arrangements were made for Danny to be gone from work for a few days. The new Stocking and Filing Shop was still being erected on the armory grounds and the need for workers was less until operations were fully reestablished.

It was April now and the roads were dryer as the snow had long since melted. Maple and birch trees were speckled with light green tips on every twig and robins searched frantically for worms.

Polly's baby was due to arrive in a week so there was a growing urgency to return to the small town northwest of Springfield as soon as possible. Mr. Dobbins arranged for a comfortable two-seater carriage to transport the four of them to Deer Run.

Susannah carried her clothes-filled portmanteau out to the waiting carriage and handed it to her father. Polly carried the basket she had arrived with a few weeks prior and Danny nestled it in the compartment near their feet. He very carefully helped his sister manage the step upward onto the back seat of the carriage. Plunking down onto the pillow they had brought to cushion her ride, her eyes suddenly widened.

"Oh! I forgot the reticule that Susannah made me. I must have left it on the chest of drawers."

"Stay here. I shall go find it." Danny raced back inside and took the steps at a faster-than-usual pace.

Opening the guest room door, Danny scanned the room for the small drawstring purse that Susannah had made for his sister. Smiling, he picked up the silk piece and sniffed it.

The lovely scent of Susannah.

Sniffing it once more to savor her fragrance, Danny turned to leave. His eye caught a small folded parchment on the floor. Leaning over to pick it up, he noticed that it was more than one parchment—it was a small pile of letters tied together that had slipped under the edge of the quilt along the floor.

At first he hesitated but then, compelled by curiosity, he pulled one out. It was a love letter from Jonathan. Sitting on the bed, he quickly scanned its contents and took in a deep breath.

"Polly, he wanted to come back to you! Why did you spurn him? Were you so beset with guilt you could not accept his love?" Danny thrust his hand through his hair.

Susannah had told him that Polly had lied to Jonathan, making him think Polly had found another man she loved instead. Danny had been furious when Susannah told him, but she had gently calmed him down.

"Let God touch her heart to reveal this grievous mistake. She knows it was wrong. But the Holy Ghost can penetrate through Polly's pride better than you or I." Susannah's words clung to his thoughts.

When did my future wife become so wise?

But reading Jonathan's letters, it was obvious that the

father of Polly's baby was completely in love with his sister and wanted to return to her. Until, of course, she sent Jonathan the deceptive letter. After that communication, his declarations of affection to her ceased.

He searched the most recent one for a return address. *Connecticut!*

Jonathan was not that far away. Picking up a quill at the writing desk, Danny hurriedly wrote out the address last given. He refolded the letters, tied them together, and placed them exactly where he had found them on the floor.

He knew as soon as they arrived in Deer Run, he would send his brother James on a mission to find him.

I pray God he is still there.

Chapter 31
Home

It was dusk when the horse-drawn carriage with two rows of seats pulled up the road toward the Lowe cabin. Susannah anxiously peered through the waning light to see the home in which her future husband had grown up.

It was a modest log cabin with only two windows that she could see, and an addition on one side with a sloping roof, likely added as the family grew. The front door burst open with a frenzy of sisters welcoming Polly back with open arms. Daniel followed the fluttering bevy of females and Susannah saw an older woman in the doorframe, haloed by the light of an indoor hearth behind her. A dog came running out, barking and wagging its tail, and Susannah grinned.

I always wanted a dog.

Daniel Sr. approached the carriage, reaching up to help Polly's unwieldy frame manage the steps to the ground.

The father gently encased his oldest daughter in his arms. "Welcome home." Polly clung to him for several moments, silent tears winding in streams down her contorted face.

The four younger sisters smiled shyly at Susannah and Mr. Dobbins still seated in the carriage. The girls curtsied and whispered to each other about the "fine carriage." Little Betsey stroked the muzzles of the two horses.

Susannah greeted them warmly and Mr. Dobbins doffed his felt hat and grinned. "You have a lovely family, Daniel."

Daniel released his grip on Polly's shoulder and addressed the man. "Thank you, Charles."

He looked at his daughter with concern. "Come inside and rest." The sisters, arms embracing Polly, led her carefully toward the cabin, fussing over who would carry her basket of clothes.

Glancing up at Mr. Dobbins and Susannah, Daniel gave a bow. "Thank you for bringing my daughter home. And welcome. My sister-in-law Sarah and her husband have a much larger home we thought would provide more comfort for you both. Danny, of course, can stay with us but he will guide you to the Eaton farm forthwith."

The middle-aged woman in the doorway shyly approached the carriage. Mr. Dobbins grinned. "Mrs. Lowe. You are as lovely as your husband described."

Even in the waning light, Susannah could see the woman's skin tone redden. "That is kind of you, Mr. Dobbins." She curtsied then addressed Susannah. "And you must be Susannah. Welcome to our home. Please stay in Deer Run as long as you are able."

Her gracious welcome warmed Susannah's heart. "Thank you kindly, Missus Lowe. I am so pleased to meet you. I feel as if I know you already, Dan speaks so often of you."

"You must be tired from your journey. I know that my sister Sarah has food aplenty for you both. We will all sup here together tomorrow after you are more refreshed."

Mr. Dobbins grinned. "Thank you, Missus Lowe. And please call me Charles."

"Then you must call me Mary." Danny's mother grinned, making her countenance bloom with the beauty reminiscent of her youth.

Danny stepped down so he could hug his mother. "I'll hasten home after I take them to Aunt Sarah's." His mother touched his face. Susannah realized it was the first time that she had seen him since he was so seriously injured. She saw in the mother's eyes a glistening of relief that her child, now taller than herself, was indeed safe. Mary kissed Danny's cheek tenderly and said, "Hasten home, son."

"I shall." Hugging her quickly, he climbed back into the carriage and directed Mr. Dobbins to the Eaton farm.

Susannah turned to look at him in the back seat. "Your family is lovely, Dan. Or should I call you 'Danny'?" She teased a grin.

Danny rolled his eyes. "All my efforts to sound more grown up, now dashed in one visit to my youthful abode."

She laughed at him and then gasped as she was jerked to one side as the carriage tilted from a rut in the dirt road. Clinging to the wooden seat, she breathed a sigh of relief that she had not tumbled out. In the meantime, Danny had grasped her arm to keep her securely in place.

The strength of his grip was a comfort. It also sent warm shivers up her spine as he held it there a moment longer than necessary and caressed her shoulder with his thumb.

"Now, see there, Miss Dobbins. That must be a sign that you must respect your future husband by calling him by his adult name."

"Perhaps I should call you 'Mr. Lowe' and follow you from room to room, waiting on your every need."

She saw him sit up straight in the back seat. "That is an excellent idea, Miss Dobbins. You should respect your consort, treating him as the man of the house." He folded his arms and nodded his head.

Grinning, she turned to look at him and fluttered her eyelashes, eliciting a laugh from the man who would soon be her husband.

By the time they arrived at the Eaton farm, Susannah was yawning. She smiled at the friendly greeting of Dan's Aunt Sarah and Uncle Nathaniel. The boys were already in bed, as was Grandmother Eaton, they told her.

Sarah put her arm through Susannah's and led her toward the front door. "You look so tired, Susannah. Come let's show you a nice warm bed with Mother. We have a guest room for your father where the boys will not disturb him in the morning."

Susannah felt Danny give her a kiss on her cheek and she vaguely heard him say that he would see her in the morning.

Aunt Sarah's arms guided her to a room off the main living area. Entering the cozy chamber, Susannah could hear the gentle snoring of Grandmother Eaton on one side of a large bed. Sarah helped Susannah remove her bonnet and pelisse, and then pulled the bedcovers down.

"Here, my dear. Settle in and make yourself at home. I'll have a breakfast ready first thing in the morning. I can see you are too weary for anything to eat tonight."

"Yes." Susannah yawned and fell down onto the bed. She felt the covers being drawn over her body and she smiled at the comforting quilts wrapped snugly around her.

The gentle snoring of the grandmother lying next to her lulled her to sleep.

* * *

Awakened by the boisterous song of a house wren, Susannah lazily opened her exhausted eyes. Streams of early morning light poured through the uncovered window panes and, squinting from the glare, Susannah threw the quilt over her eyes.

Sounds of small voices from the next room and the hushed tones of older voices trying to subdue the enthusiastic chatter of little ones made Susannah grin. An occasional clatter of a plate on a wooden floor followed by an admonition from the parents, prompted her to roll onto her side and push the covers away.

Her body ached from the long ride over country roads and she stretched out her muscles to work away the tautness. Sitting on the edge of the bed, she noticed that she still wore her muslin travel gown of yesterday.

Oh, my. So many wrinkles.

Sighing, she pushed herself up from the feather-filled mattress and stretched. Lazily removing her outer gown and chemise, she shivered as she went to the chest of drawers where the pitcher and bowl sat. Pouring chilled water into the bowl, she splashed it over her face and under her arms and dried herself with a linen towel. Covered with goose bumps, she scurried toward her portmanteau and unlatched the over-filled bag, searching for her bottle of lavender water. She gratefully splashed the liquid onto her neck and her underarms. Recorking the bottle, she found a clean chemise and slipped it on over her head. Grabbing a corset, she tied it fairly loosely for comfort and then placed her dimity gown on over her head.

There. That should do.

She did not wish to dress in too much finery in front of Dan's family.

Walking toward the looking glass, she combed her hair and placed a few pins to keep it up off of her neck and set a sheer cap over the bulk of her hair, leaving several visible curls to sweep forward along her cheeks.

She adjusted her bodice a little higher, hoping that her full bosom was not exposed too much. She did not know what was considered appropriate here in the hill country.

Lord, I pray that they will like me.

Taking in a deep breath, she walked bravely to the door and unlatched the handle.

"She's up!" The excited voice of a child about four years old broke the silence of the rest of the family.

"Yes, I am finally awake." Susannah smiled shyly.

Carrying a large bowl of gruel in one hand, Sarah came over to her and hugged her with one arm.

"Come, sit down."

The four-year-old shouted, "She can sit next to me." He scooted to the side to make room, bumping into his older brother.

"Benjamin, be careful. Remember your manners." Sarah gave him a stern look.

Susannah smiled at the boy. "Thank you, Benjamin. I am most grateful." She slid onto the bench next to the boy, who could not take his eyes off of her. After inspecting her gown from top to bottom, he leaned toward her and sniffed. "You smell like flowers."

Laughing at his comment, she squeezed his dimpled cheek and leaned over to sniff him back. "And you smell like...sunshine."

Little Benjamin grinned. "I do?"

"'Tis true." She tugged at his long blond hair, pulled back with a ribbon.

Sarah laughed. "You have a new friend. Boys, this is your cousin Danny's lady friend, soon to be his wife. Her name is Miss Dobbins."

"They can call me Susannah, if that suits you."

"That will be all right." Sarah plopped a spoonful of warm gruel into Susannah's bowl, which was placed in front of her. "Here is maple syrup for sweetening. Just harvested last month. Your father has already eaten and he is visiting with Daniel—Danny's father that is."

Nathaniel was at the head of the table. "So, Susannah, I pray your trip was uneventful. Traveling such a distance can be quite the trial." He swallowed a drink from his tankard.

"Oh, it went quite well. I think it was the most difficult on Polly."

Sarah sat down with one-year-old Rachel on her lap. "I am certain it was, in her condition."

"What is a 'condition'?" Benjamin wiped some gruel from his face with his hand.

"That means she is with child, Benjamin. Now please eat."

Nathaniel pointed a finger at the two oldest boys. "Joseph and Myles, time to get the oxen ready for the field. Time's a wastin'. Benjamin, you carry the satchel of seeds today."

"Yes, Father."

The boys pushed away from the table and prepared to go out the door. Starting to head toward the door, Benjamin stopped and returned to Susannah. Leaning toward her, he sniffed in deeply and smiled. "See ya later, Miss Susannah."

Susannah covered her mouth to keep from bursting out in laughter.

Sarah looked at Nathaniel. "He is quite the romantic, like his father." Sarah pulled her homespun shift down and let Rachel nurse.

Staring at the child nursing, Sarah swallowed, fascinated by the sight. "I've never seen a child nurse before."

Sarah's eyes widened. "Never? Well you will see lots of it here I assure you." As if in response, one and a half-year-old Ethan sauntered over to his mother, pulled down the other side of her shift, crawled onto his mother's lap and attached himself to her other breast.

A flush of warmth filled Susannah's cheeks. Sarah laughed. "They are like twins. Rachel was born when Ethan was a few months old. When James's wife died, I became Rachel's wet nurse. We are quite attached to her now — she is our only girl amongst the troops." She rocked them slightly as she suckled both toddlers. "I shall wean them after the summer — when the danger of the fever is past."

Nathaniel finished his tankard of drink, walked over to Sarah and kissed her cheek while standing behind her. He stroked the top of one of her rounded breasts and whispered something in her ear. Sarah turned red and said, "Go on with you, Nathaniel."

He grinned and picked up his hat. "Good day, Susannah."

"Good day, Nathaniel." Susannah's voice was strained and she shifted in her seat.

She had never viewed such intimacy before. Feelings that were so personal arose in her own breast. Grasping her tankard, she swallowed a mouthful of cider, desperate for any distraction from the scene she had just witnessed.

Country life is so — earthy.

Pushing aside her discomfiting yet pleasurable thoughts, she hurried to finish her breakfast. "What can I do to help, Sarah?" She stood up and carried her plate to the wash basin. "I can clean these, if you like." Staring at the pile of dirty bowls, Susannah almost regretted her offer.

So many dishes!

"That would be most helpful, Susannah. Today will be planting day, so I can get started in my garden sooner with you washing."

"When I finish the dishes, I will come help you in the garden." Susannah did not have the faintest idea how to plant a garden — but she knew she needed to learn.

By the time she had cleaned and dried all the dishes, Susannah looked down at her hands in horror.

Red and wrinkled!

She caught her breath, wondering how long they would look like that. Covering them up with the apron Sarah had handed to her to wear, she headed for the door and the garden.

Ethan and Rachel looked adorable, barefoot and toddling around on the softly turned earth.

Susannah breathed in deeply of the warm spring air. The weather was perfect, not too hot, and rich with the smells of damp earth and budding flowers. Closing her eyes, she suddenly realized how quiet it was. The trills of birds, the digging sounds of Sarah making holes in the garden, and the giggles of the toddlers were the only sounds wafting to her ears. No carts in the street, no yells of the merchants, no bantering in the crowds.

It was blessedly peaceful.

Shaking out of her reverie, she walked toward Sarah and stood with hands on hips.

"Ready to work, Madam." Her voice was exaggerated and low, as though a sailor speaking to a ship's captain.

Sarah laughed. "Thank you, matey." She handed a pouch of seeds to Susannah. "You can start over there. Place about four or five seeds a few inches into the middle of those mounds over there. They will bring us a nice pumpkin harvest come fall."

Taking the pouch of seeds, Susannah headed for the sunny area that Sarah had pointed to. Stepping carefully around each mound, she wrinkled her nose.

Cow dung!

Bravely bending closer to the mound, she dug a hole with the planting stick that Sarah had given her and placed the seeds into the dark brown mixture of dirt and fertilizer. Her nostrils burned from the aroma, but she determined not to complain.

Country life is most definitely, earthy.

* * *

As was promised the previous evening, Susannah and her father were invited to eat the midday meal with the Lowe's at their cabin.

After a morning of working in the garden followed by Missus Lowe's rich meal of chicken, vegetables and biscuits,

Susannah's eyelids grew heavy.

"I think I'd best take Susannah for a walk before she falls asleep." Danny teased her as the rest of the group chuckled at their guest.

"I am sorry." She felt her cheeks burn.

Mary smiled. "Nothing to apologize for, Susannah. You've had a long journey yesterday and, as I understand, a work-filled day at Sarah's. Enjoy your walk."

Danny and Sarah excused themselves from the long tableboard at the Lowe's home after the meal.

Grabbing her straw hat from the hook on the wall, Sarah walked out the door with Dan.

"Thank you for rescuing me from embarrassment." She tied the ribbons on her bonnet as they strolled.

Dan grinned. "It gave me an excuse to be alone with you. There's something I wish to show you."

They ambled through the woods, Susannah lifting the skirts of her gown to avoid the clinging brambles.

Danny took her arm and helped her traverse the terrain, guiding her around rocks and bushes that stood in their path.

"So where are you taking me?" Glancing at her companion, she noticed the ruddiness of his cheeks after working in the field with his father and brothers all morning. His deep-set green eyes glistened with mirth in the shaded sunlight of the woods as he enjoyed her predicament.

"You will see."

Walking for what seemed a long journey in her sleepy state, Dan suddenly slowed down. "Here. This is what I wanted to show you."

Large, dark boulders, some covered in moss, climbed upwards several feet into the air. Occasional openings in the mass of rocks appeared to draw his eyes to dart from one to the next, youthful excitement dancing in them.

"This is where my brother and I played as lads. Those holes we called 'caves,' only large enough for a child to fit in." He plopped onto a circle of soft grass. "And here is where I would dream. You see how there is an opening here for the sunlight? It allows the grass to grow in this one spot, surrounded in a circle by trees and boulders. It was my one place of refuge. My thinking place."

Susannah carefully sat down on the grass next to him, trying to keep her dress as neat as possible. Shielding her eyes from the sun, she stared upwards at the clouds visible in the blue sky. She stroked the soft new grass emerging from the earth.

"I can see why you loved coming here. It is so peaceful." She felt Dan staring at her.

"You look — so lovely." Leaning over he kissed her on the lips. His kisses became more moist and passionate and, without her resisting, he placed her onto the ground. He began to caress her and she reveled in his touch. When he started to move even closer, she gasped.

"Dan." He paused, his eyes heavy and his breathing rapid.

Sitting back up, he put his hand on his forehead. "What am I doing? I am sorry."

Susannah sat up and pulled her bodice higher, still thrilling at the heat of passion from his fingers.

"Dan, can we marry — tomorrow? I do not wish to wait any longer."

His eyes narrowed but his lips smiled. "Here? In Deer Run? I thought you wanted to marry in Springfield?"

Leaning in seductively toward him, she spoke into his ear. "I wish to be with you — as your wife. It does not matter where I become your wife."

His lips consumed hers with hunger until he pushed her away. "I cannot keep doing this. We must return to the house." He drew his hands nervously through his hair.

He drew in a deep breath. "Yes, I shall make arrangements and we will marry tomorrow." He pushed himself up from the grass and pulled her hands up. Drawing her closely to himself, he hugged her tightly.

"Until tomorrow then."

"Until tomorrow."

Chapter 32
Wedding

The announcement caused near panic—as well as great joy.

"A wedding with one day's notice—well! We have managed greater challenges before." Sarah smiled at Susannah. "Don't you worry about a thing. We will all work together." She hugged Susannah, who gave her a relieved and grateful look.

Susannah bit her lower lip. "I hope Dan's mother will not mind. I am certain she has much else to be concerned with at the moment—with Polly and all."

Sarah held Susannah's arms and squeezed them gently. "'Twill be a pleasant diversion for Mary and Daniel. This is a joyful event." She hugged Susannah. "Now, let us figure out about the food—and the wedding night." Sarah put her finger thoughtfully on her cheek. "I have it! You can use the small cabin on our land. We only use it occasionally. I will fix it up forthwith, if you can help me watch the little ones."

"Of course, let me help out in whatever way I can."

Nathaniel and the three boys walked in from the fields covered with sweat. Little Benjamin squeezed a bunch of dandelions between his fingers and handed them dramatically to Susannah.

"I brought you some flowers, Miss Susannah." He grinned as he thrust them before her.

"Oh, they are lovely." She bent down to take them from the child. "Thank you so much."

"Benjamin, Miss Susannah and Cousin Danny will be married tomorrow. Is that not lovely?"

The child furrowed his brow. "Must you marry my cousin?"

Susannah bit back a giggle. "I must. Your cousin insists."

"Has he ever brought you such lovely flowers?"

"No, I must say, never any so beautiful as these. But he does love me and I love him." The boy looked at the floor. Susannah lifted his chin up. "I would be most honored if you would pick flowers just like these for my wedding tomorrow. Could you do that?" She had placed both her hands on his small arms.

He looking up, grinning. "I could do that."

"Wonderful. And Benjamin, some day when you are much older, you will meet a lady to marry."

"Will she smell like flowers?" He squinted doubtfully.

"I am certain she will."

"Good." He looked at his mother. "I'd best go find flowers for the wedding, Mother."

As he ran out the door, Sarah shook her head. "He is just like his father."

She walked over to Nathaniel, who was drinking a tankard of cider, and kissed him on the cheek.

He grinned. "What was that for?"

"For being such a romantic." Sarah smiled at Susannah.

* * *

Susannah had not seen Dan since they made the announcement. She was beginning to get nervous as she prepared for bed that evening. Sarah had shared some intimate instructions about the wedding night with her in order to prepare her. She was eagerly anticipating the pleasure — but also extremely nervous about the first encounter.

The door opened while she was walking about in her thin chemise and she thrust a gown in front of herself.

"Grandmother Eaton." Susannah had not had much of a chance to visit with Danny's grandmother since the midwife had been gone most of the day, delivering an infant. "How lovely to finally meet with you."

The elderly woman sat wearily on the bed. "It is lovely to meet with you as well, my dear. I am sorry, I have not been here to visit with you — get to know you better." She stopped to catch her breath and then grinned. "I understand we are to have a wedding tomorrow. ''Tis marriage season after all,' as my late husband would say."

Susannah looked at the floor self-consciously. "Yes. I am most anxious to marry your grandson. I love him so much."

"Good. 'Tis a long life together if there is not love along with respect."

Susannah set the gown on the wall hook. "I respect Dan greatly. He is so honest, godly, kind, courageous — everything I would wish for in a husband."

She noticed Grandmother Eaton scrutinizing her form. "You should do well, my dear."

"Do well?"

What is she talking about?

"In childbirth. Your hips are well formed for a birthing — wide and set the right distance apart. That is a blessing since you are marrying a Lowe man. They are quite — fruitful in progeny, shall we say." She raised her eyebrows and smirked.

Susannah's cheeks burned. Such frank talk was unknown to her and she did not know what to say. She held her arms tightly across her large bosom.

When she had finally found her voice and was ready to change the topic, she heard a gentle snore. Grandmother Eaton had slipped under the quilts, and fallen into a deep sleep.

Susannah unfolded her arms. Pulling her sheer chemise across her hips she bent forward and side-to-side to view the hipbones that protruded outward at angles. Releasing the material, she blew out the single burning candle and climbed under the covers.

Grabbing her pillow into her arms, she pretended she was hugging Dan and smiled as she fell into a deep sleep.

* * *

The birds provided the music in the trees overhead in the meadow near the Lowe's farm. As the justice of the peace administered the wedding vows to Susannah and Danny, numerous cousins and family members stood watching. Susannah held her bouquet of dirt-covered dandelions provided by little Benjamin.

Susannah glanced at Daniel Sr., who had his arm around Mary. Tears glistened in her mother-in-law's eyes, as Daniel Sr. gave her a gentle hug. All the children were quiet, even little Rachel, who played with a dandelion in her chubby fingers.

The only missing sibling was Polly, who waited inside the Lowe cabin. She was accompanied by Hannah, who would be her midwife and who stayed with the young pregnant girl. Hannah's husband James had gone on a mysterious mission and no one knew when he would return. At least, that was what Danny had told her.

Susannah's gaze wandered back to her soon-to-be husband.

He looks so handsome.

His chest had returned to its normal muscular tone following the attack that had weakened him for so long. His hands that held hers were sure and steady; only a hint of moisture told her that he might be nervous.

Moving her gaze upward, she breathed in sharply at the look in his eyes. It was sheer love and admiration. Perhaps there was a gleam of passion in his eyes. It made her blush and look downward at her hands enveloped by his.

"By the power of the law invested in me by the Commonwealth of Massachusetts, I now pronounce you man and wife." The justice of the peace closed his book. "You may now kiss your bride." The round-faced man grinned mischievously.

"I believe I shall." Danny leaned forward and planted a moist kiss on Susannah's lips. As he pulled away, he whispered. "There are more to come."

Susannah grinned as the crowd cheered.

James shook his brother's hand. "Well done, Brother."

Dan spoke closely to his brother's ear. "Has Uncle James set off yet?"

"Yes, I gave him the note. His boys were able to do the planting so he could leave but it was important that I stay and help Father."

"Thanks. Let us pray he is successful."

Confusion filled Susannah's thoughts. "Successful in what."

"I shall tell you later." Danny greeted the rest of the cousins and Sarah called the group over to eat from a table brought outdoors. She folded the muslin cloth that protected the food during the ceremony. Cousins swarmed the table laden with breads, cheeses, salt pork, and dried fruits.

Susannah was not hungry. She was far too nervous to think about eating, although she had not had anything since breakfast. Since everyone was practically a stranger to her, she clung to Dan and searched the crowd for her father.

He caught her eye over the swarm of attendees and gave her a grin. He seemed sad, she thought.

His only daughter is now married, after all.

Working his way through the crowd, he approached her and gave her a fatherly hug. "Susannah, you have never looked lovelier. I am overwhelmed with emotion." He wiped a tear away. "Forgive an old man."

She patted his lapel. "You are not old, Father." She reached up and pecked him on the cheek. "And I do love you so. Were it not for your guidance, I might have chosen a man that was completely wrong for me."

He smiled and kissed her hand. "I can tell how happy you are, my dear. That is all the thanks I need."

"I love you, Father." Tears erupted unexpectedly.

"And you will always be my little girl — even when you have a little girl of your own."

Susannah blushed. "Thank you." Her voice whispered.

Dan interrupted them. There was excitement in his voice.

"Excuse me, sir. I wanted to give something to Susannah."

Mr. Dobbins smiled sadly. "Of course. She is your wife after all."

Danny struggled to maintain his excitement. "Susannah, please come with me. I have something to give you."

Curious, Susannah followed him as he drew her into the woods. Everyone was so busy visiting, it seemed as if they slipped away unnoticed.

"Dan, can this not wait?" She hiked up her delicate muslin, hoping it would not catch on the twigs and thorns.

Before long, they had arrived at Dan's special boyhood haven—his "thinking spot." Bright sunlight warmed down upon her head.

Danny swallowed. "Susannah. This is for you. My father just gave it to me." Opening a small blue velvet pouch, he poured the contents into the palm of his hand. Sunlight glistened across the shimmering gold ring in which was set a ruby stone that sparkled like fire. Its edges were cut in dramatic slants that showed its color to the best advantage.

Susannah caught her breath. "Dan! It is exquisite. Where is it from?"

Dan looked at her in a manner that drew her breath away. "It is from England. My grandsire left it as a gift to me on my wedding day. As my father's oldest son, it was to go to me. It belonged to my grandmother in England." His eyes welled with passion. "It will look lovely on you."

Slipping the ring onto her left index finger, he cupped her hand closed. "The vein in that finger carries the blood strait to your heart. So you will always remember my love that flows through you. It belongs to you alone."

Susannah's pulse surged as he embraced her, kissing her with unbridled passion, his hands grasping every part of her. She did not want him to stop. She reached up to untie the cravat at his neck. Unbuttoning his coat, then his waistcoat, she reached across his linen shirt, groping his waist.

His kisses swarmed her neck. She shivered with pleasure as his mouth sought that which was still covered. Gasping, a craving rose deep within that she had long smothered until now.

"Lay with me." She could barely breathe. He paused long enough to meet her eye.

"Here? Now?"

"Yes."

Dropping to their knees, they laid down in the warmth of the sun, cushioned by the soft grass below as he covered her with his love.

Chapter 33
Regrets

Daniel opened the solitary window of their bedroom as wide as he could to allow a slight breeze. The air inside the cabin was stifling and he removed his linen shirt before crawling into bed next to Mary. Her eyes were wide open, flitting back and forth.

"Not sleepy? Thinking about today's wedding?" Daniel stared at his bride of twenty-three years. Family weddings always brought back reminiscences of their own day of marriage.

Mary rested her eyes upon him. "My mind is galloping from today."

"I know." He put his hands behind his head and stared at the ceiling, before he broke out in a grin. "Did you see Danny and Susannah come back from the woods? It seems they were as anxious for their wedding day as you and I were."

Giggling, Mary rested her hand on his chest. "And who could blame them, after all they've been through? I thought poor Susannah was going to faint when little Benjamin asked her where she and Danny had gone. I have never seen a woman turn so many shades of red in such a short span of time!"

"'Twas amusing. But Danny looked quite — pleased." He stared at Mary. "I know I was. I still am."

Mary kissed his chest. "I am as well." In the moonlight streaming through the window, he could see her eyes narrow. "I am so saddened that Polly will not know this pleasure. The joy of her wedding night — experiencing love for the first time." Tears welled in her eyes.

Renewed guilt flooded Daniel's thoughts like a surging river in spring. "I still cannot believe it. My own daughter —

raised to know right from wrong — yet driven to sin because of my own lack of forgiveness. 'Tis I who should be in front of the congregation confessing my sin on Sabbath next. My sin is just as wicked — it's just hidden, unlike Polly's obvious wrongdoing."

Mary was silent for a moment. "We have not discussed what to do once the baby comes. Can we raise another child — our grandchild? Polly cannot do this alone."

Daniel's eyes searched the low ceiling of the room addition but he could find no answers written on the wood. "We will have to. We have no choice."

Mary swallowed audibly. "Can you love this child, despite the circumstances? Especially being Josiah's grandchild?"

Stroking the long tresses streaming across her shoulders, he met her gaze earnestly. "Yes. I already do love the child."

She touched his cheek with a trembling finger. "Thank you, Daniel." She leaned down to kiss him.

Feeling her bare skin against his chest excited his desires. Pulling her closer he embraced her, swept up in passions that still ignited easily after so many years.

* * *

The next morning was Saturday — the day appointed for Daniel, Mary, and Polly to visit with Reverend Hollingsworth. It was a meeting that Daniel had long dreaded. It was to prepare Polly for standing in front of the congregation to confess her sin of fornication during the next Sabbath service.

The writ from the church deacons sat on the tableboard as a cruel reminder of her sin. But Polly had said she was willing to face it now and she reread the script at breakfast. The letter said she must confess her sin in public and the church would decide if she was sufficiently repentant. If they deemed she was not, they could excommunicate her from the body of believers.

Daniel's heart ached as he watched his daughter read the

letter that occasionally jolted upwards, apparently from the active baby in her belly.

If only I had not been such a fool.

"Polly, it is not necessary to read the writ again. Why do you not put it aside and enjoy your breakfast?"

She set it down. "Yes, Papa." Folding the parchment, she tucked it inside her pocket. Taking a small bite of gruel, she swallowed it with obvious difficulty then sipped from her tankard. "Everyone else must have eaten early today." She looked down the long empty table that was usually bustling with ravenous Lowe children.

"Yes. I suppose they are in the field." He did not tell her that he had asked the rest of the children to eat early so he could have some time alone with her.

"Polly, I want you to know how very sorry I am that I let my hatred for Jonathan's father overrule my better judgment. My sin has caused you great grief and I am ashamed of my bitterness. I offer no excuse — but I ask that you forgive me."

His daughter stared down at her gruel without speaking, but tears fell onto her hands. Looking up, her face contorted in pain. "Thank you, Papa. But my sin of rebellion against you was equally wrong. And that led to my sin. I am truly a sinner who deserves no mercy."

Daniel lurched to his feet and went to his daughter. Wrapping his arms around her shoulders, he let her cry against him. When she finished, she sniffed and wiped her eyes with her kerchief. "I must compose myself, Papa, and prepare to speak with the reverend."

Tilting her chin to look at him, Daniel whispered, "I am also a sinner who deserves no mercy. We all are. I am so sorry you must make this public confession. In truth, we should all be up there confessing our transgressions before God and each other."

Polly looked at him gratefully. "Thank you, Papa." Sniffing, she resumed taking a few bites of gruel while Daniel sat down.

This will be a long day.

* * *

Approaching the meetinghouse an hour later, the trio appeared somber. Mary's arm wrapped around her daughter's shoulders and Daniel walked with his hands in his pockets and his head looking downward. Polly stared straight ahead, determination on her features.

She is braver than I am. Daniel was amazed at his daughter's strong resolve and courage.

Polly took the stairs slowly, assisted by her mother. The five steps seemed like a journey up a tall mountain peak.

As they entered the meetinghouse, Daniel opened the door, cringing at the noise of the creaking metal hinge. The building seemed to echo every sound. Usually it was a bustle of activity, with congregants at Sabbath service or town meetings overflowing with boisterous discussions from residents. Today, even the smallest steps of Polly's or Mary's shoes seem to be exaggerated in the stillness of the nearly empty building. Besides Daniel, Mary, and Polly, the reverend was the only other attendee.

Turning around to greet them, Reverend Hollingsworth waved them closer. He had found a pew to sit upon and he moved aside to make room for them.

At least he is smiling.

"Thank you for coming, Miss Lowe. Daniel, Missus Lowe. I am certain this is not the easiest time of year to put aside fieldwork for a morning."

Daniel watched Polly carefully navigate the tight pew and sit down awkwardly. The cedar squeaked when she landed on the seat, causing a rush of redness into her face.

"Thank you for visiting with us, Reverend." Daniel removed the hat that he had forgotten to take off upon entering. "We are grateful you have taken the time to meet with my daughter before...before the service tomorrow." He cleared his throat.

Reverend Hollingsworth loosely folded his hands with one arm across the back of the pew. He stared directly at Polly, who sat closest to him.

"Miss Lowe, I am pleased that you have decided to reconsider the public confession. As you are aware, I am sure, fornication is a most grievous sin both against you, the young man involved, your family, but, most importantly, against your God. Do you understand this?"

Staring down at her hands as they rested atop her large belly, Polly spoke in a low voice. "Yes, I understand."

"And do you repent of this wicked act?" The reverend stared directly at her.

Taking in a shuddering breath, she replied, "Yes." Looking up at the reverend for the first time, her eyes implored him. "My act of fornication was evil. But my child is not." Tears brimmed her eyelids.

The reverend looked down, then gazed upward. "No, Miss Lowe, the child is not evil. But this child must now grow up without the benefit of knowing its father — the nurture, care, and support that a father can provide. I understand that the father has disappeared?"

Polly bit her lip. "I no longer know where he is. I...I must confess another sin to you." She inhaled sharply. "I did not inform the father of my condition. He does not know about our child. The last time I heard from him was after I...I lied to him. I told him I had found another man." Tears poured down her cheeks at this admission.

Stunned, Daniel's voice caught in his throat. "Polly! You knew where he was?"

Why would she do this?

"Because my sin was so wicked, I would not make him take the blame. I took advantage of his grief. I knew exactly what I was doing and I did not care. I was angry with my father, grieving that Jonathan would be leaving because Papa could not accept him. I was filled with lustful passion." She sobbed. "It was my sin against Jonathan. I loved him too much to make him pay for my wickedness."

Daniel put his head into his hands and closed his eyes. He could feel Mary's trembling hand on his arm.

Hearing the reverend sigh, silence followed for several minutes. When Reverend Hollingsworth spoke, Daniel lifted his bleary eyes.

"Miss Lowe, you have confessed these many offenses before God and the rest of us in this room. I believe that you are truly repentant and understand your wrongdoing. I want you to remember that every sinful desire is a rebelling of your will against the will of God. God has placed your earthly father in authority over you. No matter the reason for his decisions, you rebelled against him, which in essence, is your rebellion against God Himself. Do you understand this?"

"Yes."

Daniel took in a breath. "Reverend, I must confess that my reasons for disallowing this relationship were wrong. They were based on my bitterness toward Jonathan's father. I am not guiltless in this sin."

Reverend Hollingsworth sighed. "'Tis a truth that one sin doth lead to another. Your bitterness, Daniel, led to your daughter's rebellion, which led to this fornication, followed by her lie to the father of the child. Sin begetting sin. How easily we are deceived by the evil one.

"But let us focus on this sin of fornication, which was birthed from lust in your heart, Miss Lowe. Men—and women—come into the world with many strong and violent lusts in their hearts. We are all exceedingly prone to transgress, in even the best of circumstances. So how can we defend ourselves against these evil inclinations? Let me give you an example by comparing this danger of falling into lust with a simple example in Scripture."

The preacher stopped for a moment and took a deep breath.

Is this as difficult for him to say as it is for us to hear?

Reverend Hollingsworth continued. "Consider with me the way the ancient Israelites provided for protection from falling. But instead of falling into sin, we shall compare it to falling off their flat roofs that were the common design in those days. So how did the Israelites protect themselves as they wandered around on their rooftops, which was their custom? They created battlements along the sides—a defense against falling to their deaths. If a man stands upon a roof or precipice without something to keep him from falling, is he not more likely to fall?

"So we who dabble in lusts of the imagination that lead to the precipice of sin, are not our minds more likely to cause us to fall into the valley of wickedness? As we feed and promote our lust with the very actions of stirring up our appetites, do we not thus wander toward the edge of sin?"

Polly stared quietly at her hands. After a moment, she replied, "Yes, we dabbled in our lust—quite often before we fell into the precipice."

The reverend shook his head. "Many of the practices of our young people today only increase the lustful passions so anxious to be fulfilled. The defenses in this war are weak. As it says in the Holy Scriptures, 'Keep thy heart with all diligence; for out of it are the issues of life. Put away from thee a froward mouth, and perverse lips put far from thee. Let thine eyes look right on, and let thine eyelids look straight before thee. Ponder the path of thy feet. And let all thy ways be established. Turn not to the right hand nor to the left: remove thy foot from evil.'"

"I know that I must seek the Lord's forgiveness, as well as that of the townspeople. I shall do so tomorrow." Polly's voice was weak.

Daniel stood up. "Reverend Hollingsworth, my daughter is fatigued. She will fulfill her obligation to the church tomorrow."

"Yes, Daniel, I understand."

Mary helped Polly stand up in the narrow pew. Walking toward the door, the two women gasped as the door flung open. Filling the doorway, the large man whose features were obscured in the shadows thundered with a bellowing voice.

"Miss Polly Lowe?"

"Yes?" Polly's voice quivered.

"I am sheriff of Hampshire County." Unfolding a rolled parchment, he began to read:

"You are forthwith charged by the Commonwealth of Massachusetts with a crime against chastity. You are hereby ordered to appear before the justice of the peace to hear evidence of said crime. Should you be found guilty, you may be sentenced to up to two months in gaol or be required to pay a fine of thirty dollars."

Mary held onto Polly to keep her from falling to the

floor.

Daniel stood between the sheriff and his daughter. "This is outrageous. You cannot imprison my daughter!"

Before anything further could be spoken, Polly collapsed to the floor.

Chapter 34
Friends

Mary almost felt sorry for the sheriff when Hannah arrived.
Almost.

Sitting inside the meetinghouse with her arm supporting a revived Polly, Mary stared in awe at the scene through the open door. Her best friend and sister-in-law Hannah, one of the local midwives, had her finger in the sheriff's face. Reddened and practically spitting as she screamed at him, Hannah was a fiery force that no man would wish to reckon with.

"How dare you upset my patient! *You* should be the one in gaol, forcing your way into the minister's personal meeting, endangering my patient's child with your vexatious declaration. I ought to report you to the higher authorities in the Commonwealth of Massachusetts." Hannah put her hands on her hips as she stood mere inches from the man.

"Now see here, madam, I am merely performing my duty as sheriff of this county. My office received a complaint from a concerned citizen and we were forced to issue this writ."

Hannah turned even redder, if that were possible. "Your duty, sir, is to protect the citizens of this county and *not* endanger them. You have been informed, sir, that my niece will be appearing before the deacons in church tomorrow. The justice of the peace will already be present, and *he* is the one who determines if there is to be retribution. In the meantime, my niece and her child are *my* concern and you will do *nothing* to cause ill to either of them. Is that clear?"

The sheriff thrust his hat down on his sweating head. Glaring at her, he walked off in a huff. "Nagging, irksome woman." Turning back to her, he pointed his own finger from a safe distance. "Your husband should repent of the day he married you!"

Mary tried not to laugh as Daniel walked in the door carrying a drink for Polly. He was obviously caught up in the exchange between the two and as he turned toward Mary and Polly, his face bore an amused look. "We could have used Hannah in the war."

Scowling at him, Mary asked, "On which side?"

"Well, let me put it this way. If she had been on the side of the King's army at Saratoga, history's outcome might have been quite different." He grinned while handing the drink to his daughter.

Polly guzzled the amber liquid and sighed with satisfaction. "Thank you, Papa. I was so thirsty."

"Are you all right now, Polly?" Mary stroked her shoulder tenderly.

"Better, thank you." Polly's eyes widened. "I have never seen Aunt Hannah so enraged before. She was quite the bulwark, was she not?"

Daniel snorted. "More like a cannon set to fire."

"We can be grateful for her fiery defense of our Polly." Mary hugged her daughter closer. "Hannah has become far stronger since losing her own little one years ago. Baby Samuel helped her to become unafraid to stand up for her patients. She will do anything to protect them."

Hannah walked into the door of the meetinghouse. "I wanted to be sure that rapscallion was well on his way." She touched Polly's hand. "How do you fare, Polly?"

"Much better, Aunt Hannah. But I need to know. Papa, was what he said true? Can they put me in gaol for up to two months? How would I take care of my baby?" Tears filled her eyes.

Daniel cleared his throat. "'Tis true there is such a law. However, each case is decided by the justice of the peace. He is a member of our congregation and he will witness your confession tomorrow. Let us pray that he will provide mercy in this situation."

Polly looked at her hands. "I am not certain that is much comfort." Her voice filled with despair.

Hannah put her hands on her hips. "Now, let us not wallow in the mud that that rogue was trying to fling at us. Should anyone try to put you in gaol, they will have to get past my musket."

All eyes in the room widened. Daniel smirked. "I believe you." Turning toward Mary, he feigned a shocked visage. "Does your brother know how dangerous his wife is?"

Mary playfully slapped his arm.

Daniel acted as if he were hurt. "You are both dangerous women!"

By now, even Polly was laughing.

Hannah wiped the tears of laughter from her eyes. "Oh my, I needed that respite. Speaking of respite, why do you not take a day off and go visit Sarah and her family? Polly can come home with me and rest while the young men work in the field."

"When is James expected home? And where is he?" Mary stood up from the pew and stretched her arms.

"On an important mission, he says. I am not certain where but he said he would explain later. Good thing I trust the man!" Hannah grinned.

"You did not frighten him away with your musket, did you?" Daniel stood back as if afraid.

Mary and Hannah rolled their eyes as they each grabbed one of Polly's arms and pulled her up from sitting on the pew. Polly pressed her hand into her lower back and Hannah looked closely at the girl's belly. "It should not be much longer, Polly."

"I hope not. I do not think I can bear this much longer."

Mary kissed Polly's cheek. "Take care, dear daughter. And Hannah, you send for us if her time draws near."

"You know I will." Hannah put her arm around Polly's arm and they exited the doorway.

Mary stared up at Daniel. "Perhaps I will take Hannah's advice and go visit Sarah. Would you like to come with me?" She wrapped her arms around his waist.

"I would enjoy a respite, but the fieldwork awaits. I'd best return to it." He held Mary tightly for a moment. "We will get through all this, will we not?"

"Yes, Daniel. With God's help we will. I love you."

"I love you, Mary. I will survive this with God's help — and yours. You are far stronger than I in these matters. I cherish you." He held her for a long moment.

Mary pulled away just enough to meet his eyes. "And I cherish you. You are my one and only love."

Hands pressing against her back, he drew her even closer. "Perhaps we can do something about that love later this evening."

Mary grinned. "'Tis Sabbath at dusk, you know." She drew his body closer to hers.

"Well, my wife…that has never stopped us before." Kissing her deeply, he pulled away and doffed his hat at her as he put it on his head. "We shall discuss this further…after dusk."

Mary laughed. "After dusk then."

* * *

The walk to Sarah's was a refreshing diversion for Mary.

So much is happening and I am weary. Thank you, Lord, for the gift of your beauteous nature coming alive once again in this season.

Inhaling deeply of the warm spring air, Mary neared the road that led to the old Stearns farm. She could see Sarah leaving a covered basket on the stoop and saw her sister dragging Benjamin away before he could knock on the door. She could hear Sarah scolding the four-year-old as they drew nearer.

Sarah noticed Mary and waved. "Good day, sister! So good to see you!" She held tightly to Benjamin's hand, who squirmed to loosen her grip.

"Why cannot I knock on the door?" Benjamin's voiced dripped with childish indignation.

Sarah gave an exasperated sigh. "Because, young man, Danny and Susannah are busy."

Benjamin scowled. "Busy? Doing what?"

Mary smothered her laughter.

Sarah sighed. "They are busy...talking about making a family."

Benjamin tilted his head. "Why cannot I talk about it with them?"

"Because they must discuss this alone." Dragging the small boy home, Sarah sighed wearily. "Questions!"

Approaching the Eaton farm where Sarah and Nathaniel's family lived with Widow Eaton, Mary was surprised to see an elegant carriage parked in the yard near the carriage belonging to Charles Dobbins.

"Sarah! I nearly forgot it was time for Missus Bainbridge to visit from Boston! You must be so excited to see her!"

Sarah gave a conspiratorial glance at Mary. "I am not just excited to see *her*. She has traveled here with Nathaniel's youngest sister, Abigail!"

"Abigail? Well, she must be all grown up now!"

"She is three and twenty. Just a year older than your twins." Sarah giggled.

"So what are you saying, sister? I recognize that mischievous look."

Sending Benjamin on ahead to their house, Sarah turned closer to her sister, keeping her voice low.

"When Missus Bainbridge arrived with Abigail, I was astonished that such a lovely lass was as yet unmarried. As I spoke with her, she began to ask about your son, James. She had met him several summers ago on another trip to Deer Run. Do you remember that they were sweet on each other?"

Mary put her finger on her chin. "I must have forgotten."

"Probably because it did not last long. Then, of course, she went home to Boston. The miles separated them for months and then James met Anne." Sarah paused to take a breath. "So apparently, Abigail was heartsick when she heard that James had married and she never returned here for a visit. Until now." Sarah squeezed Mary's arm.

"You are quite the romantic, Sarah. But then, you always were." Mary put her arm through Sarah's. "So perhaps we should send for James."

Sarah stopped and bit her lip. "I already have. I hope you

do not mind me taking him from the field work."

Mary burst out laughing. "Sarah, you are a conspirator! But a loveable one."

Arriving at the house, Mary walked indoors expecting to see everyone. But James and Abigail were missing.

Missus Bainbridge stood up and greeted Mary. "Missus Lowe, so pleasant to see you. I was just telling Charles here how happy I was that his daughter married your son, Danny."

"Yes, we are so pleased." Glancing around, she asked, "Where are James and Abigail? I understand Nathaniel's youngest sister came with you."

Missus Bainbridge gave a knowing look to Charles and they both smirked. "I do believe they have taken a short walk." Missus Bainbridge grinned.

"I see. Does Nathaniel yet know that his sister is here?"

"Yes, he was most excited to see her."

Sarah interjected, "It seemed as if someone *else* was excited to see Abigail as well."

As she spoke the door opened and the flushed face of James stuck his head through the partially open doorway. "Mother! I did not know you were here."

"Well, I might say the same to you, James." She held back a teasing grin.

James opened the door wider and an equally reddened face young woman with upswept brown hair covered with a straw bonnet came inside the portal. "Mother, you remember Uncle Nathaniel's youngest sister, Abigail?"

Mary curtsied politely. Abigail curtsied back graciously and lit up the room with a brilliant smile. "So pleased to see you, Missus Lowe."

The young woman's gown was a blue striped and open in the front, revealing an elegantly ruffled petticoat that showed through. Her empire bodice flattered her shapely form but was not so low as to cause Mary embarrassment.

"And I am most pleased to see you as well, Miss Stearns. Welcome, once again, to Deer Run."

"Thank you, madam."

"And how are your dear parents faring, Abigail?"

"Quite well, Missus Lowe. My father still suffers some from pain but the doctors do what they can to manage it. I think his best medicine appears to be my loving mother. 'Tis inspiring to see their love."

I like her already.

James shifted on his feet. "Mother, I was hoping to show Abigail our farm."

Mary smiled. "Yes, that sounds pleasant. Have a lovely walk."

Smiling, the couple exited slowly out the door, engaged in conversation interspersed with smiles and giggles.

James's daughter, Rachel, toddled toward the open door, but Sarah stopped her. "Oh no you don't, little one." Scooping the one-year-old into her arms, she spoke to her in a high-pitched voice and waved at the couple. "Say 'Bye-Bye, Father.' Say, 'Go fall in love, Father.'"

Rachel giggled and pointed at the couple in the distance. "Da-da."

"That's right, little one." Kissing the child on her chubby cheek, Sarah closed the door and sighed.

Smiling at Missus Bainbridge, she drew closer to the woman and hugged her. "You have once again saved the day, Missus Bainbridge. Bringing Abigail and all."

Mary laughed. "You are certainly putting the cart before the horse, dear sister."

Sarah gave a self-satisfied grin. "Sometimes, one just *knows.*"

Grinning, Mary thought that her sister could be right. But what she truly wished that she could know—without any doubt—was that tomorrow would turn out well for Polly.

Dear Lord, please let it be well for my dear daughter—and her baby.

Chapter 35
Confessions

Danny lifted his languid eyelids. When he focused his gaze on Susannah standing at the window, delight energized him. The long curls draped across her shoulders and back did not hinder his appreciative vision of her curved form illuminated by the sunlight through the thin chemise. Passion surged through all of his senses.

"Good morning, Missus Lowe." He grinned as he patted the quilt next to him. "Perhaps you would care to join your husband."

Turning to face him, she simpered. "Perhaps."

Leaning down to kiss him, he pulled her toward himself and enveloped her in his embrace.

Susannah giggled. "I thought we had to get ready for Sabbath service."

"We do." His kisses persisted as did his passionate caresses. "But you must see to your husband's needs first."

Her breath caught in her throat. "Very well then. If you insist."

"I do." Leering at his wife, who did not resist his advances, he threw the quilt over them both as he was consumed in her love once again.

* * *

"Must we get up?" Danny stared at his wife who sat up on the edge of the bed. He stroked her back with one finger.

Hair disheveled and leaning to kiss him again, she whispered, "We must—even though I would like to stay here with you, as well. Today is your sister's confession. You promised you would be there for her." Susannah stroked his arm. "Your strong arms tempt me to stay here all day with you but I am certain you would not be pleased with yourself if we missed Sabbath service."

Fixing her gaze upon his scar below his ribs, her eyebrows furrowed. She stroked near the red, uneven ridge and shivered. "I cannot bear to think I almost lost you."

Danny stared at the recently healed wound. "When I think that I came so close to missing the pleasure of our wedding bed, I am so grateful to God for sparing my life."

Susannah's thoughts drifted to that painful incident of three months before. Fear tried to gain a foothold in her heart until she resisted the frightening memories.

"Let us speak of this no more—'tis too painful for us both. I love you with all my heart, Dan. My love just seems to grow more each day until I cannot even describe the depths of my feelings for you."

Dan reached for her hand and kissed her fingers slowly. Drawing her down, he could feel her warm, feminine curves against his skin. Kissing her deeply, he released her abruptly. "We shall be here all day again if we do not cease." Dan pushed himself up from the quilt and stared appreciatively at his bride. "You are the most beautiful sight."

Leaning over to kiss him, she stood up with resolve. "I shall get dressed now. We must hurry."

* * *

The pews seemed full this Sabbath service. Even the infrequent attendees jammed into the overflowing rows. Word had apparently spread about Polly Lowe's public confession and there were no extra seats to be found.

Insufferable gossipmongers. Danny could feel his pulse surge with anger at the leering looks on several faces and the pompous whispering nods amongst several in the congregation.

Ah, Missus Endicott. Of course she would not miss a chance to observe my sister's pain. She will likely relish it.

Memories of her hateful words at the funeral of James's wife a year before galled his spirit like the sharp point of a quill. His anger was soon supplanted with shame at his own vindictiveness.

Is my anger any more noble than her prideful gossip? They are both sin. God, forgive me.

He resisted tears of sympathy for Polly, while at the same time, was immersed in self-reproach.

I should have been looking out for her more. I should have intervened somehow. Why did I not do more to save her from this sad state of affairs?

He knew it was far too late for regrets. It was time for them all to bear their guilt with humility and dignity. It was time to help Polly get through this.

Danny felt Susannah's hand squeezing his. She drew his gaze toward hers and mouthed, "I love you."

He squeezed her hand in return and whispered the same words back to her.

A commotion in the crowded room drew Danny's attention to the door. A pale and weak looking Polly came in on the arm of their father, Daniel. Staring at the floor, she gripped her father's arm as if she might fall over without his support. Her large belly stood out as confirmation of her crime against chastity. There was no room for anyone to deny the charge against this unmarried woman.

Danny fought back tears again at the sight of her. He drew strength from Susannah's hand gripping his.

Thoughts of growing up with his little sister flooded Danny's memory. Always the responsible oldest sister, Polly had kept everyone and everything in order. She filled in with cooking meals and cleaning when their mother was ill. She was the defender of the younger ones when they were mistreated by anyone. She was stubborn and strong and filled with love for her family. Looking at her now, Danny agonized at the look on her face. Her spirit appeared completely broken and trampled.

Dear Lord, please help my sister through this.

Reverend Hollingsworth straightened out the white collar draped across his shoulders and stepped up to the podium. His face was somber but his voice bellowed throughout the meetinghouse of 200 congregants.

"As many of you appear to already know..." He glared

at several of the infrequent attendees, who squirmed at his stare. "As many of you know, we will be hearing a public confession this day from one of our church members. I ask that you listen with judgment infused with mercy. Our justice of the peace, Hiram Rowe, will be sitting in to determine the outcome of this confession and the resulting punishment." Meeting the reverend's gaze, the justice of the peace signaled to him with his finger that he was there to perform his duty. "So without tarrying further, please allow Miss Polly Lowe to state her confession."

Her father interrupted. "Reverend Hollingsworth…if I may please speak first."

The reverend's eyes widened, but he swept his arm to indicate that Daniel Sr. could stand at the podium.

Danny could see his mother sitting near the front, clasping her hand over her mouth, reddened eyes contorting with pain. Large tears rolled unhindered down Mary's cheeks.

Daniel Sr. led Polly to a chair in the front before releasing her arm. Polly crumpled into the wooden seat, staring at the floor.

Clearing his throat, Daniel stood with shoulders held back in resolve, pain etched across his countenance. "Before my daughter speaks, I have my own public confession to make."

Gasps were heard across the congregation, as numerous hands covered mouths and whispers filled the otherwise silent room. Daniel waited for the whispers to cease before he resumed speaking.

"Whilst my daughter, Polly, is the church member required to speak a public confession, I must confess my own sin in the matter."

Other than a few gasps from the crowd, silence lay like a smothering pillow dulling all noise. Danny's heart raced. His father continued.

"'Twas my own bitter soul—my lack of forgiveness— that has led to this more obvious sin by my daughter. I truly hated Josiah Grant for transgressions in his past against me.

I…I thought I had forgiven him. But when he returned to Deer Run with his son, Jonathan, my hatred toward Josiah had not ceased. No, it had grown, infesting my soul with evil that corrupted my thinking." Pausing to swallow, he wiped his eyes. "Jesus has said that if you hate someone, then you are guilty of his murder. So in my heart, I murdered Josiah Grant. But since I could not actually kill him, instead, I tried to kill my daughter's affection for his son, Jonathan. In doing so, I have nurtured sin in my family."

Leaning against the podium for support, Daniel looked down for a moment. His gaze lifted toward the congregation, and his eyes filled with tears. "So I beg of you to forgive me and to have mercy upon my daughter in this her transgression. I beg of you to give her grace."

Pushing back from the wooden stand, he limped down the one step and walked toward Polly. She stared at him with tears in her eyes as she stood up. Aided by her father's arm, she waddled with difficulty toward the stair leading to the podium. Daniel stood beside his daughter, holding her arm in support.

Although visibly trembling, Polly stood as resolutely as she could.

Danny smiled through his own tears. *Dear Polly. Always so brave…even now.*

Clearing her throat, Polly's voice was small and shaky. Congregants leaned toward the front to hear her words.

"My fellow church members, I humbly come before you as a sinner. I confess to you my sin of fornication that has deemed me worthy of your most severe judgment." She paused and took a deep, shuddering breath. "I wish you to know that I have confessed my sin before God, before the reverend, and before my parents. I now confess it before you and ask humbly for your forgiveness as well." She swayed to the side and Daniel held her arm tightly to keep his daughter upright. She gripped the side of the podium and took a deep breath again.

"I also wish to tell you that this wickedness was entirely of my own doing. I hold no one else responsible for my willful act against a man. This evil deed was a darkness upon my own soul and I take full responsibility for this sin against God."

"That is not so." A man's voice from the open doorway drew everyone's attention. "This sin of fornication is my transgression against you, Polly Lowe."

Danny watched his sister's face contort into tears.

"Jonathan!" Polly covered her mouth with her shivering hands as the young man ran to her side and embraced her.

Pulling back to gaze at her face, Jonathan stroked her cheek then looked at her large belly cradled between them. "Why did you not send for me?" His own face contorted with emotion as he clung to Polly.

No one spoke a word but there were numerous sniffing sounds across the room. Danny looked gratefully at his Uncle James, who was removing his hat and sitting down next to his wife, Hannah. Daniel released his daughter to Jonathan's grasp.

After several moments of stunned silence, Reverend Hollingsworth cleared his throat and stepped forward. "Mr. Grant, is there anything that you wish to say?"

Keeping his arm around Polly's shoulders, Jonathan wiped tears from his face with one hand and stood at the podium. "If anyone needs to confess sin, 'tis I. I alone am responsible for Polly's condition. I confess my sin of fornication against her and I beg this congregation's forgiveness." Turning toward Daniel, he said, "And sir, though I am most assuredly not worthy of her, I beg you for your daughter's hand in marriage."

Daniel stood as tall as he was able and slowly extended his hand to Jonathan. "Yes, Jonathan, you have my blessing."

"Thank you, sir." Jonathan shook Daniel's hand, then held Polly's cheek tenderly and gazed into her eyes. "Please, Polly. Please forgive me, and be my wife."

Fresh tears flooded Polly's cheeks. "Yes, Jonathan. I will gladly be your wife."

The reverend cleared his throat again. "Hiram Rowe, we are in need of your services for a marriage ceremony." Everyone looked around when no one stood. "Hiram Rowe!"

Danny saw the man sitting next to the justice of the peace nudge the snoring man.

Hiram Rowe jerked awake. "Huh?"

The reverend contorted his face. "Mr. Rowe, please refrain from sleeping in Sabbath service. We need you down here forthwith in official capacity."

The justice of the peace slowly stood, the cedar pew creaking, and made his way to the aisle. Walking toward the front of the meetinghouse, he stopped and scratched his head. Staring at Jonathan, he said, "When did you get here."

Reverend Hollingsworth shook his head in annoyance. "Long enough to confess that he is the father of Polly Lowe's child. And they now wish to be married, sir."

"Oh." Mr. Rowe smothered a yawn. "Very well." Looking at the couple, he instructed them to hold hands, even though they already were. "Do you, Jonathan Grant, take this woman, Polly Lowe, to be your wife?"

"Yes." Jonathan stared intently at Polly. "By all means, yes."

"And do you, Polly Lowe, take this man to be your lawful husband?"

Tears spilling down through her smile, Polly shook her head in agreement. "Yes." Her voice whispered. "With all my heart, yes."

"Then by the power invested in me by the Commonwealth of Massachusetts, I now pronounce you man and wife. You may kiss the bride…even though it appears you have already done so some time ago."

Jonathan tenderly kissed Polly.

Thank you, God. Danny's emotions were in a whirlwind of gratitude toward Uncle James, Jonathan, and especially toward God, Who had answered this heartfelt prayer.

Thank you.

He turned toward Susannah, who had tears rolling down in streams onto her cheeks. Clinging to her hand, they gazed at each other with eyes brimming with love.

Suddenly, Daniel Sr.'s bellowing voice from the front of the meetinghouse interrupted Danny's reverie.

"We need the midwives!"

Chapter 36
Storm

Mary's heart clenched with concern as she leaped out of her seat to hurry toward Polly. Watching her daughter grab her belly, Mary knew Polly was clearly ready to birth. The mother tried to calm herself, but her own breathing was nearly as rapid as her pregnant daughter's.

Hannah and Widow Eaton were there in an instant, much to Mary's relief. Mary had never been one to gravitate toward being a nurse; medical emergencies sent her into spasms of nausea and anxiety. She was grateful her sister-in-law Hannah had become a midwife. Deer Run had far too many birthings now for her mother to handle the practice alone.

The women assisted Polly out the door, while Mary noticed another woman mopping up the puddle of water that was on the floor where Polly had stood.

Dear Lord, this is truly happening. Please help my Polly.

Widow Eaton, Mary's mother, took over directing. "Let us take Polly to the Sabbaday House. 'Tis the closest shelter."

Approximately one hundred yards from the meetinghouse, the Sabbaday house stood as a haven for need. The building was a small wooden house much like other dwellings, built with a central fireplace that served two rooms. The two chambers were completely separate for men and women, partitioned by a wall and with separate entrances. The house provided warmth as well as a clean bed in case of emergency or illness during a Sabbath service. It was certainly needed now, and Mary was thankful that the town selectmen had voted to build it two years prior.

Wind stirred the tree branches filled with newly opened leaves. Mary held her bonnet onto her head, afraid the occasional gusts would undo the loosely tied ribbons holding her hat in place.

Mary felt helpless walking behind Polly, who was supported on either side by the two midwives. Occasionally, Polly had to stop as she gripped her belly with two hands and clenched her teeth, red infusing her cheeks. The pregnant woman moaned deeply with each contraction and Jonathan, who was following the group of women, held his wool felt hat down onto his head to keep the wind from carrying it off. His eyes were filled with distress. Mary turned to him, pity for the man flooding her heart.

"Jonathan, she will be fine." Mary reached out to his arm and gently held it.

Moisture filled the man's eyes that were deeply shadowed underneath. "Can you know that for certain? I can never forgive myself if — anything happens."

Mary stopped him while the others proceeded to the Sabbaday house. "Polly is young and strong. Women have birthed babies since creation itself. She and the baby should do quite well." She tilted her head and gave him a reassuring smile.

"Thank you, Missus Lowe." He licked his dry lips. "I am...so tired from traveling and still in such distress discovering this news. Imagining Polly carrying this burden alone all these months...it makes my heart break." He stared at the closing door of the Sabbaday house, a look of pain filling his countenance. "Once again, I cannot be with her."

Mary gently patted his hand. "Polly was so ashamed of her sin. She felt that she took advantage of you in your grief. She could not forgive herself and refused to make you carry the consequences."

"But 'twas not just *her* sin. Does she think I did not carry equal blame? I am more responsible for lack of controlling my passions than Polly ever was." Looking at her nervously, he added, "Forgive my blunt speech, Missus Lowe."

"There is naught to forgive in your explanation. I am so grateful that you came forthwith once you heard the news from my brother."

Jonathan looked at Mary with intensity. "How could I

not come? I have never stopped loving Polly. I thought she had found another. I was heartsick…" His voice trailed off.

Mary squeezed his arm. "There was no other, Jonathan. Only you." Looking toward the Sabbaday house, Mary's eyes narrowed. "I must hasten to her now. We will keep you informed."

"Thank you."

* * *

Daniel saw his wife go inside the Sabbaday house while Jonathan stood by himself, staring at the place where his new wife had been taken. Sympathy tugged at Daniel's heart as Jonathan's shoulders slumped. The man looked so alone.

Approaching him from behind, Daniel spoke quietly. "'Tis always a frightening time for husbands."

Jonathan spun to face his father-in-law and anger was visible on his face. "'Twould be less frightening if I'd been here all along." He wiped his hand across his face, and looked at his shoes. "I am sorry. I am so overwhelmed by it all. First, I think I have lost her forever, then I find she carries my child. Then we marry and now…" He shook his head slowly.

"I cannot imagine the distress of all this." Putting a fatherly hand on his shoulder, Daniel pointed to a tree stump. "Come, let us sit on the old chestnut."

Jonathan followed Daniel's leading and all but fell onto the low stump. Putting his face in his hands, he sighed. "I am exhausted. We rode all night to get here."

"Where did James find you?"

"In East Haddam—in Connecticut. James said that Danny found old letters from me in Polly's room and the address where I was schoolmaster." Jonathan shook his head. "I will never be able to teach again with this 'sin against chastity' hanging over me. But I am not complaining…I deserve whatever punishment is given."

Daniel stared at his new son-in-law with admiration. "You are much like your grandfather, Jonathan. You have integrity and honesty even when you know you have done wrong. I was wrong to have judged you harshly. And I...I pray that you can forgive me for how I wronged you and Polly."

Jonathan was quiet for a moment. He stared at Daniel with weary eyes. "I forgive you. But 'tis difficult to forget the time that Polly and I have lost together — and the pain of our separation. Nothing can replace that loss."

A chill swept through Daniel's heart.

Lord, I deserve this. But please — mend these wounds that I have caused.

"I deserve your condemnation." Daniel stared into the sky quickly filling with dark clouds.

"I do not condemn you." Jonathan met Daniel's eyes. "But I wanted to marry Polly before all this happened. You never gave me a chance." Jonathan's eyes moistened. "I deeply apologize for what I did — I was wrong. But, had I known Polly wanted me back and was with child, I could have taken care of her while she awaited the birth. I would have loved Polly as I wanted to — as she wanted me to. Nothing can bring that time back to us."

A dull but deep pain sliced into Daniel's heart as he realized the ramifications of his bitterness. How would he have felt if his love with Mary had been denied by her mother? If Mary had become pregnant and he had not been there to anticipate the birth? Prepare for the twins? Treasure the future together?

"I have no words to express my sorrow about what I have caused. Please understand what I deprived you of grieves my heart. I have no words..."

Daniel stared at the leaves blowing in circles on the maples. Swirls of gusts carried his hat several yards distance across the green. Jonathan leaped up from the tree stump and reached for the felt farmer's hat before the wind could carry it further.

As he stood up holding his father-in-law's hat, the door to the Sabbaday house burst open. It was Hannah.

"Daniel!" Her voiced shouted above the wind. "Get Dr. Burk! Hasten. Get Sarah and James as well."

Daniel saw Jonathan blanche. "No. No. Please Lord. No."

Jonathan sat down on the ground weakly.

Daniel did not have time to comfort the young father but raced as quickly as he could, limping as he went, toward the meetinghouse.

I will not think about what is happening. But Lord, please spare my daughter and her child.

Pulling himself up the steps by using the handrails for support, he thrust the heavy door of the meetinghouse open.

Gasping for breath, he could barely get the words out past his dry tongue. "Dr. Burk, Sarah, James — to the Sabbaday house. Hasten!"

The entire congregation stared at him and he saw the three he had called hurrying toward him.

Sarah reached him first. "What is wrong?" Her eyes widened and panic filled her voice.

"I know not." Daniel craved water on his dry throat.

Sarah, James, and Dr. Burk raced on to the Sabbaday house, then Danny, his brother, James, and several others stood up and exited the meetinghouse. Danny paused at the door. "Father, what is it?" Fear filled his voice.

Daniel shook his head and turned to go back to the Sabbaday house. He had no breath left to speak but gestured for Danny to accompany him. Susannah, Abigail, Missus Bainbridge, and Mr. Dobbins all joined the group.

Mr. Dobbins paused with his hands on Daniel's arms. "What is it? What can I do?"

Shaking his head, Daniel's voice croaked. "I know not."

Suddenly, they looked toward the Sabbaday house and saw Dr. Burk and James carrying a woman out. It was not Polly.

Mother Eaton!

The men carried her by her shoulders and ankles toward the men's side of the Sabbaday house and kicked the door in. They heard voices yelling inside. "Mr. Hansford, get up off the bed, we have an emergency."

Soon a rumpled elderly man walked out. As soon as he put his farmer's hat on his head, the wind carried it away, sending him on a mission to recover it.

Daniel hurried toward the group standing outside the

house. They were discussing who would stay with Polly and who would attend Widow Eaton.

Dr. Burk walked toward them. "Mary, Sarah, you might wish to visit with your mother." The look on his face spoke of the gravity of the situation.

Mary and Sarah both turned white and clung to each other as they hurried toward the other entrance of the building.

Thunder rolled overhead and soon rain began to pour from the sky, blending with everyone's tears.

Chapter 37
Life

Mary and Sarah gripped each other's waists as they approached the bed where their mother lay. Covered with sweat and pale in appearance, the midwife's typical ebullience was replaced by a weakened woman panting for breath.

Struggling to keep calm, Mary leaned toward her stricken mother and stroked her shoulder. "We are here, Mother." Mary was shocked at the fear she heard in her own voice.

Ruth Eaton flickered her eyes weakly and attempted a smile. "Mary." She closed her eyes again and struggled to take a deep breath.

Mary drew Sarah closer to their mother. Sarah, obviously fighting tears, managed to vocalize a few words. "Mother, 'tis I…Sarah."

Without opening her lids, Widow Eaton managed to smile. "Sarah." Her hands suddenly moved toward her youngest daughter and weakly gripped Sarah's hand. "Sarah. I am sorry I was…so harsh on you."

Tears poured down Sarah's cheeks. "You were not harsh, Mother. I'm afraid I was quite a handful. I know now how difficult my stubbornness was when I see that same strong will in my own boys." Sarah's arm impatiently wiped the tears from her face.

A gentle smile emerged on the mother. "They are just like…your father, James."

Sarah's eyes widened. "They are?"

"Yes." Widow Eaton attempted another deep breath. Sweat increased on her forehead. Forcing her eyes open, she gazed directly at her youngest child. "Love them, Sarah…and know...how much I love you."

"I love you, Mother." Sarah kissed her mother's hand, covering her fingers with warm tears.

"Mary..."

"I am here, Mother." Mary got closer so her parent could see her without effort.

"Mary...I nearly...made a terrible...mistake."

Shaking her head, Mary stroked her mother's clammy forehead. "Do not labor so, Mother."

Sharp crackles of thunder exploded overhead. Although midday, the room grew darker.

"Mary...please...forgive me. You chose...the right man."

When Widow Eaton's color grew paler, Dr. Burk hurried to her bedside and felt her pulse. He whispered to Mary, "She does not have long."

Mary's lips trembled as her face contorted. Moving closer to her mother again, she held tightly to her hand. "Do not strain yourself, Mother. There is no need to apologize. I know I chose the right man."

Smiling faintly, Widow Eaton opened her eyes half way, connecting with Mary's. "Love Daniel, Mary."

"I do, Mother, with all my heart."

Widow Eaton's breathing increased, interrupted by spasms of inhalation. She gasped, "James."

Her oldest son, James, hurried to her side. His face was reddened and awash with moisture from crying. Grabbing his mother's hands, he could barely speak. "Mother."

After a moment, she managed to gather her strength. "James." Her voice was a mere whisper. "So...proud of you." Another pause. "I love you."

James gripped his mother's hand tightly and held it against his face.

Suddenly Widow Eaton gasped. Her eyes opened wide and her voice was suddenly stronger. "Myles. Asa. James." She reached toward the ceiling then suddenly relaxed. She exhaled briefly then breathed no more. A slight smile appeared on her relaxed face.

A deluge of rain hammered the shingled roof of the

Sabbaday house. Dr. Burk hurried toward the deceased woman and took her pulse.

Standing up straight, he spoke the words he had likely said hundreds of times before. "She is gone."

Mary, Sarah and James sobbed without reserve as they each gathered around the body of their mother, draping their arms across her still form.

Although Mary knew that her mother's spirit was now reunited with so many who had gone before, her heart broke for the loss of the woman who had given her birth.

As the group wept in unison, a high-pitched sound from the adjacent room rose above the wails of grief.

It was the cry of a newborn baby.

Chapter 38
Passages

The next day, Daniel and Mary walked arm-in-arm back to the Sabbaday house. They were returning from the Thomsen family graveyard where Widow Eaton had just been buried next to her first husband, James.

Mary's pale face, covered with dried tears, lifted toward the clear sky overhead. "I am so grateful that Mother did not have to suffer for long. But I do so miss her."

Daniel squeezed her shoulder. "Yes. I do as well. Despite our difficult beginnings, I believe we grew quite fond of each other through the years."

Mary curved her lips upward. "The last words she said to me were, 'Love Daniel, Mary.'"

Squinting in the sun, Daniel replaced his hat, surprised. "She did? That amazes me," he said, remembering their initial confrontations and disagreements. "She was a fine woman, Mary. You are much like her."

"Thank you, Daniel. I suppose I am like her in some things—although I shall never be drawn toward midwifery."

Daniel laughed—and the mirth refreshed him. "You never wished to help birth other women's babies. You just wanted to keep the local midwives busy delivering ours."

Hugging his waist, she chuckled. "You are right, although that part of our lives is now past. 'Tis time to watch our children bear the next generation."

Daniel grinned mischievously. "We just get to partake of the pleasures of the marriage bed—without the midnight feedings."

Mary blushed and glanced around. "Daniel, please keep your voice low."

As they neared the Sabbaday house, they could hear the new baby crying inside. Mary placed a hand upon Daniel's chest. "Wait here whilst I see if Polly needs help with anything."

Daniel stopped and waited for Mary to emerge from the door again.

After a few minutes, she stuck her head out and grinned. "You may come in, Grandsire."

Carefully opening the door, Daniel awkwardly entered the large room, careful to make as little noise as possible.

Polly was cradling the swaddled baby in her arms and touching his small lips with her finger. Looking up, Polly grinned at her father.

"Come see your grandson, Papa."

Grandson.

It was difficult to grasp the reality that the next generation of young men was beginning.

Walking quietly toward Polly, he was amazed at the transformation in his oldest daughter. Although tired looking, her smile radiated joy.

When was the last time she had looked so happy?

Jonathan stared with unabashed admiration at the newborn. His countenance filled with fatherly pride. But Jonathan's face seemed to radiate far more than parental bliss — his pleasure at being with Polly seemed to emanate a fulfillment of his deepest desires for love. Daniel winced inwardly at how he had nearly dashed the young man's dreams — as well as his daughter's — on the rocks of his own pride.

Leaning in toward the sleeping infant, Daniel recognized the features. "He favors you, Polly. Remarkably so."

His daughter blushed. "That is what Jonathan says, as well."

Jonathan leaned toward his wife and kissed her cheek warmly. Polly turned a deeper red.

Daniel stood with his arms folded. "So, have you decided upon a name?"

Polly and Jonathan looked at each other with furrowed brows. Polly glanced at her father. "We cannot decide. We have a middle name decided…Thayer, after Grandmother's surname."

Mary covered her quivering mouth with her hand. "That is lovely, Polly."

Daniel cleared his throat. "Well then. I think Josiah Thayer Grant sounds like a splendid name. What say you?"

Polly removed one hand from the baby long enough to touch her husband's. "I think it is a splendid name, as well."

Jonathan stared with grateful eyes at his father-in-law. "'Tis the perfect name. Thank you, Mr. Lowe."

Daniel grinned. "I do believe that you may call me 'Father Lowe,' if you so choose."

Grinning, Jonathan reached for Polly's hand that was still cradling the baby. "Yes...Father Lowe."

There was a knock on the door and Hannah peaked around the corner. "'Tis time I examined Polly. You men may wait outside."

Daniel threw his hands in the air. "Once again, the men are not wanted."

"Out with you." Hannah shooed Daniel and Jonathan toward the door while chuckling.

Putting his hand on Jonathan's shoulder, Daniel breathed in deeply of the rain-freshened air outside. "He is a fine lad, Jonathan. I know you will be a good father to him."

"With God's help I will." Jonathan put his hands in his pockets and stared at the ground.

"'Tis a wise sire who looks to the heavenly Father for guidance. He will give you wisdom, if you ask for it."

"Then I shall be on my knees quite often." Jonathan stared into the distance.

"Best place for a father to be."

A voice from the direction of the meetinghouse caught their attention.

"Good day, Mr. Lowe. Mr. Grant."

Tension gripped Daniel's heart.

Hiram Rowe!

The rounded stomach of the justice of the peace preceded the rest of the man's frame as he half-waddled toward the two men. Daniel noticed Jonathan's hands clench tightly next to his side.

"And how is the new mother doing—as well as the wee

babe?" Hiram grinned with his small mouth.

Jonathan swallowed in apparent difficulty. "They are well, thank you." His eyes viewed the man with distrust.

Hiram took out a kerchief and wiped the sweat from his forehead and reddened face. "'Tis certainly warm today."

Daniel's eyes narrowed. "Yes, it is."

"Well then, let us settle the matter of the charges against Miss Lowe...er, Missus Grant. She has been charged with the sin of fornication, punishable by up to two months in gaol or thirty dollars."

Jonathan interrupted. "Why am I not being charged with the same crime against chastity?" He folded his arms.

Hiram scratched his head and looked downward at his protruding waistcoat. "Well, let us see. The sheriff served the official writ to Miss Lowe...er, Missus Grant. But...under the circumstances, I am certain we can assume that you, sir, are a person involved in this crime. So, I will assume the sentence is for you both."

Daniel saw Jonathan's face turn pale.

The justice of the peace continued. "Now, how long is this woman's lying in to be?"

"At least two weeks, perhaps three." Daniel also folded his arms.

Hiram gave a jolly laugh. "Excellent." Pulling a parchment from his pocket he leaned down with difficulty and picked up a rock.

Setting the paper on the narrow sill of the casement, he placed the rock on top of the parchment to keep it from falling off.

Daniel and Jonathan walked closer in order to view the words: Gaol.

Their eyes narrowed as they looked at each other.

"Gaol?" Jonathan put his hands on his hips and faced Hiram.

"I am declaring this side of the Sabbaday house to be a temporary gaol. You and Missus Grant are hereby sentenced to two weeks in gaol, starting today."

A smile crept its way from Jonathan's mouth to his eyes.

"Thank you, sir." Extending his hand to the portly justice of the peace, Jonathan shook his hand with enthusiasm.

"And visitors will be allowed." Grinning, Hiram Rowe plopped his hat back onto his moist, balding head. "Good day, gentlemen."

Daniel watched him waddle back toward the meetinghouse. "Thank You, dear heavenly Father."

"Amen." Glancing at Daniel, Jonathan started for the door. "I must tell Polly!"

Daniel grabbed him by the shirt. "Hold on there, son. Let Hannah finish first, unless you wish to be slain by the midwife. I know her. You do not wish to raise her ire." He laughed at his son-in-law.

"Sound advice. I suppose this is women's territory after all."

"Without a shadow of a doubt."

After a few moments, Hannah came out. "You may return, gentlemen."

Jonathan raced past Hannah into the room.

Daniel closed his eyes for a moment, overwhelmed by the events of the past few days. He heard his daughter and son-in-law laughing excitedly. It was a laughter filled with relief. Mary's arm looped through his.

"We must go to Sarah's. 'Tis time for Danny and Susannah to return to Springfield. Mr. Dobbins, of course, as well."

"Yes." He glanced down at his wife. "I hate to see them leave."

"'Tis so easy to become accustomed to their presence. Then, all of a sudden, they are gone again."

Strolling silently toward the Eaton farm, Mary stared straight ahead. "'Twill never be the same there with Mother gone."

"No. Not that there is want for babies to fill the rooms."

"So you know?"

"Know what?"

"That Sarah is with child again?"

"No. I am usually the last to be so informed." Grinning,

he shook his head. "That Nathaniel—he is quite the lover."

"No more so than you."

He patted her derriere.

"Daniel! What if the justice of the peace is nearby?"

"Then perhaps he will put us both in gaol together for two weeks. Sounds like a honey-month to me."

"Daniel!" Mary laughed.

"'Tis good to hear you laugh, Mary."

Hugging his arm, Mary looked admiringly at her husband. "'Tis good to be in love."

Arriving at the Eaton home, Daniel saw Charles Dobbins carrying a portmanteau out to the awaiting carriage. The horses were nodding their heads and shifting their hooves as if anxious to get back on the roadway.

"Good day, Charles. We are sorry to see you return to Springfield."

He doffed his hat at Daniel and Mary. "It has been a most eventful week, Daniel. I am sorry to have to return, as well. And by the way, in all the hubbub, I do not know if I congratulated you on your new grandson. He is a fine lad."

"Thank you, sir. Yes, he is." Daniel shook his extended hand. Swallowing with difficulty, Daniel asked, "Where are Danny and Susannah?"

"Inside. I shall give you time to bid farewell."

"Thank you." Daniel took Mary's arm and helped her up the steps. Upon entering the main room, it somehow seemed emptier with Widow Eaton gone, despite the bustle of five children moving about. The Lowe's five other children would be along soon to say good-bye to Danny and Susannah.

Family faces were still stained with tears from the burying of Grandmother Eaton, but Sarah kept busy feeding everyone a meal before Danny and Susannah left.

James and Abigail sat at the table. Daniel noticed his son occasionally touch the young lady's hand.

How much longer before the next wedding?

Although their now-deceased daughter-in-law, Anne, would always be missed, Daniel smiled at the thought of his son, James, finding happiness once again.

Missus Bainbridge sipped tea and looked elegant as always.

Such a gracious Christian woman — she brings an atmosphere of peace amidst our stormy lives.

Just as Daniel ruminated about family chaos, the rest of the Lowe children arrived and were soon followed by James and Hannah and their large family of eight children.

God, you are bounteous in blessings — as well as loud children!

Mary stared at him. "What are you grinning about?"

Daniel placed his arm around her. "About how much noise God's blessings can create."

She burst out laughing and yelled above the chatter. "Most assuredly!"

Danny and Susannah emerged from the bedroom, carrying the last of their bags. "Well, 'tis time to return to Springfield. We must not tarry."

Daniel saw Mary's eyes well with tears and he fought them back, as well. Mary walked toward the couple and first embraced Susannah. "I am so pleased you are a part of our family now, Susannah. I know that you are the perfect consort for Danny and we rejoice that the Lord has brought you two together."

"Thank you, Mother Lowe." Susannah hugged her new mother-in-law warmly. "I must say, I knew I was in love with your son. But I did not expect to fall so in love with his home and his family as I have." Wiping a tear from her eye, Susannah kissed Mary's cheek. "Thank you, for everything."

Danny approached his father and held out his hand. Daniel could see that his son was struggling with the emotion of the last few days. Daniel pulled his oldest son into a warm embrace and patted him on the back. "Take care of your new wife. And keep making excellent armaments to help protect America." Daniel pulled back and viewed his son through blurred vision.

"I shall, Father."

Susannah reached up to Daniel and kissed his cheek. "Thank you, Father Lowe, for raising such a fine son." She smiled warmly.

Daniel felt humbled by the compliment. "'Tis truly God's

guidance that raises a child to His best purpose. I shall not take all the credit for my fine son. But we are most proud of the man he has become."

"As am I." Susannah quickly hugged her father-in-law and walked toward Sarah, who warmly embraced her.

Daniel looked over at his sobbing wife hugging Danny. "Be safe, my son. And know that I pray for you." Mary spoke through her tears.

"I will be, Mother. I love you."

"I love you, Danny."

Releasing her grip on his arms, she smiled bravely.

Daniel began to think his heart would break with the emotion of the last few days.

After he shook hands with Charles, everyone waved, the women all holding kerchiefs in their hands. They waved until the carriage was out of sight. Suddenly the voice of Benjamin could be heard in the now silent crowd.

"Mother, you are having another baby? Where did you get it?"

"It is a gift from heaven, Benjamin. Just like you are." Sarah kissed her son on the cheek and took his hand.

Smiling at Mary, Daniel kissed her forehead. "Ready to go home?"

"Yes…after I visit Polly and her family in gaol."

"I never thought I'd see the day that my wife preferred gaol to our home."

"Sometimes we just go where the pieces of our heart live. They are not always in one place. It helps us appreciate the times when our hearts all beat as one together, in one place."

"As long as my heart beats next to yours, I am content."

Kissing him, Mary smiled. "My heart will always beat as one with yours."

Walking arm in arm, Daniel and Mary returned to visit their firstborn grandson.

Chapter 39
Family

Mary sent Prissy to fetch Jonathan from working in the field. There was a post awaiting him at the Lowe cabin.

He arrived in mere moments, a look of hope mixed with anxiety in his eyes as he took the letter from Mary's hands.

Observing him read the parchment the post rider had delivered, she noticed the downward turn of his mouth and his narrowing eyes.

"Bad news?" Mary twisted the linen that she was sewing into baby garments.

Jonathan looked up. "I'm afraid so. The school does not wish me to return. I wrote them the reason for my delay and, I fear, my punishment for crime against chastity has rescinded my eligibility to teach." Folding the note, he threw it into the burning hearth and watched the page curl and disintegrate.

Polly's eyes grew wide as she sat in the chair, nursing baby Josiah. "What shall we do?"

Jonathan put his hands on his dirt-covered breeches. "I do not know."

It had been three weeks since the baby was born and Jonathan needed direction on where to go. He had hoped to return to his teaching position but those dreams now melted like the parchment in the fireplace.

Mary brightened. "Perhaps they will rehire you to teach in Deer Run."

Both Polly and Jonathan looked at her with doubt.

"After being in gaol for two weeks and everyone knowing about Polly and me? Not likely. What parent wants to entrust their little one to a man who cannot control his passions?" Jonathan stared out the open doorway and sighed with despair.

Polly put the baby against her shoulder and patted his back. "Besides, Mother, the way some of the townspeople glare at us, how can we expect to not always wear a badge of guilt here? Some of them are so heartless — they look at baby Josiah as if he is an evil amongst the other children. I could not bear for him to grow up with such hatred."

Mary knew her daughter was right. She had hoped and prayed that the residents of Deer Run would be more forgiving. While some were, many looked upon Polly and Jonathan with scorn. The thought of her grandson being subjected to such self-righteous judgment his whole life burned in Mary's heart. But the thought of Polly and her family moving away seared an even greater pain deep inside.

Inhaling deeply, Mary sighed. "Well then, we must pray that the Lord will guide you." Smiling as brightly as she could, the joy did not reach Mary's eyes.

"Yes." Jonathan turned toward Polly and kissed her tenderly before kissing the baby's cheek nestled against his mother's shoulder. "Take care of our little one, Polly. We shall discuss what to do tonight."

Placing his hat back on, he tramped out the portal and back toward the field.

Once he was out of sight, tears welled in Polly's eyes. "I do not know what we should do." She stared at her sleeping infant and wiped away the tears that threatened to drip onto his blond, downy head.

"Perhaps things will get better with the townspeople, Polly. Jonathan can help here with the farm. There is always much to do."

Polly's eyes filled with doubt. "I do not think Jonathan wishes to add to the family burden here. He wants to be able to provide for us — on his own. He is used to teaching and being independent." She stared into the distance, hopelessness filling her countenance.

Mary set aside the sewing and walked toward Polly sitting by the hearth.

"When I sat on my father's lap on this very chair that you are sitting upon, my father always said to me, 'Mary, when you are not certain what to do, ask God. He will show you the way.' Let us ask Him now what you should do." Smiling at Polly, she grasped her daughter's hand.

"All right." Polly wiped her nose with her sleeve. "Let us pray, then."

* * *

At the end of the workday, the weary men arrived back at the Lowe cabin. James stayed only long enough to wash up before announcing he would be eating with Sarah and Nathaniel.

Nine-year-old Betsy sent a teasing look at her big brother. "And with Miss Abigail? James's new love?" All the girls giggled at James's face that had turned redder than his sunburn.

James splashed water from the basin at Betsey, who screamed and ran away laughing. "That will teach you to spread rumors."

Mary stared at James. "So 'tis only a rumor?" She grinned mischievously while setting out trenchers along the tableboard.

James's face turned somber. "No, 'tis not rumor. But she lives in Boston and will be returning soon with Missus Bainbridge." Looking downward, he left for the Old Eaton farm, now called the Stearns Farm.

Mary bit her lower lip and stared after her son.

Prissy walked over to her side and stared after her brother. "Will he not stop her from going?"

Placing her arm around Prissy's shoulder, Mary hugged her. "That will be for James to decide." She kissed the curls escaping her daughter's cap and went back to setting out the meal.

Daniel Sr., Jonathan, and eleven-year-old Ephraim strode through the door and plopped down onto the benches.

"My weary workers." Mary leaned down and kissed

Daniel, while Prissy, Sally and Alice took turns delivering the filled trenchers from the large kettle in the hearth. After all had their plates nearly overflowing with rabbit stew, Daniel bowed his head for prayer. Everyone bowed in like manner, closing their eyes.

Daniel began to pray. "Our Heavenly Father, we are grateful for the bountiful food you have deigned to bring to our table. Bless this food, we ask dear Lord, and bless the ladies who cooked it for us. Amen."

"Amen." Everyone chorused, before picking up spoons to delve into the rich, carrot-filled dinner.

Mary's eyes narrowed at Ephraim. "Slow down, young man, or you shall get dyspepsia."

Her youngest son smiled with his cheeks bulging.

Daniel chuckled at Ephraim. "He put in a man's work today, Mother. His appetite has grown with his strength."

"I'll say he has grown. Far too quickly these days."

The late April evening air filled the cabin with a cool breeze that refreshed Mary's spirit. Polly and Jonathan had been quiet through most of the meal. Mary noticed Polly glance at the cradle to make sure Josiah was still asleep.

Jonathan finished his meal and looked up at Mary. "Wonderful supper, Mother Lowe. Thank you."

"You have earned it, Jonathan. Thank you for plowing today."

"I am a bit out of practice with farming but James helped me with handling the oxen." Looking at Polly, he took her hand. "Would you like to walk outside for a few moments? Perhaps your mother can mind Josiah whilst we discuss something."

Foreboding filled Mary's thoughts but she smiled. "Of course. I am always pleased to take care of our grandson."

A questioning look on Polly's face appeared but she followed Jonathan outside without saying a word. They walked a distance, out of earshot.

Mary questioned Daniel earnestly. "Do you know what he wishes to discuss? Did he say anything to you?"

Daniel shook his head then swallowed the last of his

cider. "No. He has been quiet all afternoon."

What is Jonathan saying? Where might they go?

Mary quelled the apprehension that played with her mind.

"Lassies, let us clean up the plates."

"I'll get yours, Mother." Prissy smiled encouragingly at her.

"Thank you, dear Prissy." She looked with loving eyes at her beautiful daughter, who was lately the recipient of more than one man's glance at the meetinghouse. Daniel had recently informed Mary that he was already on guarded watch for his second daughter's well-being. Mary grinned remembering the look on his face.

Daniel, you are such a protective father.

"Mother?"

Mary's attention was drawn to the open doorway where Polly stood with hands folded in front of her. "Yes, Polly?"

"Can you and Papa come outside for a moment? Perhaps Sally can watch Josiah for me?"

Sally glanced with narrowed eyes at her oldest sister. "Of course, Polly." Sally peaked into the cradle in the corner. "He still sleeps. I shall come get you if he awakens."

"Thank you, Sally."

Trying to remain calm, Mary walked outside, closely followed by Daniel.

The trio walked toward the edge of the woods lining the farmyard where Jonathan stared into the distance with hands on hips. As they approached, he inhaled deeply and looked at Daniel.

"Father Lowe, I have something I need to discuss with you—and Mother Lowe." He paused and drew in another breath. "My former position as schoolmaster in Connecticut has been terminated. And I know my chances of returning to this profession are less than likely. I must find an alternative to support my family."

Daniel cleared his throat. "You are welcome to stay on here—work the farm, live with us. I can always use more help."

"That is very gracious of you, sir. But I wish to provide

for my family without relying on your charity."

"'Tis not charity, Jonathan. We are family."

"I know this and I am grateful. But Polly and I know that, with all that has occurred, there are many here who would not welcome us into the community — and we do not wish for our son to bear reproof for my transgression."

"*Our* transgression." Polly placed her arm around his waist.

"Polly and I feel that we best serve our family's needs by starting over elsewhere."

Daniel swallowed visibly. "Where were you thinking?"

"Ohio. 'Tis growing and thriving with white settlers and should soon become a state."

Mary's mouth drained of moisture. "The Northwest Territory? But there are Indians…" She trembled uncontrollably.

Daniel interjected faster than usual. "The Shawnee can be quite fearsome, Jonathan. I know that you have never seen Indian warfare, but I have seen it during the Revolution. Please, reconsider…"

"Polly and I have discussed this and we feel that, if we stay close to a settlement already in existence, we have great chances of staying safe."

"Great chances?" Mary slowly shook her head. "Polly, Ohio is wilderness yet. Can you say in all honesty that you can bring up your baby safely in such dangerous territory?"

"When the settlers of Deer Run first came, it was wilderness. It was not long after that your parents came here. You were born nearby. You survived, and look at Deer Run now." Polly's face beamed with youthful adventure in her eyes.

Mary stood speechless. She wanted to scream to make them stop and reconsider. She longed to make them stay where it seemed safer. But she knew she could not.

All she could do was tremble and Daniel put his arm around her.

"Mother." Polly embraced her. "Please do not fear. This can be a new beginning for us."

Daniel spoke for them both. "If this is where the Lord leads you both, then we shall honor your decision. And we will pray for you."

"Thank you, sir." Jonathan reached toward Daniel to shake his hand. "I am grateful for your blessing in this matter."

Polly pulled away from Mary and stared with loving eyes at her husband. "Jonathan and I will begin planning and leave within a few weeks."

Grief bore into Mary as if part of her very flesh were being torn away. Watching Polly and Jonathan walk back to the cabin, Mary could only stare silently. She felt Daniel's arm wrap around her waist and he drew her close.

"We shall survive this — with God's help."

Looking up at his face she saw tears brimming in his eyes.

We shall survive this, but only with God's help.

* * *

The weeks passed by quickly, with Polly and Jonathan anxiously planning for their journey west. Occasionally Mary would see sadness in Polly's eyes and apprehension in Jonathan's, but the couple remained resolute in their plans.

Daniel seemed to be doing his best to resist his own fears, giving extra instructions to Jonathan about the best types of trees to fell for a cabin. Jonathan listened to Daniel intently, but Mary could see the uncertainty and his lack of farming skills evident in his reactions to what Daniel taught him.

Lord, how will they survive the wilderness? He is a twenty-year-old schoolmaster!

Mary held her tongue but prayed earnestly.

The day before the family was scheduled to head west, Sarah and Nathaniel invited everyone over to eat together. It was to be the last day for Missus Bainbridge as well. The Boston woman, who had provided refuge for Sarah and Nathaniel nine years before when Sarah was ready to birth, had remained good friends with the family and visited each spring, bringing clothes for the growing children. Her visits were always anticipated with joy, and her departure always dreaded.

Mary realized that this year, Missus Bainbridge's departure was especially painful for James. Since her son had heard that Abigail was to return to Boston with Missus Bainbridge, he had been more melancholy than Mary had seen him since Anne died.

Sadness was like a heavy blanket over everyone's spirits. *Lord, please help us.*

Walking toward Sarah's for the noon meal, Mary's legs felt like heavy tree trunks. Each step led her closer to saying good-bye to dear Polly, Jonathan, and the baby—perhaps forever. She pushed the thought far from her mind.

Sarah greeted them at the door, her slightly rounded belly declaring the new life within her. "Welcome, everyone."

Mary hugged her sister and patted the enlarging belly. "And how is the newest little one?"

"Apparently growing quite well." Sarah grinned and waved everyone inside.

Although the room was filled with children and several adults, silence shouted from every corner.

Everyone is so somber.

Mary had never been here before without cheerful chatter echoing off the walls. Even little Rachel seemed melancholy, holding her thumb in her mouth and clinging to Sarah's skirt.

Sarah looked around the room. "Well now, are we all hungry?" Her voice forced cheerfulness.

Suddenly Missus Bainbridge stood to her feet. "Before we eat, may I say something?" All eyes focused on the lovely middle-aged woman with the quiet, comforting demeanor. "I have a proposal to make."

Looking directly at Polly and Jonathan, she spoke to them with a gentle voice. "Mr. and Missus Grant, I have been watching you both these last weeks that I have been visiting Deer Run. I have been amazed at your gracious responses to all that has occurred in your tumultuous lives. You have born your guilt and your burdens with the utmost grace. And I commend you."

Polly's cheeks blushed while Jonathan shifted his feet. "Thank you, Missus Bainbridge." He fingered the brim of his hat nervously.

She continued. "I do not wish to embarrass you, but I would like to ask you both a question. Are your hearts truly set on heading for the Ohio wilderness? Or have you made this decision because you feel it is your only choice?"

Jonathan glanced at the floor and cleared his throat. "Madam, we have few choices." His face reddened.

Missus Bainbridge smiled. "Well, I would like to offer you another choice."

Polly and Jonathan's eyes widened. Jonathan found his voice. "Another choice?"

"Yes. You see, I am not getting younger—nor is my overseer of our factory in Boston. Our brick kiln is thriving with so much building going on and I cannot keep up with the bookkeeping as well as making certain that all is running smoothly at the factory. I need help and...I have no family." She paused and swallowed with difficulty. Standing tall and folding her hands gracefully, she continued. "So you see, if you would desire to come to Boston with me, I would be happy to embrace your family into my home and hire you as apprentice to my overseer."

Polly and Jonathan stood there, mouths agape. Mary's heart thrilled at this opportunity for them but she knew that only they could decide.

Jonathan's voice was unsteady. "You wish to invite us to live with you...and work for you."

"Yes." Missus Bainbridge smiled. "And be as a family to me."

Jonathan stumbled over his words. "I do not know what to say, Missus Bainbridge. This offer is extraordinary."

"You are part of an extraordinary family with an extraordinary heritage. I would be honored to include you in my home—as my family. If you are willing, that is."

"Yes!" Jonathan hugged Polly. "Yes, we are so grateful."

Tears rolled down Polly's cheeks. "Thank you, Missus Bainbridge." She flew toward their benefactress and embraced her.

Missus Bainbridge closed her eyes and smiled as she hugged Polly.

Thank you, God. You are amazing in your answers to prayer.

As Daniel put his arm around her, they heard the voice of their son, James.

"I have a proposal to make as well."

Mary covered her mouth to keep from rejoicing out loud.

James strode toward Abigail, who was standing near the far wall. Children scattered, making way for him to reach her.

Bending on one knee, James took her hand and looked up at the now teary-eyed young woman. "Abigail, I let you go once before but I cannot let you go again. I know that I have no right to claim your affections after I was untrue to you in the past."

Abigail laughed through her tears. "James, you were only seventeen."

"I was old enough to know that I loved you. If you can forgive me, I pray that you would consent to be my wife."

Covering her trembling mouth, she said, "Yes. I never stopped loving you."

James stood up on shaking legs and embraced her in a passionate kiss that went on long enough to make Sarah cover Benjamin's eyes.

"I want to see! Are they talking about making a family, Mother?"

"Yes, Benjamin. I believe they are."

* * *

The next morning, everyone gathered again at the Stearns farm.

Mary held baby Josiah as the men loaded up Missus Bainbridge's carriage. She had hired a local driver to manage the two horses as they rode back to Boston. The one hundred mile journey, interspersed with taverns for lodging, would take three days. In springtime, they were assured an enjoyable view with lush foliage throughout the forested trees lining the highway.

Polly tied the ribbon on her bonnet after hugging her sisters and brothers good-bye. Turning toward Mary, she picked up a sleepy Josiah from Mary's arms and nestled him in the crook of her own. "There, I think that is everything."

Mary went to kiss her good bye and clung to her daughter tightly. She wanted to be brave but her sadness overwhelmed her. "My heart is breaking, Polly."

Pulling away, Polly's eyes moistened. "As is mine, Mother. Please come and see us. We shall come each spring to see you, as well."

Mary nodded, her face contorting, too overwhelmed to speak.

Daniel embraced Polly and the baby and firmly kissed the top of her head. Holding her tightly for a moment, he looked over at Jonathan, who was waiting for Polly. "You take care of my daughter, Jonathan."

"I shall, sir."

He released his daughter and Mary watched Jonathan help Polly into the back seat of the carriage. The young man climbed upward and plopped next to her and smiled and waved at everyone.

Mary saw in his eyes relief and hope—a far cry from his countenance a few days before when he had planned to face the wilderness.

Everyone waved good-bye until the carriage disappeared down the road.

Wiping her tears away, Mary turned around and saw James kissing Abigail with great enthusiasm. She nudged Daniel's arm. "Time to prepare for another wedding."

Daniel grinned. "It looks like the sooner the better."

Waving farewell to Sarah and her family, the couple headed home along the road to Deer Run.

Chapter 40
Legacy

April 1802 – One Year Later

Danny held his three-month old daughter in his arms next to the window. Sunlight played like glittering jewels across the highlights in the infant's hair. Leaning close to her face, Danny nuzzled the girl's cheek with his nose.

"Emily," he whispered. "Sweet Emily."

The baby gurgled with delight, attempting to bring her hand toward her father's nose. As if suddenly remembering she was hungry, her mouth went from a smile to a distressed pout.

"Oh, oh, did you remember Mama was going to feed you?"

As if in answer, her face contorted and reddened in distress. Her wail, which always rent his heart, prompted him to bring her back to Susannah, who had just finished pinning up her hair.

"I want to look decent for your parents." Susannah smiled at her daughter and gently took the squirming infant from Danny's hands. Emily swirled her arms in excitement, anticipating her meal.

Pulling down her gown, Susannah offered her breast to the searching mouth of her child. Nestling into her mother's swollen, milk-filled breast, Emily suckled with soft sighing sounds of contentment.

Danny watched, amazed as always, by the miracle of his child's birth as well as by God's incredible — and beautiful — provision for his daughter's nourishment. He smiled, thinking of the pleasure that his wife provided to all their family.

"What makes you smile, Dan?" Susannah's face shone

with the special radiance of motherhood.

"The joy that you are to me — and Emily." He leaned down to kiss her warmly.

Susannah took her free hand and drew his lips to hers. Danny knelt down next to her and enjoyed the softness of her mouth for longer than he intended. Voices outside made him stop short. He was out of breath.

"They're here already!"

Susannah's gaze grew concerned. "I just began to feed her."

Standing up, he pecked her cheek. "You finish feeding her. I'll visit with them and stall. I know they are anxious to meet her but they can wait a few moments more!" Turning toward the door, he suddenly whipped back to face her. "Have I told you today how very much I love you, Missus Lowe?"

Susannah's face reddened. "Yes. But you may tell me as often as you like. I love you so much, Daniel Lowe."

Feeling like a love-sick schoolboy, he grinned and raced down the stairs to greet his parents at the door.

Opening the newly constructed portal, he saw his father touching the wooden frame with appreciative strokes. When Danny opened the door, both Daniel and Mary beamed with delight.

"Danny!" Mary hugged him tightly and kissed his cheek with enthusiasm.

He hugged his mother back and said, "Welcome to our new home."

"'Tis lovely, Danny! Such a blessing!" She stood back a few steps and looked up at the two-story frame house they had constructed the previous fall. "So many windows! You will love all the sunlight pouring through."

"Yes." He saw his father reach for his hand but Danny was too excited to see him to just accept a handshake. He grabbed his parent and hugged him. "Father! So good to see you."

He felt his father grip him tightly for a moment before releasing him. Daniel Sr. burst into a smile. "'Tis so good to see you. Some days this distance seems far more than twenty miles. Especially when a long winter keeps us apart for so many months."

"Yes. I was never so happy to see spring arrive."

Daniel Sr. shaded his eyes from the sun and stared out at the landscape. "Looks like promising land for your farm, Danny."

"I'll be working at the armory for some time yet. But this land will allow me to grow most of our food for awhile. Then when I retire I can farm even more."

Danny felt his father's eyes upon him. Daniel Sr. cleared his throat. "I am so very proud of you, Danny. This is a splendid home — with promise for a splendid future."

"Thank you, Father. Your words mean much to me." Pausing to gather his emotions, Danny glanced inside the house and then back toward his parents again. "Well then, shall we go inside?"

Daniel and Mary eagerly entered as Danny held his arm out in a welcoming gesture. Closing the door, Danny led them into the parlor. A few pieces of furniture partially filled the room.

"We are still working on getting chairs and settees. It seems to take great effort to furnish one's home."

Mary grinned. "This is lovely. And there are plenty of seats for us."

"Well, then choose your chair of comfort, Mother."

Walking toward a tapestry-covered settee, Mary sank into its softness. "This is beautiful." Looking around, her eyes narrowed. "Where are Susannah and the baby? I am so anxious to meet little Emily."

Danny thought his mother's grin took twenty years from her age. "Emily is eating and, trust me, you want her well-fed before disturbing her."

Daniel laughed at his son's words. "Spoken like an experienced father."

"So tell me." Danny sat on the edge of his seat. "How is everyone in the family?"

Mary scooted forward in her seat, grinning with

conspiratorial pleasure. "Well, let's see. Abigail is *very* great with child. Her little one should birth quite soon. She and James are enjoying living at the old Stearns farm. That is where Abigail was born, you know."

Danny raised his eyebrows. "No, I did not know. Is that not amazing?" He scratched his head. "Now, did James and Abigail take Rachel to live with them?"

"Well, only sometimes. She is quite attached to Sarah, since my sister raised Rachel from birth as her wet nurse. Rachel still calls James 'Daddy,' but I think they have decided she will mostly stay with Sarah and Nathaniel. Rachel stays occasionally with James and Abigail, as well."

Danny was thoughtful. "'Twould be difficult to know what to do in that situation."

"Yes. But I think Rachel is well loved by all, and is certainly a happy two-year-old."

"And how is Aunt Sarah's little girl, Elizabeth? She and Nathaniel finally have a lass!"

"She is a lovely thing. Fat, blond, blue-eyed and laughs all the time. They are so in love with her." Mary sighed with satisfaction. "Everyone else is well. And last we heard from Polly and Jonathan, all is well in Boston. Jonathan is well-satisfied working as apprentice and will soon be ready to be a journeyman under the overseer. He has a 'natural inclination for the accounting,' according to Polly, and is happier than she has ever seen him. And Josiah just started walking. But Polly has other happy news as well. She is with child again. Missus Bainbridge is already searching for a midwife so that Polly will be content when her time draws near." Mary's eyes welled with tears. "I am so grateful for Missus Bainbridge."

Danny's heart warmed. "She is like our Family Angel. What a blessing she has been to all of us."

A rustling on the steps drew their attention. Susannah walked in carrying a sleepy Emily wrapped in a woolen blanket.

"Mother Lowe! Father Lowe! So good to see you." Daniel and Mary stood and embraced their daughter-in-law.

Mary beamed. "You look wonderful, Susannah."

Danny hugged her waist. "She certainly does. And here is our daughter, Emily. Emily, meet your grandsire and grandmother."

"She…is so precious." Mary gazed at her new grandchild. "May I hold her?"

"Of course." Susannah placed the droopy, milk-filled infant into Mary's arms. Laughing softly, Mary whispered, "Well, she certainly seems content. Her tummy must be quite full." Mary nestled the infant in her arms and swayed from side-to-side.

Danny was overwhelmed with the comfort of being surrounded by his family's love. All four adults stared at the newest Lowe baby for several moments.

Mary looked up suddenly. "Daniel, would you like to hold your granddaughter?"

Daniel grinned. "'Twould be my pleasure."

Taking her carefully from Mary, Daniel gently embraced his newest grandchild. He gently rocked her in his arms and then paused and leaned into her chubby face.

Daniel whispered so softly, Danny had to strain to listen. He heard his father say,

"Welcome, my grandchild. Welcome to America."

Author Note

I am both excited and saddened to complete this last book in the *Deer Run Saga*. It has been an amazing journey of discovering family history, creating fictional characters based on actual individuals, and getting to know some of the most wonderful people in this adventure called writing.

The Legacy of Deer Run is a fictitious story based on my real ancestor, Daniel Prince Jr., my third great grandfather. He and his twin brother James went to work at the Springfield Armory as apprentices in 1799. They were fifteen years old at the time.

I am unsure as to the length of time that James worked there, but it appears that he left long before his twin, Daniel, and went into farming. Daniel ("Danny") stayed at the armory for 35 years, working his way to the position of inspector. Payroll records actually show that at some point, Daniel Sr., former Redcoat in the King's Army, also worked at the armory with his son, Daniel Jr. I have had the pleasure of viewing both of their signatures on work records.

I also have the pleasure of owning a photograph taken in the 1860s of the twins, Daniel and James. At the time, they were in their eighties and were somewhat famous as the oldest twins in the United States. This photograph graces my mantel in my home and bears the likeness of two very handsome, elderly gentlemen. What a joy to own! Daniel Prince Jr. lived to be ninety-two years old.

Daniel Jr. married a young woman from Boston named Sarah. Since there was already a character of that name in my story, I changed her name to "Susannah." Although Sarah did move to Springfield from Boston, I have no reason to believe that she was as uppity as the character, Susannah. But the division of classes added to the fictitious fun! The real Daniel Jr. and Sarah Prince had eleven children in all, and their first child was a girl named, Emily. I am descended from their seventh child, a son named Luke Packard Prince. He is my great, great-grandfather.

The Springfield Armory has an amazing history. It was a government-run facility to make weapons to protect the United States in the event of war. It began with limited production around 1794 but ramped up production of weapons in 1799, the same year my grandfather went to work there. The location in Springfield, Massachusetts was deemed well protected (by George Washington and Henry Knox) since it was well inland and on a hill.

By 1804, the facility produced 3,500 new muskets per year. The War of 1812 increased the demand and the armory responded by using cutting edge machinery to create even more weapons. The facility was at the forefront of the Industrial Revolution in America, continually creating newer systems for mass production.

It responded with increased production and ever-changing designs of rifles through numerous conflicts including the Civil War, WWI and WWII. In 1964, the then-Secretary of Defense decided that private manufacturers could take the place of the Armory. In 1968, after 174 years of production, the doors closed on the Springfield Armory. They are currently open seven days a week as a museum and the facility is a National Historic site.

While much of the plot in *The Legacy of Deer Run* is from my imagination, there were a few details straight from my research, including the fire at the armory in January, 1801. An account at the archives of the Springfield Museums indicates there was some suspicion that it may have been set on purpose. It actually did result in the complete loss of the Stocking and Filing Shop, as well as 500 muskets.

The incident with the shipment of coal and the disagreement between the Superintendent and the Paymaster is also documented. And the tensions between the United States and France were quite real in 1800, although I never found any incidence of sabotage at the armory from French spies. That is purely from my creative imagination.

The law in Massachusetts that the character Polly Lowe faced, however, was factual. According to research done by historian Dennis Picard, a law was passed in Massachusetts in 1789, declaring fornication to be a "crime against chastity." The sheriff would deliver the complaint to the persons involved and they would appear before the justice of the peace, who would determine the sentence of up to two months in jail or $30. Public confessions in the church were also a real consequence for sex outside of marriage.

The raising of First Church in West Springfield actually occurred in 1800—and my ancestor, Daniel Prince Jr., did in fact help raise that building. This was discovered in a newspaper article describing an anniversary celebration of the church, in which Daniel is mentioned as helping in the construction. He would have been a lad of sixteen at the time, a few years younger than the character of "Danny" in my book.

I hope that you, dear reader, have been both entertained yet informed through my Deer Run Saga that began with *The Road to Deer Run* set in 1777 and tells Daniel Lowe Sr.'s story. My prayer is that you learned more about the early years of our nation, while also were inspired by the spiritual triumphs of the characters. Life was not easy then—nor is it now. We all still face challenges in life that can either increase our faith and trust in God or lead us to despair. The choice is within our hearts and souls.

As I laid flowers on the grave of Daniel Prince Sr., Daniel Prince Jr., and Sarah Prince in October 2011, I felt the family connection with my grandparents who had faced their own severe challenges in the 1700s and 1800s. And, even though the details of my books are fictitious, I feel a deep sense of inspiration and joy when I write about their lives in those early times of our nation. Someday, I hope we can all meet on the other side of eternity.

The Road to Deer Run

The year was 1777. The war had already broken the heart of Mary Thomsen, a young colonial woman from Massachusetts. It had also broken the spirit of British soldier Daniel Lowe, a wounded prisoner of war in a strange land.

They were enemies, brought together by need. Would their differences overshadow the yearnings of their hearts? Or would the bitterness of war keep them apart?

Pages: 304
Size 6 x 9
ISBN: 978-1-4502-1919-8
Published: 3/29/2010
Also available in Ebook

Finalist: 2011 Next Generation Indie Book Awards
Honorable Mention: 2011 Los Angeles Book Festival
Best Romantic Moment: ClashoftheTitles.com, February 2011

The Promise of Deer Run is the second novel in author Elaine Marie Cooper's Deer Run Saga.

It's 1790 and the American Revolution has been over for seven years. Nathaniel Stearns, a veteran Continental soldier, still awaits the return of his father, who seemed to vanish as the battles ended. Growing embittered and isolated, Nathaniel is haunted by painful memories of war and scarred from betrayal in love. The only hope he clings to is that perhaps his father still lives.

Then he discovers his hope is shared by a young woman, Sarah Thomsen, who understands loss and the longing for a father. Their hearts are drawn together but jealousy, slander, and misunderstandings ignite a fire of doubt and mistrust— destroying their relationship.

Can two souls longing for healing and trust love again?

Best Romance: 2012 Los Angeles Book Festival
Finalist: Religious Fiction, ForeWord Reviews Book of the Year

Pages: 252
Size: 6x9
ISBN: 978-1-46203-796-4
Published: 8/16/2011
Also available in Ebook

Other Books from Sword of the Spirit Publishing

2008

All the Voices of the Wind by Donald James Parker
The Bulldog Compact by Donald James Parker
Reforming the Potter's Clay by Donald James Parker
All the Stillness of the Wind by Donald James Parker
All the Fury of the Wind by Donald James Parker
More Than Dust in the Wind by Donald James Parker
Angels of Interstate 29 by Donald James Parker

2009

Love Waits by Donald James Parker
Homeless Like Me by Donald James Parker

2010

Against the Twilight by Donald James Parker
Finding My Heavenly Father by Jeff Reuter
Never Without Hope by Michelle Sutton
Reaching the Next Generation of Kids for Christ by Robert C. Heath

2011

Silver Wind by Donald James Parker
He's So In Love With You by Robert C. Heath
Their Separate Ways by Michelle Sutton
Silver Wind Pow-wow by Donald James Parker
The 21st Century Delusion by Daniel Narvaez
Hush, Little Baby by Deborah M. Piccurelli

2012

Retroshock by David W. Murray
Destiny of Angels By Eric Myers
It's Not About Her by Michelle Sutton
The American Manifesto by Steven C. Flanders
Will the Real Christianity Please Stand Up by Donald James Parker